A large, dark figure slipped into the cabin

Kate forced back the surge of panic and gripped her makeshift club tighter. His movements, silent and deliberate as he maneuvered through the room, reminded her of a stalking panther. She searched the silhouette for a weapon, but he had none. A flicker of déjà vu swept through her. Only one person moved like that. And he was the last person she wanted to see.

Let me be wrong. Let it be a hit man on my back.

"Roman?" Kate gasped. Her mind refused to believe what her heart now recognized. Roman leaned close, putting his face inches from hers. His sharp, stony features were barely visible in the darkness. But it didn't matter.

At one time, Kate had cherished every angle, every plane....

Dear Harlequin Intrigue Reader,

As we ring in a new year, we have another great month of mystery and suspense coupled with steamy passion.

Here are some juicy highlights from our six-book lineup:

- Julie Miller launches a new series, THE PRECINCT, beginning with *Partner-Protector*. These books revolve around the rugged Fourth Precinct lawmen of Kansas City whom you first fell in love with in the TAYLOR CLAN series!

- *Rocky Mountain Mystery* marks the beginning of Cassie Miles's riveting new trilogy, COLORADO CRIME CONSULTANTS, about a network of private citizens who volunteer their expertise in solving criminal investigations.

- Those popular TOP SECRET BABIES return to our lineup for the next *four* months!

- Gothic-inspired tales continue in our spine-tingling ECLIPSE promotion.

And don't forget to look for Debra Webb's special Signature Spotlight title this month: *Dying To Play.*

Hopefully we've whetted your appetite for January's thrilling lineup. And be sure to check back every month to satisfy your craving for outstanding suspense reading.

Enjoy!

Denise O'Sullivan
Senior Editor
Harlequin Intrigue

BODYGUARD RESCUE

DONNA YOUNG

HARLEQUIN®

TORONTO • NEW YORK • LONDON
AMSTERDAM • PARIS • SYDNEY • HAMBURG
STOCKHOLM • ATHENS • TOKYO • MILAN • MADRID
PRAGUE • WARSAW • BUDAPEST • AUCKLAND

For Matthew, Cameron and Lauren
The loves of my life

ISBN 0-373-22824-4

BODYGUARD RESCUE

www.eHarlequin.com

Printed in U.S.A.

CAST OF CHARACTERS

Roman D'Amato—As a government operative, he is assigned one mission: to protect the one woman he's ever loved—or kill her. Whichever proves most necessary.

Kate MacAlister—A world-leading antimatter research scientist. Her recent development of a new energy source could revolutionize the planet—or destroy it.

Nigel Threader—Underworld arms merchant who wants the formula from Kate—and much, much more. No matter the cost.

Cain MacAlister—Kate's eldest brother, Roman's Black Ops partner, and a man with zero tolerance when someone threatens his family.

Ian MacAlister—Kate's older brother, a Navy SEAL with a reputation for getting the job done—whatever it takes.

Chapter One

The screams sought him in the darkness where he was the most vulnerable. Sinking further into the shrouded layers of fatigue, he let the murkiness surround him. Maybe this time the shadows would provide refuge. Maybe this time she'd leave him in peace.

Instead the tortured wails followed him, penetrating his sanctuary, their pitch growing maniacal as she pursued him. Didn't she realize he couldn't save her? Not now. Not ever.

Taunting his cowardice, the screams became deafening, demanding his presence. Their razor-sharp edges sliced through the darkness and forced him away from the protective shadows.

She appeared at the edge where light and dark blended into a misty vapor. Her features, contorted in anguish, softened when she recognized him.

"Help me," she pleaded, her cries turning to whimpers. The image grew clearer as the shadows receded. Her face, once exotic in its beauty, loomed before him now slashed and bloody. Her naked body, broken and mangled. Eyes, black as midnight, reflected the tortured spirit lying beneath.

"Kill me," she begged as her hands clawed at him, smearing his chest with blood. *"Please."*

"No." His own scream wrenched through the air, its rawness jarring him from his sleep. His eyes flew open and he expected to see her body lying next to his, but only the smell of her blood followed him back into reality. The metallic scent lingered in his nostrils, mixing with the sour odor of his sweat and the staleness of the cabin. His stomach heaved in protest.

"Damn," Roman D'Amato swung his legs over the edge of the berth and pressed the heels of his hands against his temples. The sledgehammer inside his skull eased into a rhythmic throb.

He'd made the wrong choice. If the nightmares were the punishment, so be it. Lord knew he deserved worse, much worse.

He grabbed a cigarette from the nightstand and shoved it between his teeth, ignoring the slight tremor in his hand when he lit up. The first drag was long and deep, allowing him to savor the taste while it filled his lungs. He waited until the burning pressure in his chest forced him to exhale, then slowly he blew the smoke out, letting it swirl around his head.

The scent of Amanda's blood faded.

Roman fell back onto the bunk and covered his eyes with his forearm. Before long, the even rocking of the boat and the nicotine soothed him. He'd bought the cabin cruiser a few years back to escape. Its long, sleek lines and comforting rhythm drew his soul like a magnet. Still, the boat couldn't save Roman from his demons or the punishment they bestowed. Nothing could.

It didn't matter, he mused. He wanted retribution, not salvation. The timing wasn't right, though, not yet.

But soon. Very soon.

A black heat pulsed in his blood, burning with revenge.

For Amanda. For himself.

The shrill ring of the telephone jolted him out of his thoughts. He grabbed the clock from the nightstand, then dropped it onto the cabin floor in disgust. Nine in the morning. Only three hours of sleep.

He got up from the bed, not bothering to put his shorts on, and walked naked to the desk where he'd tossed his cell phone. Only one person had his number, and that person would have only one reason to use it.

Automatically activating the scrambler, he answered on the fourth ring. "Yeah." Roman saw no need for niceties since the man on the other end of the line was Jonathon Mercer, Director of Labyrinth, an elite branch of the CIA.

"I've just canceled your vacation, D'Amato." Mercer didn't believe in polite conversation, either. In their business, it was a waste of time. "We have a situation."

Roman laughed, and acid burned his throat. There were always situations. He'd been a specialist too long to believe otherwise.

"I'm unavailable, Mercer. Get someone else." He bit out the words, not caring if it cost him his career. Hell, maybe it was time to retire, anyway.

"Damn it, there isn't anyone else," came the impatient reply. "Kate MacAlister walked out of Las Mesas and disappeared."

"What do you mean she disappeared?" Dread raked his gut. Cold and razor sharp.

"Exactly that," the director admitted irritably.

There was a short, tense pause while Roman swallowed an obscenity. At the mention of Kate's name, his reputed control always vanished. A truth he'd never been able to escape.

"I'm listening," Roman ground out, his voice tight. He

reached for another cigarette. The Las Mesas Institute was a nuclear laboratory located in southern New Mexico. Their security measures were the most advanced in the country. Impenetrable. The way Roman had designed them to be.

"A few months ago, Dr. MacAlister made a breakthrough on her antimatter energy research," Mercer replied gruffly. "It appears she found a way to capture the energy created when antimatter particles collide with normal matter."

Familiar with Kate's theory, he wasn't surprised she'd succeeded in proving it. Besides being Las Mesas's top physicist, the woman was a certified genius, having gotten her doctorate in both computer science and physics by the age of nineteen.

"Last night, shortly before midnight, she ran a program at the lab, destroying all her research data. Then she left."

"It doesn't make sense," Roman frowned. "The antimatter research was her baby, had been for the past five years."

"Still, her disappearance was triggered by a phone call she received at the lab." After a pause, Mercer continued, "We've reason to believe it was Marcus Boyd, her associate on the project."

Roman remembered meeting Dr. Boyd at some award banquet held in Kate's honor. The man had reminded him of an old mouse, slight in stature with a nervous disposition. He also remembered Kate's disapproving look when he'd casually offered the timid man some cheese from the buffet table.

Mercer interrupted Roman's thoughts. "We suspect she's hiding but can't verify it without tipping off the domestics." Domestics meant FBI and the local police. Labyrinth tended to avoid contact with them for security purposes.

Roman swore and pressed his fingers to his eyes, where the rhythmic throbbing metamorphosed once again into a sledgehammer. The woman had more brains than she had common sense. "I'm still listening, Mercer, but so far you haven't explained why the doc went into hiding." Roman grabbed the aspirin bottle from the desk drawer and swallowed four tablets dry as Kate's image flashed before him. The long, black hair, the startling gray eyes, the delicate lines of her face.

When he got hold of her, he'd wring her beautiful neck.

"Copies of Dr. MacAlister's latest research notes have surfaced among some of the world's leading arms dealers." Mercer's voice hardened. "Specific handwritten notes only someone working closely with her would have access to."

"Boyd," Roman supplied. The doc had been set up.

"He was the most logical suspect," Mercer agreed, "but it's going to be damn hard to confirm our suspicions—Boyd's dead." Roman smashed his cigarette between his fingers then threw the remains into a half-eaten bowl of cereal he'd left on the desk the night before. The little fool, she put herself in harm's way the moment she destroyed her research. Even if Boyd wasn't selling her work, someone was. It was only a matter of time before whoever killed Boyd went after her.

"What do you have that's concrete?"

"Not much," Mercer responded, echoing Roman's frustration. "A short while ago she contacted Cain's office from a pay phone in Raton, New Mexico. We assumed she couldn't get a signal on her cell phone and took a chance on being traced." Mercer grunted. "Which we did, of course. She hung up after Cain's secretary told her he was out of town."

Roman rubbed his face, barely noticing the whiskers

that scraped his palm. Cain was Kate's oldest brother, Roman's most trusted friend and one of the Agency's top operatives.

"He's overseas," Mercer confirmed. "Too deep undercover to reach. Hell, even if I could manage it somehow, I wouldn't."

Roman understood. If Cain found out about Kate while on an operation, the distraction might prove fatal.

Looking out the porthole, Roman squinted at the sun glaring over Chesapeake Bay. Kate was out there somewhere, alone and in danger, and he wasn't sure he could get to her in time.

Mercer continued, unaware of the emotional turmoil Roman fought to keep in check. "She doesn't know the good guys from the bad guys."

"She knows me." The words were clipped, the control back.

"Exactly."

Would she trust him? Roman was grateful the doc didn't like guns, because if she did, she would probably shoot him on sight. No, she wouldn't trust him, at least not at first. He would have to gain her confidence somehow.

Mercer's tone grew speculative. "Raton is on the Colorado–New Mexico border. We're assuming she headed north for Denver."

Cain's cabin. The ever-logical doc was heading for her brother's cabin just outside of Aspen, Colorado. A secret hideaway he had shared only with his family and his best friend.

"I'll find her," Roman kept his voice even, but his mind raced, already making plans to reach Kate by nightfall.

"Let's hope so," came the reluctant response. "It's one

reason why I need you on this. You know her as well as her family—maybe better."

"She's hiding, waiting for Cain." He didn't even consider the possibility she would sell the data to save her life.

"That's what I figured," the older man answered. "She doesn't know either of you are operatives, which means she's hoping her big brother knows someone trustworthy in the government."

Roman silently agreed. As far as Kate was concerned, Cain owned MacAlister Security, a successful international security company. Roman preferred to keep it that way.

"What about Ian?" he asked. Ian MacAlister, Kate's other brother, was a Navy SEAL team leader stationed in Virginia.

"I called in a favor. He's been shipped out to the South Atlantic with his team on training maneuvers." Roman detected grimness in Mercer's tone. "The man is a loose cannon. I don't want him finding out about her disappearance until it's too late. There's no telling what the idiot might do."

Roman knew. Ian's rage would be uncontrollable. Then again, so would Cain's. But that was Mercer's problem.

"Her parents?"

"They're in Scotland. Left a week ago and aren't due back for a few more. A combined business and pleasure trip."

Roman frowned. It didn't give him much time. Even Mercer couldn't keep something this serious under wraps for long. It was bad enough she was a world-respected scientist, but the fact she was also an heir to the MacAlister fortune made for big news. Once Kate's disappearance became public, her parents would be on the next Concorde home, complicating matters. Quentin "Mac" MacAlister had his own way of solving problems.

"You said my knowing her was one of the reasons you

called me. What's the other?" he asked, impatient now to get to her. He imagined her holed up in a cabin in the mountains. She hated the mountains almost as much as she hated him. It wouldn't stop her, though. She would wait there until she could contact Cain.

"My people found Boyd tied, hanging by his fingers to his basement rafters. From the looks of the photos, the guy was tortured then mutilated." Roman heard the shuffling of papers. "I received a copy of the coroner's preliminary report. Says here Boyd bled to death. Primary weapon used—surgical scalpel. The victim showed signs of acid burns, blunt trauma with multiple fractures and dislocations."

"Hell," Mercer said in a tone tinged with hatred. "This could be Amanda's file, the technique is that similar."

Images of Amanda's broken body flashed through Roman's mind. A cold chill gripped his insides.

"Nigel Threader," he stated with barely restrained savagery, then pushed the images away. For now.

"That's what we suspect. However—" he emphasized the word before Roman could interrupt "—we're not positive. And since you know more about the bastard than his own mother does, you're Dr. MacAlister's best bet for staying alive."

"He'll go after her," Roman said flatly, his gaze drawn to a thin pink scar on the back of his hand. He had no doubt that Threader wanted Kate. Flexing his fingers to relieve a phantom ache, he considered the arms dealer's actions. Threader might be a sick bastard, but he was a brilliant strategist.

"If it's him, he's already looking for her," Mercer agreed, then paused. "My boys got to Boyd just before he died. But he only lived long enough to warn us that Kate was in danger. We didn't get any names."

Mercer continued, his voice holding a note of impatience. "Another thing. Someone's investigating the MacAlister family. We haven't found the tie-in yet, and whoever it is hasn't left much of a trail. Could be Threader, could be anybody."

"It's Threader." A bitter certainty cemented Roman's tone.

There was another pause, this time longer, before the director said his next words carefully. "I'm not wasting my breath with lectures about the dangers of taking missions personally. You'd tell me to go to hell, anyway. But I *am* going to tell you this—under no circumstance can he or anyone else get that formula, D'Amato. Is that clear? If you can't save her—"

"I know." Roman interrupted, not wanting Mercer to finish the order. If he couldn't get her back safe, killing her himself would be the only alternative, more humane than what waited for her at the hands of a psychopath like Threader.

Even so, Kate's quick death would be secondary to Roman's true mission. If he failed to rescue her, he would have to kill her simply because she was the last known source of information on a weapon ten times more powerful than the hydrogen bomb.

It didn't matter Kate was the only woman he'd ever loved. It didn't matter he'd already betrayed that love once to keep her safe. What mattered was that millions of people could die at the hands of a madman.

Roman ran his hand through his hair and gave it a vicious yank. Another one of his nightmares had just become a reality.

Chapter Two

They'd found her.

Tossing off the quilt, Kate MacAlister slid from the cushions onto her hands and knees, letting the overstuffed sofa shield her from the front window.

How they'd found her so quickly, she would figure out later. If she lived.

She heard no sound, spotted no movement, but she sensed the threat nonetheless.

Her father would insist her Celt blood hummed the warning. Pure and blessed, it was. A gift passed down from their ancestors to a chosen few, he would say.

A few that included Quentin MacAlister's offspring.

Whatever *it* was, remained a mystery to Kate. Yet she learned long ago to accept the warnings, to trust them—just as her brothers did.

Time to move.

So when the fine hair on the back of her neck started to do a tap dance down her spine, it meant only one thing.

Blinking hard, she forced her eyes to adjust to the darkness that enveloped the cabin, keeping her panic at bay while things shifted into decipherable patterns. A solitary light glimmered from across the room as a few embers burned in the fireplace, their dim orange glow barely distinguishable.

She concentrated on filtering out the noises of the night, straining to hear her enemies, waiting for confirmation on what her sixth sense already understood. They were close.

Staying crouched below the back of the couch, Kate pushed the sofa pillows under the covers, then crawled across the room, army-style, her body tight to the floor. Her brother's dark jersey blended well with the night, although it did little to protect her from the icy dampness of the hard wood. Tremors rippled through her, but from cold or fear Kate wasn't sure.

Please God, just a few more seconds.

At the wood box by the door, she paused no more than a heartbeat, grabbed a slim log and inched up the wall before shrinking into the shadows.

Blood pounded in her eardrums, its rhythm matching the fierce tempo of her heart. She wanted to claw at her ears to make it stop. Instead she made herself take a deep, calming breath. After the second breath, the hammering eased, yet the terror remained, cloaking her like a damp wool blanket.

Soundlessly the door opened and a large, dark figure slipped into the cabin. She forced back a surge of panic and gripped the makeshift club tighter, disregarding the rough bark as it dug into her palms.

What if there was more than one? How far would they go to get the formula?

Stepping deeper into the shadows, she held her breath when the man's shape passed within a few feet of her. His movements, silent and deliberate as he maneuvered through the room, reminded Kate of a stalking panther.

Or a professional hit man.

She searched his silhouette for a weapon. He had none. No gun, no knife, not even a rope. His hands hung indifferently at his sides, empty.

Anger exploded in her head, destroying the knot of fear in her belly.

Why did she think he would bother with a weapon? After all, he probably thought she was an easy target. Some egghead doctor he could knock off with his bare hands. Some weak-kneed nonentity who would die because she had no backbone.

She glared at the man as he circled the room, obviously searching for her computer, unaware of the wrath he left in his wake. He wouldn't find it—ever. She'd worked too hard on her research to let it drop into undesirable hands.

Kate relaxed her muscles, then rolled her weight to the balls of her feet, offering up a brief prayer of thanks for her brother Ian's insistence on teaching her the rudiments of self-defense. Using the shadows to cloak her movements, she slowly raised her makeshift club, then waited—and watched.

This egghead doctor is going to knock you clear into Christmas, pal. Then you can go back and tell your boss to forget about his plans for the formula.

With his back toward her, the man paused at the couch. She drew in a deep breath as he reached for the covers concealing the decoy. When he grabbed the quilt, Kate lunged. She swung the log hard, intent on striking the back of his head, only to have it disappear in an inky blur before she felt any impact.

Twisting away, he caught the wood with one hand and jerked it from her grasp. In an instant he grabbed her and sent her flying over the couch like a bag of garbage. Her back hit the floor, cutting her scream off with a whoosh.

She bit back the pain that exploded across her shoulder blades and rolled away from the couch, using the momentum to scramble to her feet. The man dived over the furniture, missing her by mere inches. A whimper of terror tore from her lips when she bolted toward the door, her lone chance for escape.

Suddenly a hand snaked out and caught her ankle in a viselike grip, slamming Kate to the floor, chest first. Before she could recover, he was on her back, straddling her waist and locking her hands behind her.

Enraged and frightened, she thrashed about, fighting the inevitable, her body heaving and kicking, trying in desperation to buck him loose.

"Enough." The command cracked through the room. Its echo bounced sharply off the wall, making Kate cringe.

Exhausted and near collapse, she stopped struggling to lie still on the floor.

"Get off me." The low, guttural words exploded from her as she tried to gulp in oxygen while his weight crushed her lungs.

"No way, Doc." The fact he was speaking softly didn't lessen the fury behind the tone. "Not before I get some answers. *Capisce?*"

A flicker of déjà vu swept through her. Only one person owned a voice like that, husky and warm like her father's favorite scotch. He was the only person who got away with calling her that name. And the last person she wanted to see.

God, let me be wrong. Let it be a hit man on my back.

Deftly he flipped her over and snagged her hands above her head. His body straddled hers in a position far more intimate than before, one her body was achingly familiar with.

"Roman?" she gasped, her mind refusing to believe what her heart now recognized.

He leaned down, putting his face inches from hers. His sharp, stony features were barely visible in the darkness, still it didn't matter. At one time Kate cherished every angle, every plane, every...

"I'm waiting," he said, the impatience slicing through her thoughts.

His tone sent a shock wave of old memories sweeping through Kate's body—memories that aroused, then infuriated. *He's waiting.*

So what? She'd been waiting for two years, since the morning she woke up and found herself alone. No note, no explanation—nothing.

Kate tried to laugh, but the sound was so weak it came closer to a sob. "Go to hell, D'Amato."

"I'm already there, Doc." He laughed, too, the savagery in it making her stomach lurch. "So your suggestion is pointless."

"I..." Kate stopped as a wave of nausea rolled through her. Bile rose to the back of her throat and she gulped in order to keep it down.

"Roman," she whispered, the panic evident while she struggled for control. "Please." With a snap, the dam burst down at the base of her spine and wave after wave of anxiety flooded her body. *Oh God, oh God. Not a panic attack. Not now.*

"Let...me...go!" She screamed, her voice, thin and high with hysteria as she tried to break free of his suffocating hold. She was shaking violently now, almost convulsively, her hands and feet ice-cold. If she could reach the couch, she could curl up into a ball until the worst passed.

Evidently Roman was way ahead of her. He tightened his grip and lifted her into his arms, then headed for the couch.

"It's okay, Doc. Just hold on," he coaxed while he laid

her across his lap. His unbreakable but oddly gentle grip pinned her to his body. "Let me help."

At first Kate ignored the words he crooned in her ear. Time held no meaning while she dealt with the emotional turmoil within her. It didn't take long before her body, already weakened from the past twenty-four hours, gave out. Gut-wrenching sobs racked her, draining what little strength she had, finally, mercifully leaving her purged but exhausted.

She turned into Roman's chest and buried her face into the sturdy column of his neck, instinctively searching for a warm refuge from her fears. Under her lips, she could feel his pulse, strong and reassuringly steady. Kate moved her fingers over his heart trying to absorb its solid rhythm.

Roman caressed her back. The strokes felt tender and soothing while he continued to murmur soft, unintelligible words into her hair.

Gradually she drifted back to reality drawn by his voice, its husky timbre vibrating against her face. She could feel dampness on her cheek and realized it was from her own tears. *How are you going to explain this, MacAlister?*

Kate didn't want to think about explanations or make any decisions, so she pushed the question away. She'd forgotten how comforting it was to be held in a man's arms, in Roman's arms.

Strange how it had always been that way. From the first time they'd held each other to the last time, Kate had responded to Roman on more than just a physical level. From the moment their souls connected, she was lost. She'd never wanted another lover after he'd left because she knew deep down no man would ever reach her as he did.

"Thank you," she murmured. Then, unable to stop herself, she moved her mouth softly against his neck, relishing the familiar musky taste of him on her lips.

A soft hiss brushed past her ear, and his body tightened against hers. He cupped the back of her neck, bringing her face up. His warm breath fanned her lips in a light caress. A shiver of desire skittered down her spine. She squashed the feeling of betrayal that threatened to surface and closed her eyes in anticipation of his kiss, her mouth parting with an eagerness that surprised her.

A muttered "hell" was the only warning she got before he slid her from his lap onto the cushions of the couch. She blinked, stunned, as he wrapped her in the discarded quilt and stood.

"Try to relax, Doc. I'm going to stoke the fire, then find us something hot to drink—or if I'm lucky, something strong." She tried not to blanch at the coolness in his voice. It was apparent the man was not happy to see her again.

The sharp sting of humiliation traveled down to the core of her being, but thankfully she was too numb to care. Almost.

KATE GAZED into the fireplace, watching the flames lick greedily around the new logs Roman had tossed there. She tucked her bare feet under the quilt as a shiver danced over her. Even with the extra fuel, the fire did not drive away the coldness seeping into her bones.

The wind howled outside the cabin, and its agitation echoed her unease. Ignoring Roman's order to rest, she draped the quilt over her shoulders and forced herself off the couch toward the window. He wouldn't be happy, but she didn't care. While the panic attack had left her feeling drugged and unstable, she refused to succumb to the aftereffects. Experience had taught her that immobility only delayed her recovery.

Her legs wobbled but supported her well enough to get

her across the room. Once there she peered into the pitch-black beyond the cabin, careful to remain concealed behind the slightly parted denim curtains. How much time did she have before they found her? Were they out there now, watching?

The faint clatter of pans reached her from the kitchen, and reminded Kate of her unwanted company. What was Roman D'Amato doing here? More important, how was she going to get rid of him? Or did she want to? As much as she disliked the man, she wasn't sure she dared risk his safety. She sighed and adjusted the edges of the curtains together. Placing another human being in jeopardy, even a questionable one like D'Amato, went against her nature.

She hugged her arms tight to her chest, knowing she wasn't in any shape to do any more strategizing tonight. Under the quilt she rubbed her arms with her hands. In the few minutes by the window, the tremors had stopped, leaving her legs feeling quite a bit steadier, but the iciness still lingered deep within her joints. It would, she was sure, until her nightmare ended.

"What the hell are you doing?"

Kate stiffened at the militant tone. He'd missed his calling when he'd chosen computer consulting over the Navy as a career. Well, she wasn't a subordinate he could order about. Relaxing her features, she planted a wide smile on her stiff lips and swung around.

"Looking outside," she said, being deliberately obtuse.

The light from the kitchen flooded the living room, allowing her to see every harsh, irritated angle of his face. Her smile almost faltered.

Up to an hour ago no one had ever seen her fall apart,

not even her family. She would be damned if she let it happen again.

Roman walked toward the couch, a coffee mug in his hand, his eyes narrowing as they took in every detail. The dark brown of his irises reminded her of tarnished copper, flecked and ringed with gold she knew turned molten amber with anger or desire.

Now they glinted with suppressed annoyance.

"You look like hell, Doc." Deftly he placed the mug on the end table, and in two strides he was standing in front of her.

She had a good idea what she looked like. She'd caught a glimpse of her image in the rearview mirror of her sports car, right before she deliberately drove it into a ravine. The dark smudges. The pale skin. "Thanks, I wish I could return the compliment," she retorted, not trying to hide her sarcasm.

Almost forty, Roman was in better physical condition than most males half his age. The man oozed masculinity, not that it surprised her. His broad shoulders, well defined under his dark T-shirt, tapered to a lean, narrow waist. A worn pair of blue jeans sheathed his muscular thighs. Her eyes followed the snug fit, setting off a heat in Kate's stomach. Uncomfortable, she forced her gaze back to his face.

He kept his dark, curling hair longer then she remembered, with the ends brushing casually against his shirt collar. The thick mane now showed signs of silver shimmering in its depths, but instead of detracting from his looks, it added to the rugged hardness of his features.

Distracted, she missed the determination reflected in those same features until it was too late. Before she realized his intention, she was off the floor and against his chest.

"*Stupido*," he muttered over her head.

Stupid. *Nobody* called her stupid. She tried to escape his iron grip, but the covers acted as a cocoon, thwarting her attempts. Furious, she resorted to verbal abuse, calling him every vile name she'd learned from her brothers over the years.

"Shut up." The words were clipped, their sting sharp enough to cause her to flinch. "I can't believe you kiss your mother with that mouth." He dumped her onto the couch and stood away, his hands on his hips. "When's the last time you ate?"

She blinked. Ate? When *was* the last time she ate? Long before the phone call from Marcus…

"Never mind." He let out a sigh and shoved the cup toward her, forcing Kate to drop the quilt to grab it. The warmth from the ceramic felt good against her cold hands.

"Drink." He squatted in front of her. "It's canned, but it'll do."

Irritated, she hastily sipped the warm broth, not really tasting it. "I'm—"

"All of it," he commanded, placing his hands over hers before lifting the mug to her lips again. Inwardly seething over his high-handed approach but afraid he would notice her hand trembling beneath his, Kate drank most of the soup in one gulp.

It slid down easily. So easily in fact, she disregarded the vague, bitter taste it left behind on her tongue. Vegetable. She should have guessed. Cain was addicted to vegetable soup.

The warmth filled her stomach, then slowly mushroomed through her body, diminishing some of the hollowness and leaving her strangely comforted. She smothered a yawn.

With a soft grunt of satisfaction, Roman stepped away. He took the iron poker and stoked the fire. "What are you doing here, Doc?" he asked, glancing her way.

She paused, just a fraction. The lift of his eyebrow indicated he saw her hesitation. The man was too perceptive. With a shrug, she managed to say, "Taking a break from work."

Roman regarded her, his gaze burrowing into hers. Seconds ticked away while Kate, refusing to fill the uncomfortable silence, waited with what she hoped was a blank look. He could wait until the next ice age as far as she was concerned. It didn't matter Cain trusted this man. It didn't matter that her parents loved him. She wouldn't. Ever.

"Let's try again." He returned the iron to its stand and leaned against the fireplace brick. "What are you doing here?"

She wasn't fooled. His tone was friendly, even mildly pleasant, but the man was angry. Not seething, but infuriated enough to harden his jaw. Why?

"I'm on vacation," she replied, shocked at how easily the lie slipped over her tongue. "I wanted time to myself and decided to use my brother's cabin. When I called Cain, his secretary said he was out of town indefinitely." She waved a hand in the air. "Some overseas business complication."

"So you decided to come anyway, is that it?"

Kate glared down the censure in his eyes. "That's it."

"What about the attack?"

"What about it?" she returned, covering the defensiveness by setting her mug on the end table and gathering the covers around her. "My nerves are shot from working too hard, and I certainly didn't expect to be scared out of my mind by you creeping around." She eyed him shrewdly. "What's your story?"

"The same, it appears. Cain loaned me the cabin because I wanted to relax and do some fishing, since I'm in between projects." One shoulder rose in a negligent motion. "I thought you were some local kids trying a hand at vandalism."

"Quite a coincidence," she murmured. What were the odds? It went against her nature as a scientist to believe in coincidences.

"That would explain how you opened the locked door so easily. Cain must've given you his key. I took the spare from under the porch." She frowned. "When did you talk to my brother?"

"A few days ago," he said, then changed the subject. "It still doesn't make sense."

A sharp thwack sounded against the outside wall of the cabin and Kate jumped. Cautiously, Roman straightened from the hearth and lifted the curtain. Kate watched in tense silence as he studied the outside, a short prayer whispering through her mind. A second thump sent a small cry of alarm from her lips. "Roman."

He let the curtain drop back into place. "It's just a tree branch, Doc." As he spoke, he started toward her. "But this proves my point. We both know you're more of the moonlit-beach, soft-breeze and Calypso-band type. So why choose the wilderness?"

Because it was the safest place to hide. "Because I wanted a complete change." Uncomfortable with his prodding, she decided to switch the subject. "What makes you an expert on my likes and dislikes?" she quipped. He was right, of course. She would've traded anything to be lounging dreamily on a nice, flat beach right now, free of her nightmare. Trade anything, that is, except millions of innocent lives.

"I know you." Leaning over, he placed one long finger under her chin and tipped her face up toward his. "Better than you know yourself."

There was a time when that was true, right before he'd gotten bored with their relationship. She *was* a different person now, mostly because of him. "Be careful, D'Amato, your arrogance is showing." She jerked her head away and was immediately sorry when the movement made her light-headed. "You might've known me two years ago, but times change and so do people."

"Yes, people change. Just not you."

Another insult. Scottish pride stiffened her spine. "Don't assume that because we were once—" She groped for the word, but her mind fumbled.

"Lovers?" He inserted, his voice dipping huskily.

"Close," she corrected. At one time, the possessive-ness in his voice would have liquefied her insides, now it raised her defenses. She tried to slide toward the end of the couch to put some distance between them, but her body suddenly felt denser than lead, making her move-ments cumbersome.

As he watched her retreat, amusement glinted in his eyes. "'Close' or not, I understand you. And you wouldn't be caught dead in the wild unless you had no other choice."

He sat down beside her, successfully pinning her be-tween him and the arm of the couch. He gathered her close, ignoring the stiff resistance of her body.

"Let me help you."

"Help me?" Awareness rippled through her as the warmth of his body seeped inside the quilt, increasing the lethargic haze that had settled over her. She shook her head to clear her mind, but the dizziness continued to assail her, muddling her thoughts.

"If I did need help—which I don't—you would be the last person I would turn to." She emphasized each word by trying to poke her finger into his chest.

He started to say something, then changed his mind. Abruptly he released his hold and leaned back into the cushions. "I'm not going to rehash the past with you. I admit I could have handled the situation a little better."

"A *little* better?" She bumped him with her elbow and snorted. Not very ladylike, but she didn't care. "Even King Kong treated his woman better."

He responded in Italian, a habit he had when he was angry, but she ignored him. She was fluent in five languages, Italian being one, along with Spanish, Russian and two others she seemed to have forgotten for the moment. Even trying, she couldn't focus on the translation— something about his knowing what's best.

Her eyes burned with fatigue, and she rubbed them with the heels of her hands, releasing a long, audible breath. Lord, dealing with a hardheaded Italian left her even more drained—something she'd considered impossible. She wrestled with the fatigue, trying to maintain her train of thought while her head continued to swim.

"Look, Roman, you can do whatever you want," she said, interrupting his tirade. She tugged the covers up to her chin, not quite ready to let go of their protection, and slumped toward the edge of the cushion. "Just do it away from me." Checking first to see that the quilt sufficiently covered her legs, she struggled to stand up, praying her limbs wouldn't give out.

"I'm going to bed." She looked slowly around the cabin. Where in God's name was it? She shut her eyes briefly trying to concentrate on her surroundings, but the fog grew thicker, enveloping her mind.

"Is something the matter, Doc?" The question sounded distant and muffled in her ears. She tried to face him, but couldn't quite make it. Still, she could feel his gaze on her, intent while he watched her confusion.

"I can't seem to remember where the bedroom is…"

Her voice trailed off as her tongue grew thick, taking up most of her mouth. She tried moving it to the side.

"Upstairs." Quiet amusement laced the word, but she barely noticed because the room blurred. Upstairs. She remembered now. Sleeping up in the loft would have left her vulnerable, that's why she'd chosen to sleep on the sofa. She nodded, and the room began to sway. She grabbed for the couch in an effort to gain her balance, but that was a mistake. Her feet tangled with the quilt, causing her to fall back onto the cushions with a bounce.

Kate heard a soft, masculine chuckle over her head, but her eyelids refused to open so she could glare. He would just have to wait until morning. She could feel her body floating, snug and protected. It had been so long since she'd felt safe that she gave in to the exhaustion and leaned into her warm haven. A deep voice drifted over her, its tone gentle and comforting.

"Sweet dreams, babe."

Chapter Three

Isla de El León (Island of the Lion), Gulf of Mexico.

Poised at the edge of the diving board, the ebony-haired beauty smiled up at Nigel Threader. Her classic features softened with feline pleasure before she sliced cleanly into the kidney-shaped pool. From the private balcony, he watched in fascination as the blue glow of the underwater lights cloaked her dancer's body with ethereal radiance beneath the rippling water. Exquisite.

It was an illusion, of course, but nonetheless magnificent because it hid the imperfections he knew existed. Like a brilliant but flawed diamond.

Pity.

Marina Alexandrov's pedigree as the prima ballerina of the Paris Ballet was above reproach. With Russian royalists for parents, her upbringing was exemplary, her social status assured. She reached the end of the pool, planted both hands on the edge of the tile and hauled herself upward in a cascade of water, her nude body arching gracefully in the night air.

He returned her seductive smile before walking back into his office. Yes, it certainly was a shame. Even her baser needs matched his. They could have shared a future together full of limitless possibilities.

Unfortunately, with her great beauty and ancestry came a lack of intellect. Marina was a woman of average intelligence, an intolerable flaw his employee had overlooked and which Nigel hadn't discovered until it had been far too late. A disappointing situation indeed.

The man paid for his incompetence, of course. What little pleasure Nigel gleaned from the kill was still too small a compensation for the time he'd wasted on seducing Marina.

He frowned and felt the familiar stiffness pull at his right eye. Resisting the urge to touch the cause, he tugged at his sleeves instead, automatically running his fingers over the yellow diamond cufflinks as he entered his office. Naturally he would enjoy her tonight. After all, it would be their last evening together. Loose ends were untidy.

Sitting behind the massive, seventeenth-century ebony baroque desk, he reached for the bottle of cognac that sat at the corner. Nigel glanced at the label, pleased to see that Quamar had brought him his favorite French vintage, and then poured a healthy dose into the snifter.

A red light flashed across the room, drawing his attention to the bank of closed-circuit televisions on the opposite wall. He warmed the cognac, swirling the amber liquid against his palm. Their guest had arrived. Leaning back into his plush throne chair, he studied the silver Jaguar while it followed the winding curves of the sleekly paved drive to the villa.

The estate itself was more than fifty acres of enclosed land overlooking the Gulf of Mexico. The three-story villa, originally designed by a French architect, was built of adobe, mosaic tile and imported marble. A masterpiece of French-Mexican culture. As he watched, the car came to a halt in front of the wrought-iron gates set in the twelve-foot wall surrounding the villa.

He pushed a button under his desk activating the automatic gates and then swung around in the chair to press the intercom on his desk. "Quamar. Our guest has arrived, please escort him to my office."

Several moments later the oak doors opened. Nigel glanced up from his glass when Quamar entered.

"Mr. Hiram Alcott, sir."

Nigel nodded at the huge man who stepped aside to allow their guest through the doorway.

"You may stay, Quamar." The bodyguard bowed but said nothing, closing the doors behind him.

"Has Pheonix reported in yet?" Nigel spared only a flickering glance at Alcott.

"No, sir."

"When she does, tell her I need to see her."

Again Quamar bowed.

Only then did Nigel turn his attention to his guest.

"A pleasure to meet you in person, Mr. Threader." The wiry little man crossed the room, set his briefcase down, then leaned over the desk to offer his hand. The scent of cheap cologne saturated the air. "Nice place you got here." His watery eyes scanned the elegant room before returning to Nigel, hesitating only slightly on the puckering scar tissue that pulled at Nigel's right eye. "Very nice place."

Dirt caked the underside of the man's overgrown fingernails. Ignoring the outstretched hand, Nigel placed his drink on the desk and gestured to the chair beside his guest. "Have a seat."

Alcott cleared his throat, bringing his hand back to smooth his tie, then slid into the high-backed leather chair. "You disappoint me, Mr. Alcott." Nigel rose slowly from behind the desk, well aware of the effect his deliberate movement had on the man across from him. "I've paid you a great deal of money to perform a mediocre task and, so far you've failed to live up to your end of the deal."

Alcott didn't flinch. Instead the man sat back and crossed his legs. The casual pose didn't quite mask the tension in his body.

"Finding a woman on the run isn't a mediocre task, believe me."

Nigel picked up the Buddha from the desk corner. The size of his fist and carved from pure white jade, the statue symbolized enlightenment.

"I *believe* you claimed expediency, accuracy and complete confidentiality. I have yet to witness either of the first two." Nigel observed his guest's face muscles tighten with apprehension at the statement. "And I have my suspicions about the third."

Carefully, he set the statue back in its place, then continued. "But since my time is limited and your tracking skills came highly recommended by our mutual business acquaintances, I've decided to allow you to continue with your efforts. Provided, of course, you start showing me results."

Alcott's expression eased a little as he ran a hand over his lacquered gray hair then wiped his palm on the chair. Nigel's eyes narrowed in disgust.

"I promise you, I won't require much more time, Mr. Threader. A week on the outside. Dr. MacAlister has proven to be an unexpected challenge, but I'm closing in." He shifted his position, his hair leaving a grease mark on the back of the chair. "These things can be tricky, if you know what I mean."

"I see." Nigel kept his expression noncommittal as he leaned against the desk pretending to consider Alcott's excuses.

After a significant pause, he said, "I believe you, Mr. Alcott."

Alcott visibly relaxed. "I appreciate that. After all, we aim to please. But it's nice when a customer understands the difficulties of the job, if you know what I mean."

"Hmm," Nigel murmured while brushing a blond hair from the arm of his silk suit. Over the years, the natives on the island began calling Nigel "El León," or the lion, because of his thick, tawny mane of hair.

"I trust you had a pleasant trip to my island."

"Oh, yeah, slept like a baby through most of the plane ride." The investigator reached into his coat pocket and pulled out a cigarette, obviously taking the change of subject as a good sign. "That Jag you left for me at the airport was one impressive number."

He waved the cigarette in the air as if it were a baton. "It's quite a setup you got here, Mr. Threader." Alcott grinned, revealing a row of tobacco-stained teeth. "Owning your own island and all," he added, before lighting his cigarette.

"Yep, one sweet setup." Leaning back into the chair, Alcott tucked his lighter back into his jacket pocket. "One a man like me could appreciate." He exhaled a stream of smoke that turned into a low whistle when he noticed the Renoir on the wall. "Classy."

Nigel's gaze followed his to the painting. "I'm glad you like it," he said, his smile not quite reaching his eyes. "We aim to please, also."

"Yeah, I'll bet you do." Alcott flicked his ashes off to the side and onto the Persian rug.

Irritation scraped against Nigel's nerves, but he forced the emotion down. "Did you bring the dossier on Dr. MacAlister?"

"Got it right here." Leaving the cigarette dangling from his mouth, Alcott grabbed the case and pulled out a manila folder. "You know at first I couldn't understand why you wanted a profile on the dame. I got the impression you already knew who she was." He slid a color glossy of Kate MacAlister out of the folder and took a long, appreciative look. "Once I got this, I figured it out real quick."

He shoved the picture into Nigel's hand. "Now, there's a good-looking broad. It doesn't hurt that her daddy's an international tycoon. Or that he manufactures the best damn scotch known to mankind. Money, brains, looks and an unlimited supply of booze. Wouldn't mind getting to know her better myself. If you know what I mean."

Nigel studied the photograph, ignoring Alcott's suggestive laugh. No matter how abhorrent the man appeared, as an investigator he did excellent work. The woman in the picture was dressed in a light T-shirt and jeans but the casualness of the dress didn't detract from her natural beauty. A perfect oval face, the elegantly defined nose complemented her classically high cheekbones. Her black hair, tied back into a long, silken tail, accented her flawless skin. Nigel resisted the urge to run his finger over the image. Her pale gray eyes flashed brightly with amused intelligence, taunting him, daring him, with an impudence reflected in the generous curve of her mouth and delicate arch of her eyebrows.

Oh, yes, even the great Michelangelo himself would've been in awe.

"Interesting." He maintained a noncommittal coolness as he placed the folder onto the desk, preferring to peruse the rest at his leisure where he could analyze this new development alone.

After taking a linen handkerchief from his pants pocket,

he wiped his hands. "Now about your timetable, Mr. Alcott. More than twenty-four hours is unacceptable." He meticulously folded the material and tossed it into the wastebasket.

The other man blustered. "Look here, Mr. Threader. I thought we had an agreement. It's like I told you. I'm close, but a job this sensitive takes time."

Nigel sighed and nodded to Quamar, who immediately came over and grabbed Alcott from behind, pinning him to the chair with one arm braced against the little man's throat. The bodyguard ignored Alcott's shriek of surprise and slammed the man's left arm down on the desk, exposing his palm. The investigator struggled briefly but was no match for the well-muscled giant.

"What the hell is going on?" Alcott's eyes widened in alarm, his face etched in desperation. "Listen, we can discuss this like civilized gentlemen. There's no need to get heavy-handed."

Nigel responded in a bored voice. "You are an ill-mannered cretin, Mr. Alcott. Please do not insult my intelligence by trying to convince me otherwise."

Without waiting for a response, he walked behind the desk, opened the top drawer and pulled out a pair of surgical gloves.

Alcott watched, his face reflecting a numb horror as Nigel snapped on the gloves. The sound ricocheted through the room. Out of sheer desperation, the small man fought against his captor. "What the hell is this? You can't do this."

"This, Mr. Alcott is a warning." His dark blue eyes turned arctic. "And make no mistake—I do as I please. I make it a point never to deal personally with brutish, ignorant people such as yourself." Nigel withdrew a cigar from the rosewood humidor beside the desk and rolled it between his fingers. It was his own personal blend, hand-made on his plantation in Cuba. "But time and circum-stances have forced otherwise." He picked up the guillotine cigar cutter lying beside the humidor. Its silver blades flashed in the light.

Alcott whimpered.

"I believe you are aware of my reputation," Nigel said while he placed the end of the cigar into the guillotine cir-cle and squeezed. The twin blades sliced together, deftly cutting the tip of the cigar off.

He studied the decapitated end for a moment, pleased with the clean edge. "You have until midnight tomorrow to locate her and notify me." His voice took on a hard edge. "Or I will kill you." He placed the cigar on the desk beside him. "I consider myself a fair man. Moreover, to prove it, I will loan you some of my staff to help with the search. Remember, Mr. Alcott, expediency, accuracy and confidentiality." Nigel leaned forward and lowered his voice to a conspiratorial whisper. "After all, we would not want to put a permanent black mark on your reputation, would we?" Leaning back, he tossed the cutting instrument in his hand, like a child would a coin. "If you know what I mean."

The sweat poured off Alcott's face soaking the grimy, white collar of his shirt while his gaze fixated on the blade in Nigel's hands.

Nigel glanced at Quamar and nodded toward the desk. The bodyguard grunted in approval before he grabbed Al-cott's neck from behind and slammed his face onto the desktop, leaving it pinned there.

Nigel stood to the side, a small, inhuman smile creas-ing his lips. "Think of it this way, Mr. Alcott," he said softly as he inserted the pinkie into the cutter. "You might be leaving here with a whole new perspective on the phrase 'Close but no cigar,' but at least you'll be leaving." Nigel squeezed the cutter. "If you know what I mean."

THE UNMISTAKABLE HUM of helicopter blades woke Roman. The sound, out of place in the quiet mountain wilderness, had him off the couch. Within seconds he grabbed a pair of binoculars from the peg beside the back door, his senses instantly alert. Damn. Whoever it was, was circling low and easy. After unstrapping the 9 mm Heckler & Koch from his ankle, he stepped barefoot onto the porch, staying hidden in the midmorning shadows of the eave.

A slight turn of the lens's dial placed the helicopter in focus. It was a civilian bird, brand-new with no call numbers and definitely high tech with its sleek lines and stealth capabilities. Roman's grip tightened reflexively around the binoculars as he released a soft whistle between his teeth. Big bucks.

The helicopter banked left, hovering for a split second before it increased its speed and headed west. Through the lenses, he caught a glimpse of two men dressed in outdoor gear, viewing the area through their own scopes before the helicopter disappeared beyond the farthest ridge.

Helicopters were a common enough sight in the Rockies, but not one hovering so close to the treetops. Since the cabin was located in prime terrain for hiking and rappelling, a logical explanation could be that these boys were outdoor enthusiasts with more money than brains, scouting the area for new trails.

Roman's lips twisted back in a feral grin. Sure, and he'd just bought some swampland in Florida to start a Putt-Putt business.

It was more likely Threader's people were mapping the

cabins in the area for a ground-level search. Not hard to do when the pilot doesn't file a flight plan.

He stuck his head through the doorway, listening for any movement upstairs. Silence greeted him, which meant the doc was still asleep, undisturbed by the helicopter.

Over ten hours now. The mild sedative he'd slipped into her soup the night before had done its job.

He ignored the twinge of guilt over drugging her. It had been necessary. Obviously, Kate had been living on raw nerves for quite a while. The paleness in her face, the hunted look in her eyes, but most of all the fact she'd attacked him instead of running, told him that she wasn't thinking straight.

At first he'd been enraged, knowing how foolish it was for her to stand and fight anyone Threader sent. Damn it, she knew better. The thought that he might have been one of Threader's thugs and what they could have done to her—what they could still do to her if they found her—scared the hell out of him. He'd regretted it almost immediately, though, when his fear had turned to anger and caused what little control she had left to snap.

Suddenly feeling a need to check on her, Roman tucked the gun into the waistband of his jeans, its coolness reassuring against his naked back, then took the loft steps two at a time, stopping short at the top.

The bedroom was dim in the midmorning light. Faint streaks of sunlight sliced through the partially open slats of the wooden blinds. Kate lay sideways on the rustic pine bed. The tartan flannel sheet lay tangled across her chest while Cain's faded football jersey rode high around her rib cage, leaving her stomach and legs exposed. The comforter he had wrapped snugly around her the night before lay in a heap at the side of the bed. Even the drug-induced sleep couldn't stop her habit of wreaking havoc on the bed linen during the night. Sharing space with the doc was like going ten rounds with a steroid-enhanced octopus.

He smiled at the memory.

Assured she would sleep a few more hours, he started to turn away then caught sight of a wisp of peach lace. His mouth went dry.

The fluff of underwear, while accenting her slim hips and long, supple thighs, did nothing to protect her from his gaze. Roman's throat tightened. He'd forgotten her fondness for sexy lingerie.

His conscience nudged him to turn away, but he ignored it. In the diffused light her skin reminded him of some fresh cream he'd gotten once from a Slavic farmer, warm and rich with the texture of liquid velvet. He feasted like a starving man.

Then he swallowed, willing his glands to work again while he devoured her with his eyes. They traveled down her sleek, smooth legs, stopping briefly on the gentle curves of her calves, before finally resting on her toes—each nail painted a deep, decadent red.

He held his body tense, anticipating the heavy blow of desire. And it came—like a wrecking ball catching him in the solar plexus.

She muttered something, drawing his attention to her face. Her brows furrowed, then smoothed, but she didn't open her eyes.

Her midnight hair fell in shimmering waves around her face, mussed by the pillow. Her ivory complexion had an elusive pink hue, like the flush of sunset on snow. She looked warm and feminine and so damn inviting he wanted to submerge himself in her softness and not come out, ever.

Years of need and longing twined tightly within him,

forcing him to fight his urges. He remembered the way she felt in his arms, the gentleness of her touch, her sweet shyness that always gave way to an even sweeter surrender. He could still feel her lying in his arms that last night, her cheek resting against his heart when she whispered she loved him.

Swearing under his breath, he jerked around and went downstairs. His desire for her was as strong as ever.

He slipped out the front door, too agitated to stay within the confines of the cabin. He was here to do a job, damn it. The situation was complicated enough without allowing his emotions to overrule his mind.

He wrenched his gun from his waistband and circled the cabin, moving silently through the aspen and pine.

Cain, never one to leave anything to chance, had designed his little vacation getaway out of native rock, using little pine, making the structure impervious to most guns and nearly impossible for anyone to burn down.

The rear of the cabin butted up to shale, with two propane tanks that provided the fuel for heat off to one side. The rock wasn't impassable, but if someone rappelled from the top of the mountain, it would be damn difficult to remain undetected.

Roman patrolled the perimeter twice, assuring himself they weren't under surveillance. Not because he sensed anything unusual—the normal sounds of the forest had already told him they were safe—but because he wasn't ready to face what waited for him inside.

Last, he checked the rented SUV, parked a few yards away. It, too, rested undisturbed and well hidden beneath the thicket of trees.

After sliding his gun back into his back waistband, Roman sat down on the front porch steps and lit a cigarette.

He glanced briefly at his lighter. To the untrained eye, it looked like an ordinary disposable lighter. To Roman the homing device hidden in the plastic cylinder was a lifeline connecting him to the one person who might be able to liberate them if the situation became too explosive. Cain.

Roman tucked the lighter into his pocket. They would be safer lying low in the cabin for the day before he moved Kate. If he was right about that helicopter, Threader's men would hit town late tomorrow. He could get Kate out and keep her relatively safe before the search reached the cabin.

That would also give him a chance to break down her defenses and gain her trust.

Last night hadn't been the time to tell her the true reason for his appearance. She'd been in no condition to handle any more shocks to her system, and finding out her ex-lover was a government operative ranked high on the emotional Richter scale.

Even as the lesser of two evils, lying to her had been a calculated risk, one that could quite easily blow up in his face.

Unless he controlled the explosion.

Roman leaned back against the pine railing, occasionally taking a drag on his cigarette.

With Kate it might work.

She had a hidden sensitive side, but she definitely possessed her father's volatile temper, too. Making her angry was easy, but could he convince her to turn that anger toward Threader long enough for her to forget about their past and to trust him? Long enough for him to keep her alive?

"*D'Amato!*"

Chapter Four

The shriek of rage came from inside. Its intensity rocked the porch rafters, causing Roman to flinch. It had taken her less time than he thought to work through the events from the previous night. His lips twitched with amusement. He should've known.

He field-stripped the cigarette, then stretched, rolling his shoulders to ease the tension in his neck just as another scream, this one sounding more like a screech, rent the air. He stepped inside.

She stormed down the stairs barefoot and wearing only a jersey. A Scottish warrior princess. Regal. Graceful. Lethal.

"Hungry, Doc?" he asked smoothly, suffering her glare with equanimity before entering the kitchen.

A search of the cupboards the night before had revealed filter packets containing coffee and some canned corned-beef hash. He started the coffee first, knowing it would be his greatest ally.

"You drugged me." The accusation jabbed at him from the doorway behind.

"Yes, I did," he answered, deliberately keeping his

voice calm. "Want some breakfast?" Opening the can of hash, he dumped the contents into the sizzling frying pan.

He heard the sharp intake, felt the pause as she absorbed the shock of his admission.

"You, you—"

The anger was back. Good. Roman shut off the burner and counted to two before turning around to face her.

She clenched her fists to her sides, but he knew it was only because he wasn't close enough for her to take a swing.

"You deceitful, two-faced…" Her eyes blinked with unshed tears. "Jerk."

Christ, he hated tears. He leaned his hip against the counter and crossed his arms. "Tell me, is that a scientific fact or just your everyday off-the-cuff hypothesis?"

"Oh, it's fact, all right." Her gray eyes turned into finely etched diamonds of white fire at his tone, evaporating the tears. "You actually thought I wouldn't figure it out?" She spat out the words before her gaze skimmed the counters.

"I wouldn't have cleared the kitchen of all possible projectiles last night if I'd thought that. So you might as well stop looking."

She glared at him, her hostility palpable.

Kate hadn't realized she'd been searching for something to throw until he'd pointed it out, but the idea held tremendous appeal. If she had a knife right now, she would gladly aim for his heart.

She'd been on overdrive since she'd awakened with the strange feeling of being watched nagging at her subconscious. She'd lain there for a while, letting an unfamiliar dullness clear from her mind. Almost immediately the events of the past twenty-four hours came rushing back. The frantic call from Marcus. The destruction of her work

Bodyguard Rescue

and her desperate flight to the safest place she knew. The difficult hike to the cabin after ditching her car.

The fear. The fatigue.

Roman's unexpected arrival.

Quickly, the facts formed into a well-developed theory. The slurred speech. The dizziness. The bitter-tasting soup. Stunned, all she could do was lie there. Roman was a lowlife, but he would never sink that far into the bowels of deceit.

But he had. He'd just admitted it, and the hurt made her strike back.

"Don't tell me you have to drug your women now." Giving up on the weapon search, she propped one shoulder against the doorjamb, her body stiff, her voice dripping with acid.

The muscle in his jaw flickered, telling her she'd scored a hit. But he didn't respond to the barb. Too bad.

"Was it good for you?" she taunted, not willing to let it go. She watched with satisfaction as his eyes burned amber and his body grew tense. "I mean, it was basically the same for me," she continued, ignoring the warning signals. "Forgettable."

He gave her a long look that showed how close he was to unleashing his anger, but his voice remained silky smooth, the sound chilling her to her marrow. "Do you want me to prove you're lying?"

She managed to keep the fury and humiliation out of her voice, just, "What I want is for you to tell me why you found it necessary to drug me." Her balled fist hit the counter.

He shrugged with indifference, somehow leaving Kate with a vague feeling it was partially feigned. "You needed it. I told you last night you looked like hell."

"Your concern for me is touching, but it's coming just a tad too late for me to believe it's sincere."

"It's sincere," he said, the words low and even.

For a moment she almost believed him. Then suddenly he relaxed with an easy smile and turned his attention back to cooking the food.

Kate let the air out of her lungs with a huff. "The last time I checked my driver's license, I was a grown woman, D'Amato. I can take care of myself."

He laughed. "Why don't you pour us some brew?"

"Why don't you go straight to——"

The sputtering of the coffee machine cut off her retort. For the first time she smelled the tantalizing aroma coming from the far corner. Her throat constricted.

And he knew it. Without looking up from the stove, he said, "Go on. Your brother stocked the kind you both like. Brazilian."

Addiction won over indignation. Grudgingly, Kate reached into the cupboard above the coffeemaker for a mug, and then poured coffee to the rim.

He could damn well get his own.

Taking a sip, she released a sigh of unadulterated pleasure.

Perfect.

"I'm surprised you didn't make me drink first." Startled, she glanced up to find him watching her, his eyebrows raised in a mockingly polite question.

She'd always hated it when he gave her that superior, all-knowing look. "The thought crossed my mind," she bluffed, irritated because the thought *hadn't* crossed her mind. "But even you wouldn't stoop so low."

"So you're beginning to believe that I did it for your own good?" He reached around her to grab another mug from the cupboard, brushing against her shoulder and effectively locking her between his arms. Kate, startled by the contact, turned, inadvertently placing her face inches away from his granitelike chest. She could smell his scent, feel the warmth of his body.

There was a jagged, raised scar just under his right shoulder. She focused on that, trying to clear her head. From a rock-climbing accident, he'd told her once. The whiteness of the scar stood out against the otherwise tanned skin of his chest. A chest covered with a thick pelt of crisp, sable hair. Hair tapered into a thin line, down his flat, muscled stomach, disappearing into the waistband of his jeans.

She couldn't stop herself from inhaling deeply.

"Drop something, babe?"

Jolted out of her trance, she jerked her head up in confusion, catching his chin.

His grunt of pain had her scooting around him and resuming her place in the doorway, somehow feeling safer with the exit at her back.

"Am I supposed to believe that you carry sedatives around with you now?" She sipped her coffee in an effort to stabilize her system with caffeine. "I seem to remember the only substances you allowed in your body, Roman, were some of my dad's good scotch and the occasional nicotine fix." She quirked her eyebrow. "It's hard to accept that you've graduated to taking narcotics." Kate flashed back to the time he'd been overseas on business and suffered a couple of cracked ribs in a traffic accident. He'd endured days of the excruciating pain rather than take a drug for relief.

"I still don't. Doctor gave me a prescription since I've been having some trouble sleeping. I filled it in a moment of weakness, thinking I might need them. When I saw the shape you were in, I snagged them from my sport bag in the car where I'd tossed them."

She didn't believe him. To her knowledge he never allowed himself a moment of weakness. From the time Cain had introduced them, Roman had been suave, intelligent, funny and arrogantly attractive but never, ever weak.

His gaze clinically skimmed the length of her body. "They seemed to have done the trick."

She bristled over the perusal, before the rest of his previous comment caught her attention. Roman had always moved like a cat, swiftly and silently. A trait that had intrigued her when they'd first met and unsettled her as time went on. Still, it was hard to believe he'd walked out the door and returned unnoticed. "I didn't see you go outside last night."

He swallowed some coffee, disregarding the handle and grasping the ceramic in his fist. "Doc, the state you were in last night, a nuclear explosion would've gotten past you," he said with surprising gentleness.

So much gentleness that his next question almost caught her unaware.

"How often are you having panic attacks?"

Every time I'm more than ten feet above the ground and looking straight down. "That was my first one." She placed her mug on the counter and crossed behind him to stir the breakfast. The first one she'd ever experienced not related to her acrophobia.

Again he sent her a disbelieving look. She pretended not to see it and nodded toward the food. "It's done if you want to grab some plates."

Instead Roman grabbed her hand and gently twisted her around. He watched in fascination while Kate studied their hands twined together, a silk curtain of hair covered her face, making it impossible for him to read her expression. He found himself studying their hands, also—his firm and brown, hers softer and pale with their strength masked by the slight bone structure.

As if sensing his thoughts, she looked up at him. He caught the full force of her inner turmoil. Something in her eyes softened, then deepened, revealing a flicker of her vulnerability hidden beneath.

A sharp stab of guilt made him drop her hand as if it held a grenade. She stiffened briefly over the abruptness of the move but recovered swiftly and swung back to the stove.

Roman swore.

"It's obvious you didn't bargain on me when you decided to use Cain's cabin." Her tone brought him up short. "I can't help that, it's important I stay here for a while." Kate snagged the plates and served up breakfast, quietly, efficiently. "I have to go to town. Since I'll be gone for a few hours, it should give you time to relax a little before leaving." She handed him his plate.

Grimly, Roman accepted the food. "Even if I wanted to go, I wouldn't leave you up here stranded." Not bothering to explain how he knew, he pointed out her biggest problem. "How do you expect to get into town when you don't have a car?"

She flushed, obviously ill at ease. "I have a car." Her voice faltered. "I...I had a little trouble on the way up from New Mexico and left it at a garage in town to be checked." She took a swallow of food. "I'll walk into town."

Another lie. While she'd been sleeping the night before, he'd followed her tracks until he'd found the ditched black sports car, surprised that she'd done a reasonably good job at camouflaging the trail and the car.

He'd improved it.

"It's at least a three-mile hike." The statement was hard and brooked no argument. "I'll drive you."

He was right, of course. It would be ridiculous for her to hike all that way. Damn it. If she had a choice, she wouldn't be making the trip, but the cabin didn't have a telephone and her cell phone was useless in the mountains. There was no way to contact Cain without going to town.

Frustration fueled her anger. If only Roman had made his offer a suggestion and not an order, she might not have lost her temper. But he hadn't.

Kate slammed the plate onto the counter. "I got here by walking," she snapped. "I can damned well get myself down again the same way."

"You walked…" His eyes narrowed. Her attitude about hiking a second time set him off. "How long did it take you—two, three hours?" In his rage, he switched to Italian. "Do you realize how dangerous that was? How utterly stupid it was? What would you have done if you'd been injured or attacked?"

Kate advanced, met him toe-to-toe. "Since you arrived, you've been insulting my intelligence by pretending you care." Her eyes became shards of ice. "Or just simply insulting my intelligence." Brandishing the fork like a weapon, she waved it in front of his face. "And I've had it. I want you to leave. You did it once before without a backward glance. I'll bet your technique isn't so rusty that you couldn't do it again." She raised herself up on her toes, almost putting them nose-to-nose. "And I promise not to look."

"You've got a smart mouth, Doc," he snarled thickly, this time in English. Tossing his plate next to hers, he caught her wrist, took the utensil and threw it against the wall. He captured her flying fist with ease, before he pinned both arms behind her, pulling her body against him, hip to chest. "Let's find another use for it."

His mouth, hard and hot, consumed hers, causing her to gasp in surprise or anger. Roman didn't care which. It was too late to stop, he'd tasted the spicy sweetness of her and his craving erupted into a rampage of hunger. He swallowed the gasp, slanting his mouth over hers, his tongue rough and insistent as he plundered the forbidden.

She quivered, flexed and then caved under the onslaught, her body going pliant while her teeth parted, allowing the unrelenting probing of his tongue. He growled and dove into the recesses of her mouth, stroking, petting—taking.

"Roman." Kate tore her mouth away, her breath coming in pants. He slid his hands up under the loose sleeves to her shoulders, using the callused pads of his thumbs to soothe her.

"I'm here," he murmured against the swollen curve of her lips. Then he skimmed his mouth down her jaw and explored the soft skin below her ear, savoring its sweetness. "And here." Following the arch of her neck, he opened his mouth, tasting, suckling until he reached the base of her throat where he nibbled gently at its delicate hollow. "And here."

She moaned, sending a vibration humming against his tongue before it shot down his body and exploded in his groin. "Feel for yourself," he demanded, pleaded.

Obeying, she put her palms against his chest, flexing them in the thick hair, then curling her fingers against his heated skin and allowing her nails to scrape lightly over his nipples.

He shuddered and gathered her closer, his own painful groan mingling with hers at the contact of her thighs between his. He could feel the swell of her breasts beneath the slickness of the jersey. *"No fermata, mi amore,"* he rasped against her ear, his voice gravelly with restraint as he begged her not to stop. "I want it all."

She stiffened against him, and he knew at once that her anger had resurfaced. She shoved herself away, staggering to the other side of the kitchen, her eyes shooting daggers from a face flushed with desire. "I'm not *your love.*" Her chest heaved with emotion. "And I won't be a diversion."

Roman gripped the counter on either side of his hips, taking several unsteady breaths to gain control. Better that than grabbing her to finish what they'd just started.

She hugged her arms over her chest, a self-protective move that sliced through him. Looking up at the ceiling, he gritted his teeth and ignored the pressure between his legs. Oh, he wanted her. He also wanted her to be loved unconditionally, to have children, to grow old with someone. Everything he couldn't give her. "Doc, I had no right—"

"I agree," she interrupted, her voice cool, the control back in place. "You don't. Once, I gave you the right, but you handed it back." Her chin tilted with an academic arrogance. "No, you did worse. You tossed it aside on your way out the door. I won't give you the opportunity to do it again."

She swung away. When she reached the bottom step to the loft, she stopped, not bothering to face him, her spine rigid, her hand curled tightly around the railing. "It was ridiculous of me to turn you down earlier. I'm not going to make excuses for my behavior, but I do apologize. If the offer for the ride is still open, I accept." She started up the stairs. "But don't expect me to thank you."

His gaze followed her until the bathroom door closed with a quiet emphasis. He rubbed his hand over his chest, trying to ease the tightness. So much for the trusting approach.

KATE STEPPED from the shower, wincing when the cool air stung her heated skin. How could her emotions have gotten out of control so quickly?

She had scrubbed her lips with trembling fingers, washing away the last of his taste as she faced the harsh truth—she was no more immune to Roman now than she had been two years ago.

The humiliation swarmed over her, making her skin crawl. In spite of their past—the animosity she felt—Roman could still arouse her passion to a fever pitch, defying all logic.

It was difficult to believe that his kiss had been little more than a means to punish her. Then their lips met and she simply hadn't been prepared for the onslaught of emotion that emerged.

If her instincts were right, neither had he.

With quick, jerky movements, she dried her body with a bath sheet, rubbing hard to erase the imprint of him from her skin.

If she hadn't felt so safe and protected, she wouldn't have given in to the raw passion that surged to the surface. But when his strong arms surrounded her and she felt the steady, reassuring rhythm of his heartbeat against hers, she'd folded into him.

Again.

Despite it all, she had to admit she was terribly relieved he'd shown up yesterday when he did. His presence made her feel less vulnerable, more secure.

Common sense told her the safest option would be to stay here with Roman until she could contact Cain. Still, could she trust Roman? And did she have the right to put his life in jeopardy? From what Marcus had told her on the phone, this Nigel Threader was a dangerous man. A man who wouldn't hesitate to kill to get what he wanted.

Realistically, having an able-bodied male around gave the formula more protection. Roman was resourceful, intelligent and too chivalrous to turn away from a damsel in distress—or an ex-lover in distress, for that matter.

He was also connected. Most of Roman's jobs were government contracts. It was very possible he would know someone who could be trusted enough to help her out of this situation.

Kate wrapped the thick bath sheet around her, anchoring it with a knot between her breasts and stepped onto the earth-toned tile.

A quick search in the bathroom cabinet produced a half-used tube of toothpaste. Smiling at her small discovery, she finger-scrubbed her teeth while studying her reflection in the mirror.

Grudgingly she admitted the drugged sleep had done its job. She looked much better than she had the day before. The dark smudges under her eyes were almost transparent against her skin. But the signs of stress remained, visible in the tightness around her mouth and the pinched area between her brows.

It wasn't until she searched her eyes, finding the terror lurking in the depths of her pupils, that Kate made her decision. "You can't trust him with your love," she said to her reflection. "It will be up to you to keep your heart safe."

Tapping the mirror for emphasis, she ignored the smears of paste left on the glass. "But right now you've only one option if you want to save the world, and he's downstairs."

Five minutes later Kate pitched her beige skirt and matching vest into the bathroom wastebasket. The clothes were grimy, and too battered from her trudge up the mountain to be of any use. After a few minutes of scrounging in the bedroom closet, her search revealed only one other wardrobe choice—her brother's frayed Naval Academy T-shirt, a pair of his sweats that had been cut off above the knee and an old, shriveled pair of ladies' canvas shoes, a half size too big.

She tied the drawstring of the sweats tightly around her waist, rolled the cuffs, then donned the T-shirt and shoes. Her ponytail, tied with some extra string from her shorts, swished damply against her back as she descended the stairs.

After steadying herself, she noticed the unusual silence that filled the room. Uneasily she scanned the cabin.

"Roman?"

No answer. The nape of her neck prickled and her unease took a quantum leap.

"Damn it, Roman where are you?" she called, keeping her voice pitched low before heading for the kitchen. Empty.

Backtracking into the living room, she took a deep breath, trying to calm her nervousness. He wouldn't leave without letting her know, she was certain. Which meant he had to be outside.

She scolded herself for overreacting and reached for the doorknob, only to smile at her silliness when the creak of the porch steps echoed through the door. Certain it was Roman, she threw it open in relief. "You had me worried."

But it wasn't Roman. Fear, stark and vivid, swept through her.

"Dr. Katherine MacAlister?"

Two men, modestly suited, stood in the doorway, both looking ridiculously out of place on the cabin porch as they presented their badges and identification. Central Intelligence Agency.

Kate remembered to breathe.

The older of the two, a tall man with trim brown hair, removed his mirrored sunglasses. His blue eyes flashed with impatience. An impatience, Kate noticed, not revealed in the politeness of his next statement.

"I'm Carl Dempsey." He nodded toward the whipcord-thin man to his side, and the faint scent of peppermint drifted toward Kate. "This is my associate, Robert Jackson. May we talk with you, Doctor?"

She didn't know what she was expecting, but calm civility wasn't it. "I'm not sure…" Kate grappled for an answer while her mind worked overtime. Where was Roman? Her gaze quickly swept the area behind the two agents, but he didn't appear. A bead of sweat tickled her shoulder blade.

"We can understand your hesitancy, ma'am, but we have reason to believe your life may be in danger." Jackson spoke, his voice liberally laced with a warm, Southern accent that matched his blond, boyish features. "Would it help to know we were sent by your brother Cain?"

She was stunned. "Cain?" Was it possible he'd found out about her situation and sent help? Like Roman, Cain's business put him in a position of making friends with high government officials. He could've learned about her disappearance.

She had tightened her grip on the door, ready to slam it shut, but now she hesitated. If they were working for Threader, they wouldn't be announcing themselves, would they?

For the hundredth time, Kate wished she had her mother's talent for reading people at a glance. Unfortunately, Ian was the only one of the siblings that seemed to have inherited that particular trait.

Kate stared into Jackson's deep, brown eyes searching

for the truth, but when he met her gaze, she saw only sincerity in their depths.

"May we come in?" he asked again, quietly this time. Sincerity and sympathy.

Nodding, Kate loosened her grasp on the door and stepped back, allowing both men into the living room.

"I'm sorry about my hesitancy, gentlemen, but I have to admit this is a little too cloak-and-dagger for me." The click of the door's automatic lock triggered a low hum of disquiet along her spine. Kate carefully positioned herself between the agents and the door.

"We apologize for that, ma'am," Jackson said, his voice showing respectful, Southern decorum. He moved to the center of the living room, taking everything in with a brief glance before he turned to face her.

"Just a minute ago," he observed, "when you answered the door, it sounded as if you were expecting someone. Do you mind if I ask who it was?"

The hum picked up its tempo.

"My brother," she responded immediately, knowing Roman was her only protection if these men were here to harm her.

"You've been in touch with him then?"

"No," Kate struggled for an explanation. "I left word for him to meet me here if his schedule permitted." She tossed her head back before pinning him with her best imitation of her father's business persona. "Why?"

"As we said, your life is in danger, Doctor," Dempsey interjected and walked to the window. He eased the curtain open, addressing his next statement to the glass. "We're here to protect you." His voice, absolutely emotionless, chilled her.

"Your brother has reason to fear that a mutual friend of yours, a Mr. Roman D'Amato, is not what he seems."

Dempsey paused for a moment while he continued looking outside. "He was right." He let go of the curtain, leaving it open and swung around to her. "But then I've never known Cain not to be right when it came to situations like this."

Slowly his gaze circled the room, his eyes searching, the look unreadable when it rested briefly on her before continuing. Kate gripped her elbows in an effort to stifle the urge to make him stop.

He did, finally, in front of the fireplace. "You know, Cain's invited me up here on several occasions, but I never could seem to make the time." He picked up the framed picture of her parents from the mantel. It had been taken the previous year, on their fortieth anniversary. "I wish the circumstances surrounding my first visit could be different."

"You know my brother personally?" She raised her eyebrow, deliberately allowing some uncertainty to show in her face.

"Over five years now," he responded absently, continuing to study the picture. "Handsome couple, your parents." He smiled before putting it back, an easy good-ol'-boy smile that set Kate's teeth on edge. "I haven't had a chance to meet them yet."

It was obvious Dempsey wanted her to believe that Cain and he were friends. Cain had many acquaintances but few friends. Her brother never allowed anyone, with the exception of family, into his inner sanctum of trust. As far as she knew, his only close friend was Roman.

As if sensing her suspicion, Dempsey continued. "We met when he was working on a security job for the Agency. Hit it off right from the start. He called me when he started to worry."

"I don't understand," she said, furrowing her brow in feigned confusion. "Why is Cain worried about me?"

The men shared a subtle look before Jackson took over the conversation. Kate saw the pass, tough agent to sensitive agent, but chose to ignore it for now.

"Your brother told us about your history with Roman D'Amato, so this might be difficult to accept." He hesitated, clearly uncomfortable. "Several weeks ago Cain started becoming suspicious of D'Amato's business activities. At your brother's request, we did a little digging. It turns out that the man you know as Roman D'Amato is a man the Agency's been tracking for a few years now. He calls himself Cerberus."

He pulled out a small notebook from inside his jacket and flipped to a middle page. "We also believe he operates under the aliases of Xavier Roman, René Arneau and Ramon Cordova. He's wanted by our government, and several others, for selling illegal contraband to foreign countries." After closing the notebook with a snap, he placed it back into his pocket. "He's considered unstable and extremely dangerous."

The hum rushed through her ears and the floor started to give way under Kate's feet. She dug her nails into the backs of her arms to offset the shock.

"Contraband? Do you mean drugs?" This time she didn't have to fake her confusion.

Her question had been directed to Jackson, but it was Dempsey who answered, his voice grave. "Weapons mostly. Some drugs."

She was suddenly cold, as if her blood had stopped pumping. Roman? An arms dealer?

"Do you need to sit down?" Jackson asked the question, his concern apparent.

Yes, her mind screamed, but Kate shook her head, not trusting herself to speak yet.

They were lying. They had to be. Roman wouldn't hurt her. Or would he? Logic conceded that his appearance could've been more than a coincidence, and his concern for her an act. Her heart contracted painfully against her mind's reasoning.

What if they *were* telling the truth?

"Dr. MacAlister," Dempsey prodded. "Besides being an expert on weapons and demolition, Cerberus has extensive knowledge in martial arts, communications and cyber-intelligence." He paused, his gaze assessing. "The man is a cold-blooded killer. He's taken credit for twenty-three deaths—and those are just the ones the Agency is aware of."

Kate put her shaking hands to her temples and pressed hard, struggling to calm her rioting thoughts. She remembered the loving touch of Roman's hands when they'd first made love and he'd realized it was her first time ever. The reverent way he'd held her afterward while she cried softly, overwhelmed by the sweet beauty of the experience. No matter how hard she tried, she couldn't match that image with the monster they described.

Jackson continued, his attitude more compassionate than his partner's. "After your disappearance from Las Mesas, Cain suspected you might come here and contacted us again. He asked that we keep you safe until his return later tonight." The younger agent rubbed his forehead, obviously searching for the right words. "We know this is hard for you to believe, but the only way we can prove our story is to put you in contact with your brother once we reach our office." His eyes gentled with persuasion. "If you could trust us until then, Cain will verify everything."

Her brother. If what they said was true, Cain would be devastated over Roman's betrayal. And her parents. They would be heartbroken. Her mother especially.

Alarms went off in Kate's head. Big foghorn alarms that nearly blew the top off her skull. Her mother. If what these men were saying *were* true, Christel MacAlister would've never trusted Roman all these years. She would've seen through his ruse almost immediately.

Dempsey broke into her racing thoughts. "We don't want to make you any more afraid than you already are, Doctor, but time is of the utmost importance." The two men shared another unspoken message. Kate's stomach clenched at the deception she now saw lurking beneath their glances. "We believe D'Amato is searching for you as we speak."

An icy fear twisted around her spine. She might not trust her own instincts anymore when it came to Roman, but she trusted her mother's. The man might stink at relationships, but that didn't necessarily make him a psychotic murderer—just a jerk.

"Why?" she asked, just managing to keep the tremor out of her voice. "What would an arms dealer want with me?"

The man hesitated, clearly not sure how to proceed. Jackson came to his partner's rescue. This time his soft accent rang fraudulent in her ears. "Look, Doctor, we are going to be totally upfront with you. We know about your research. We know you destroyed it before you left the laboratory. We also know that Marcus Boyd called you right before your disappearance." He paused, his dark eyes suddenly intent. "But what *you* don't know is someone killed Boyd the night you disappeared."

Sheer willpower kept Kate standing. That and the fact she was sure these two men were somehow involved with her colleague's death. She closed her eyes for a moment, hoping to blot out the searing pain that engulfed her chest. Another lie? Possible, but she doubted it. Marcus had told her himself that he'd be lucky to live through the night. All because he'd underestimated the power of this Threader person.

Poor Marcus. He hadn't deserved to die for his greed. Especially when he'd ultimately realized his mistake and had warned her.

"You think…" Her throat was so dry that speaking was painful. If these were Threader's men, why did they want Roman? Unless Roman worked for the government. The fine hair on Kate's neck prickled. Yes, she could see Roman as an agent.

So why didn't Jackson and Dempsey take her, now that they'd found her? It didn't make sense.

She cleared her throat and started again. "You think Roman killed Marcus?" Somehow she needed to keep them talking until she could figure out a way to escape and warn Roman.

"Yes," Jackson answered. "And so does your brother. When Cain's secretary notified him of your phone call, he immediately thought of the cabin."

Dempsey took over, his impatience finally breaking through his calm facade. "Look, Doctor, I don't think you get it. We could bring you in forcibly, but we would rather have your cooperation." He shifted slightly back, putting more space between them. "A lot of people are looking for you, but as a favor to your brother, we haven't told our superiors you've been located." He paused, taking a deep breath. "I guess you could call it an act of faith on our part. Cerberus wants the formula and we want Cerberus."

Kate couldn't stop herself from flinching at the viciousness reflected in his stare. This man wanted Roman, badly. But why?

"We can't capture him without your help," Jackson interjected solemnly, his college-boy features carefully blank. "We need a bargaining chip to lure him into a trap."

"The formula," Dempsey prompted. "If you could give us the formula, after we get you somewhere safe, of course, we would take care of the rest."

Kate pretended to consider their suggestion for a moment, desperately searching for a plausible reason not to go with them. "I'm sure what you are telling me is the truth, gentlemen. Nevertheless, what we are talking about is classified information. Even if I wanted to, I don't have the authorization," she said, her voice steady as she made her choice. "I need verification. High-level verification."

"You need—" Dempsey made a strangled sound, deep in his throat. "We don't have the time. I can make book on the fact that Cerberus knows you're on the run. We're sure he got the information from Boyd before he killed him."

The muscles in the agent's neck bunched with the effort he used to maintain some control. "Cain assured us Cerberus knows about this cabin, which means he's on his way here to get you. How long do you think it will be before he comes knocking on your door?"

A distinctive click sounded from behind the two agents, causing them to freeze. A tense silence filled the room as Roman stepped from a trapdoor beside the fireplace.

"Knock…knock."

Chapter Five

Cerberus, the watchdog of hell.

Whoever had chosen the name for Roman had chosen well.

She sensed the danger from across the room. An aura of controlled violence surrounded him like a tight leash. Outwardly he appeared to be the Roman she'd loved, dressed in a pair of khaki pants and T-shirt. But the clothes failed to conceal the constricted muscles or the rigid stance. His clean-shaven skin, bronze against the whiteness of the shirt, was drawn taut over his cheekbones. The muscles in his jaw flexed, almost as if he were holding back the desire to bare his teeth and tear into his adversaries, feasting on their evil carcasses.

Kate shuddered. With the late-afternoon light casting sinister shadows over the planes and hollows of his chiseled features, she could almost see Cerberus's huge serpent tail whipping fiercely behind him, ready to strike against whoever tried to escape from his world.

A world she'd never known about.

His unblinking gaze moved over the two men. The dark, incandescent orbs reflected a lethal aloofness that lowered the temperature of the room by several degrees.

Kate studied him as his gaze flickered over her. In that millisecond, she saw the cold starkness of his rage, the unbending integrity and something else she couldn't identify before it disappeared under a hood of indifference.

His words from the previous night came back in a rush.

Let me help you.

With breathtaking clarity, she understood that the Roman she'd loved never truly existed. He'd been the glossy surface to this other being, this Cerberus. One sent on a mission to recover a formula for his government, not a man who just happened to run into an ex-girlfriend. She stiffened, trying to control the spasmodic pain that rippled within her, but she was unable to prevent the gasp of anguish that escaped her lips.

Roman heard the soft cry, like the sound of a wounded animal. As the realization dawned, clouding her clear gray eyes, he saw it, absorbed it. He knew that what she'd doubted a few minutes ago, she now accepted as the truth.

"Why?" She barely whispered her question, but he heard it. Hell, he would have heard it a mile away. It hit him like a sonic boom forcing him to steel against any outward reaction.

Why what? Why did he lie? Why did he choose to keep the dark side of his nature from her? Why was he cursed to bring them both pain because he was driven to eliminate the Threaders of the world?

"Tell me," she whispered again. He saw her muscles tense before she took the damning steps toward him, her distress making her oblivious to the danger.

"Stay there!" Roman snapped, fear keeping his tone terser than he'd intended. "It's you they want."

She stumbled back from the harshness of the order, her look of pain instantly transformed into sheer terror. A tight knot of fear squeezed against his lungs.

Because the warning came too late.

Dempsey snatched her from behind, giving her no chance to struggle, giving Roman no time to react. In a fraction of a second he had her pinned to him with a Glock leveled at her temple. The position put her up on her toes, immobile, her body covering most of his.

"You're wrong, Cerberus." Dempsey drew the syllables of the name out, his tone dripping with venom. "We want you both."

Carefully, to conceal the frustration burning in his eyes, Roman shifted his gaze lazily from Kate to Dempsey, who met it with icy contempt.

Roman was sure Dempsey wasn't the man's real name, but it didn't matter. Aliases were a necessity that he'd used himself over the last decade and a half. More than they'd listed for Kate. Dozens more.

Roman responded with practiced ease, his voice was low and filled with amusement. "Threader couldn't be missing me already?" His shirt clung to the dampness between his shoulder blades, but he ignored it, subtly shifting his stance to allow for a better angle on his target.

"I believe he feels your last visit ended prematurely," Jackson responded congenially, his lethal smile leaving all pretenses behind. The younger man hadn't moved during the scuffle, his hands splayed carefully at his sides. From the bland look that crossed the college boy's face, Roman suspected Jackson was willing to let Dempsey play out this hand with the gun while he tried conversation. So be it.

Jackson nodded toward Roman's weapon. "But considering our current circumstances, I might be able to persuade him to forgo your company for that of the beautiful doctor here."

Roman laughed, a harsh laughter that sounded more

like metal grinding in his throat. Jackson's sincerity could've enticed many of the politicians Roman knew out of their campaign money. No wonder Kate had let them into the cabin. The fact that she had seen through their charade at all impressed him.

"Your strategy needs work," he said, deliberately not looking at Kate. "Or haven't you heard that this lady's IQ is registered somewhere with *Guinness*." His lips twisted cynically. "She was on to you boys halfway through the first act." Roman just barely kept the admiration out of his voice by covering it with a tinge of scorn.

Jackson conceded the point with a shrug. "My associate became overeager when he boasted of a friendship with her brother," he said, his mouth tight and grim. "Regrettable but not irreparable. I admit it would've been much easier to deliver her if she had believed us, but we won't let a bit of poor luck—" he studied the fireplace for a second, where the trapdoor stood ajar, before shifting his attention back "—deter us."

"To hell with this," Dempsey jabbed the gun into Kate's temple, eliciting a small gasp of pain. "Drop the pistol or I'll leave her precious IQ spattered across the floor."

"Shut up, Carl," Jackson ordered, disgusted. The action triggered a vague recognition somewhere in Roman's mind. "Your ineptness has already cost us time." The younger man's eyes flickered over Kate, who returned the gaze with defiance.

The MacAlister temper was keeping her brave. Admiration tugged at Roman again.

"We would prefer to deliver her as ordered," Jackson's voice became razor sharp. "But if we can't, we'll make our explanations later."

Roman realized they wouldn't kill Kate—not without

the formula. But Roman wasn't willing to risk her life in a possible crossfire. Not yet, anyway.

"Go ahead, Dempsey, kill her." Roman spoke in soft, easy tones, though the words lay bitter against his tongue. He deliberately relaxed his stance. "Saves me the trouble. I can't allow her to go with you. I've got my orders," Roman smiled. "For the good of the country and all."

Jackson's gaze didn't waver. Suddenly Roman realized he'd seen the look before. But where? Frustration scraped at the base of Roman's spine. "You boys have to answer to Threader."

Dempsey jerked Kate closer to him, literally pulling her five-six frame off the floor, the gun pressed firmly against her throat now. "I'll take my chances, you son of a bitch."

Roman saw a tiny drop of blood seep over Kate's lip, but she didn't utter a sound over the rough handling. His dark eyes sought hers, silently telling her to be ready. The delicately curved brows drew together in uncertainty.

"It seems we have a standoff, gentlemen," Jackson said conversationally, cutting short another one of Dempsey's remarks.

Roman rubbed the pad of his thumb lightly over the grip of his gun, using the reassurance of the smooth steel to settle his impatience.

"Jackson is much smarter than you, Dempsey. He figures the only reason why I haven't wasted you and the doc yet, is that I might be interested in something else."

"That so?" Dempsey snorted with disbelief. "What, money?"

"Threader," Jackson answered, his voice silky smooth. "A small matter of personal revenge." He raised his eyebrows slightly. "Am I close?"

"You've got my attention." Roman watched Jackson's hooded expression. He reminded Roman of a cobra right before it struck at an unsuspecting victim. "My complete, undivided attention."

With fluid precision, Roman's memory snapped into place. Jackson was one of a handful of men present in the courtyard watching with sadistic pleasure while Threader tortured Amanda.

Jackson clicked his tongue. "Revenge does strange things to people." He started to slide his hand toward the waist of his jacket, unbuttoning it. "Mind if I smoke?"

"Yes," Roman answered, this time his tone was flat and uncompromising. The man would die, of course. He owed Amanda that. "Get to the point, Jackson. My arm is getting tired."

With a careless shrug, Jackson let his hand fall back to his side. "Perhaps I know the weak link in Threader's operation." Roman's gaze snapped to Jackson's. "Tell me and we deal."

The other man shook his head, his face full of humor. "I'm by nature a cautious man, unlike my partner here." A deadly look from Jackson cut off Dempsey's swearing over the insult. "I'll negotiate, Cerberus, but not in a hostile environment." He gestured toward Roman's gun. "Drop it."

The information Jackson had could be invaluable to his personal plans for Threader. For the first time Roman cursed his dark craving for vengeance, knowing ultimately it didn't weigh well against Kate's life.

She must have seen the intent in his eyes, because he heard a whispered, "No," as he let the gun fall to the floor.

"An intelligent choice," Jackson said, but Roman only half heard him. Making a noncommittal sound, he watched Dempsey out of his peripheral vision. A sudden awareness glinted sharply in the depths of the other man's eyes. Rather than releasing Kate, he tightened his hold. Time slowed the moment Roman realized he'd miscalculated Dempsey's astuteness.

Roman reached for the small 9 mm tucked into the back of his waistband at the same instant Dempsey turned to his partner in warning, extending his pistol toward Roman. Both actions came too late.

Jackson's gun was already drawn.

Death cemented Carl Dempsey's look of surprise. Marred only by the clean, symmetrical bullet hole in his forehead. Unfortunately, the exit wasn't as tidy. It shattered the back of the man's skull, showering blood on the couch behind him.

Kate screamed and fell to her knees under the full weight of Dempsey's body.

Crawling away from the smothering pressure, she felt the body slide over her and back onto the floor. The sickening thud forced her to bite back another scream. In a panic she looked up searching for Roman.

She saw Jackson first. He stood only a few feet away, holding a gun similar to Dempsey's.

"You live up to your reputation." Jackson tsked, his pistol trained on Roman. "I should've known the great Cerberus would never leave himself defenseless." He spoke in a casual, jesting way, his Southern drawl thick.

Roman had remained in front of the fireplace, both arms raised with the gun dangling from his right hand.

Jackson's smile revealed a neat row of white teeth. "You understand of course, you won't be traveling with us. I'll tell them you killed Carl. I kill you and then I *get all the profit.*"

Roman lifted his shoulders in a way that Kate was coming to associate with Cerberus. Intuitively she knew he'd try to stop Jackson with his last breath.

Her heart thumped madly. If she didn't do something, Roman would die. Not stopping to think, she braced all her strength into her legs and lunged forward, ramming her head into Jackson's groin. The man screamed and a shot discharged into the rafters.

Roman, his eyes ablaze, was on him then. He knocked the gun from Jackson's hand then grabbed the doubled-over man by the neck, slamming his face onto the floor.

Jackson growled. Whether it was from his injury or the fact that Roman had braced one of his knees in the man's back, Kate wasn't sure. Roman's face was hard and expressionless, his eyes cool. Still, she sensed the deceptiveness in his attitude while he kept his gun pinned to the base of Jackson's skull.

"Others are coming, Cerberus." Jackson turned his head, facing Kate. "And they won't fail. Threader wants her, badly."

Roman shifted, applying more pressure with his knee while he twisted the man's arm up behind his shoulder blade. Jackson grunted in a pained response.

"I want him now."

It took Kate a moment to realize Roman was talking about Threader. She thought the idea was to run from the man, not search him out.

"A professional like yourself should learn from past mistakes." Jackson's laugh rasped against the floor. "But it seems another woman has made you vulnerable. Too bad I didn't realize it sooner."

Kate was surprised that Roman didn't correct him. She'd seen his face when he'd told Dempsey her death wouldn't matter. It left no doubt Roman would've followed through on his orders. After learning he was with the government, she'd expected as much, even agreed. Not out of nobility; she wasn't that brave. It was simply the only solution, what her brother, Ian, would call a "no brainer." If it came down to it, her life didn't compare to the thousands that would be saved. She could only pray she would have the courage to follow through herself, if necessary.

Even while she'd expected Roman's answer, though, she hadn't expected the cold indifference with which he gave it to Dempsey or the acute sense of loss that hit her right afterward. It was as if his answer permanently ended their old relationship and the existence of the old Roman. Her Roman.

Jackson craned his head around in an effort to see his captor. "You think I might help you, knowing I'll be dead soon?" He let his head fall forward onto the floor and snorted. "I'll let Threader take care of you."

Roman showed no reaction to the words, but his eyes didn't leave Jackson's face.

Kate glanced nervously at Jackson. "Shouldn't we tie him up or something?"

Jackson answered, his voice filled with ironic amusement. "Why tie someone when a bullet is more effective?"

Kate gasped. Roman gave her a quick look before returning his gaze back to Jackson. The intent was there in that brief glance, and she saw it. "Why?"

"Retribution," Jackson stated calmly. "But the question is can he, with you standing there? Knowing every time you look at him, you'll see him pulling the trigger."

"Yes—I can," came Roman's unyielding response. The rage was there, bridled somewhere underneath. It unnerved her.

"You can't kill a man in cold blood, Roman!" Kate cried

and stood up, automatically tightening her hands into fists. She was ready to do something, she just didn't know what.

A percussion of shots exploded against the window. Kate jerked, expecting to feel bullets pierce her body, but for some reason the glass hadn't shattered from the force of the assault.

"Get down!"

Sharp pain exploded in her kneecaps when she hit the hardwood floor on all fours. Almost immediately, another short burst of automatic gunfire followed, but the sound seemed far off, not directed at the cabin.

"Someone just made their last mistake." Jackson's words chafed against the floor. "Whoever it was got off easy. If the bulletproof glass hadn't saved you, they would've been taken back to Threader for his own personal kind of punishment."

Bulletproof glass? Kate had no time to decipher the man's statement before Roman roared. Letting go of the arm, he jerked Jackson's head back and shoved the gun into his Adam's apple. "Tell me how to get to him or so help me God, I'll leave you alive to face your own punishment for failing."

Jackson's grin was belligerent even while his voice croaked from the increased pressure of Roman's weapon. "I don't think so. Not when both of us know that I participated in Amanda's death. In fact, I was one of the chosen few who got to finish what Threader started." He tugged once, uselessly against Roman's hold. "The whole event was extremely enlightening."

Jackson's words caused Kate's stomach to churn. She stared at both men, trying to gather her thoughts. No matter what kind of monster Jackson was, she couldn't let him be murdered. The man needed to be brought to justice. Not for his sake, but for Roman's.

With the mention of this Amanda, though, Roman's face became uncompromising, while Jackson's was accepting, welcoming the death that was sure to come. Amanda had been important to Roman. Important enough for him to willingly commit murder over the injustices done to her. How did someone logically combat revenge? Nothing in her amateur psychology courses prepared her for this, damn it.

Anxiety gnawed away at her control, and a familiar helplessness weighed her down. She couldn't fight something she didn't understand.

"You can't let me go, because we both know Amanda Salinas meant too much to you." Jackson sighed, drawing Kate's attention. "And you would never be certain that Threader had killed me."

Roman didn't respond, his face set, but she saw the pain lurking in the depths of his pupils. A jealous ache swept through her body. Roman had obviously loved Amanda.

Jackson went on, appearing not to have expected any response. "He'll kill me, though—eventually—I'm certain." He ran his tongue around his teeth before biting down hard. "Just as I'm certain that I'll see you in hell one day." He coughed, and Kate caught a faint chemical odor.

"Poison." She dived for Roman's arm, trying to pull him away, desperate to stop the inevitable. "Roman—"

"Too late," came the harsh reply as Roman let Jackson's body slide onto the floor. The agent's eyes were open and staring sightlessly at Kate. She cringed and looked away, only to have her eyes fall on Dempsey, trading one horror for another.

The scent of peppermint clung to her, laced with the smell of Dempsey's blood. Kate remembered the feel of his arm around her rib cage, his pistol hard against her temple.

She hugged herself in an attempt to stall the tremors that racked her body.

"Doc, you can't fall apart on me now." Surprisingly, Roman's tone showed no trace of his earlier anger as she found herself gathered into his arms. "It's not over yet."

He smelled of soap—basic, simple. Reassuring. Kate leaned into Roman's chest and closed her eyes, but the image of Jackson's face floated before her in the darkness.

"You would've killed him." She hadn't meant to say the words and certainly hadn't meant them to come out as an accusation.

He tilted her chin up, his eyes somber but steady. "Yes."

No other explanation, just a straightforward yes. Kate knew things weren't that clear-cut. His muscles tensed underneath her palms as if he was expecting something, like a physical blow.

Not knowing what to say, she lowered her head and nodded, her cheek rubbing against the soft cotton shirt. Wading through all the emotion and information was impossible now. It would have to wait until later, when she could think more clearly.

He must've taken the nod for an agreement, because his muscles relaxed and he gave her another quick hug before easing her out of his arms.

She felt as though her anchor had just slipped away. Trembling, she squared her shoulders, trying to keep a hold on her fragile control when what she really wanted was to be back in Roman's arms.

Outside, the resonance of automatic gunfire rent the air, followed by the sharp sound of shattering glass.

Kate screamed more from being startled then from fright. Roman swore, shooting a concerned look at her. "Are you all right?"

"Yes," she answered, her voice far from steady. She didn't have to be told that the situation wasn't good. It was there in his face. The last thing Roman needed to worry about right now was the chance she'd fall apart while he was trying to save them.

"What was it?" The possibility that another person was dying loomed in front of her.

Roman crouched under the front window and took a quick look outside. "The SUV." He slid down onto the floor and checked his gun before looking back at her. "They shot the hell out of it."

"Cerberus!" The voice came from the trees, boosted by a portable amplifier. Roman didn't answer, instead he studied the woods. How many were out there?

"We know that Dempsey and Jackson are dead."

Roman looked from the bodies to the window. He ground an obscenity between his teeth, irritated for missing the obvious. "Doc, crawl over to me," he ordered curtly. "They've got a high-powered telescope trained on you." It was close to dusk, and the shadows were growing. With the curtains closed over the other window, soon the telescope's visibility would be limited to the center of the room. They would be safe by the wall for now.

Her face white, Kate followed his order, careful to stay below the window. It wasn't until she was scrunched up against him that he noticed she was holding Dempsey's Glock.

"I don't suppose we could hold down the fort until the cavalry arrives?"

"Sorry, babe." At that moment Roman wanted nothing more than for the cavalry to come, but even if they showed up, he couldn't be sure they were the good guys. Jackson and Dempsey had known too much about his association with the government. The information they spewed to Kate could only be found in high-level security files. Their swift appearance at the cabin just confirmed his suspicions. Labyrinth worked strictly on a need-to-know basis. Not even the president had access to the field operatives' personnel files. There was obviously a leak.

"Listen to me, Cerberus!" the voice continued, its tone unusually nasal. "My name is Alcott. All I want is Dr. MacAlister." There was a pause. "You aren't part of the deal. If you come out now, you can walk away. There's no reason this has to get messy. If you know what I mean."

"Yeah, right." Roman spoke the words under his breath, wanting to laugh at the ridiculousness of the statement. The next thing you know, the guy was going to tell him the place wasn't surrounded. "Time to go, babe."

"They're going to come in after us."

It was a statement not a question, but Roman decided to answer her anyway. "Yep." No sense sugarcoating the truth. "Probably with C-4 through the front door. It's reinforced with a metal alloy, but it won't hold up against that type of explosive. It doesn't give us much time. Not answering will stall them for a while. The last thing they want to do is harm you." His face was grim as he surveyed the outside once more. "Since they can't see us, right about now they'll be wondering if I'm in a position to pick them off. That's why they want me to answer." He glanced at the fireplace before focusing on her. "The possibility of losing men might make them wait until dark before approaching the cabin, but I doubt it."

He saw it then, the fear glittering in her eyes, even though her expression remained calm.

"There comes a time when you're forced to choose retreat or fight," Roman continued. "Threader's probably sent a platoon of men to back up this Alcott character. I won't be able to hold them off once they breach the cabin."

"So we retreat." Another statement, but this time she gave him no chance to reply. She lifted the gun, holding it in both hands, her fingers white from gripping the handle so hard. "Show me how to use it." The words were soft but determined, despite the fact her hands were shaking badly. "I took a gun safety course a year ago at Ian's insistence, but the only gun I shot was Dad's .38 revolver."

The woman defied all reasoning. Instead of the hysterics he was expecting, he got a calm request for a gun lesson. The urge to hug her to him, to gently rock her back and forth was so powerful it hurt. After promising himself at the first safe opportunity he'd give in to the urge, he settled for an earlier one and placed a light kiss on her forehead. Ignoring her startled reaction, he eased the semiautomatic pistol from her ice-cold fingers, automatically thumbing the safety before placing it in his waistband. "When there's time I'll teach you, because it might save your life. Right now, we need to move."

Chapter Six

A barrage of bullets hit the side of the cabin above their heads, pelting the stones and bulletproof glass. Kate covered her ears, trying to muffle the deafening sound. Instead of easing the noise, the action emphasized the pounding of her heart.

"I'm through talking to myself, Cerberus." Alcott's voice had lost all cordiality, blasting across the din of the gunfire. "You're in a no-win situation, so don't be stupid. She's not worth your life."

Roman's profile set at Alcott's words and "a face carved from granite" took on a completely new meaning for Kate. When he'd gently kissed her forehead, she'd foolishly believed Roman had returned. One look at his hard features and she realized she'd been deceiving herself. Cerberus had never left.

"Let's go." His command, clipped and low, gave no room for argument before he grabbed her cold, clammy hand and pulled her after him. His grip was reassuring, its strength drawing her like a lifeline while they hugged the wall, circling the perimeter of the room, careful to keep hidden from view. How many times had they held each other's hands in the short few months they were together?

Hundreds, thousands. It was an intimacy they had both craved, always palm-to-palm with their fingers locked.

His hand had changed with the rest of him. Now it bore a smooth ridge just under her fingertips. Another scar, another secret.

How could she trust a man with so many secrets? A man who walked out of her life without a backward glance. But she had no other choice—fate had taken the decision away from her the moment Dempsey and Jackson walked through the cabin door.

A false-stone door, partly open, swung inward easily at Roman's slight push, catching Kate's attention. Cleverly designed to hide an entrance of approximately three feet wide and five feet high, the door revealed a small platform behind the fireplace. Beyond lay a dark hole, similar to a cellar. She peered into blackness seeing nothing. Tremors riffled down her legs.

"We're going to hide in the cellar?" It wasn't much of a plan. "They'll find us eventually, Cerberus."

He stiffened on the last word. She sensed it more than she saw it. Obviously, the man didn't care much for his nickname. Too bad, because it was much easier—safer to think of him as her personal watchdog, rather than as a man she once loved.

"It's a tunnel not a cellar." He tugged on something just inside the entrance then shoved her in front of him. "The collapsible ladder's made of steel. Steps are about a foot apart."

In the waning light, she could see a small ledge directly behind the hearth, which dead-ended at the chimney a few feet away. The cramped space didn't allow for much maneuvering room, but somehow she managed. Turning around, she started down the ladder, only to miss the second rung. Roman caught her shoulders when a small cry escaped her lips.

"Be careful." His voice was stern, businesslike. He let go once she steadied herself. "The depth is ten feet. Take a few steps back once you reach the bottom. You won't be able to see anything until I get down."

Kate descended without difficulty after her initial faltering, but still couldn't stop herself from sighing with relief once her foot rested on the soft dirt floor. Small heights, even ten feet, sometimes gave her trouble. The darkness actually worked in her favor, stopping her from seeing the depth of her descent. It was a good thing she hadn't thought to use the flashlight she'd kept in her purse.

Kate's hand tightened on the ladder.

"Roman, I need my purse. I left it in the bedroom."

"Forget it." The tone, precise and uncompromising, came from above like a command from a Greek god rather than a Greek canine. "Alcott has stopped talking. They're making their plans to break in."

"What if we need money?"

"Trust me, Doc. I've enough money for both of us. Besides, how far do you think thirteen dollars and odd change is going to get us?"

Not very far considering, but it was all she had. What did it matter to him? Thirteen dollars could mean the difference between eating wild berries and...

"How did you know what I had in my purse?"

He'd started his descent, closing the door before jumping to the floor. It wasn't until he stood somewhere in front of her that he answered. "I searched it."

"You what?"

"I searched it."

Damn it, she couldn't see her hand in front of her face, let alone him.

"Don't you have a light or something?"

She heard a faint snap, and the chamber was flooded with an unnatural green glow. In his hand Roman held an iridescent stick.

She looked around. The width of the tunnel was about seven feet with a height of ten. Roughly cut pine beams every few feet reinforced the dirt ceiling and sides. The light cast shadows onto the walls that fed into a dark passage. She shivered from the dampness that seemed to seep from the dirt surrounding them. God, how did she end up in this mess?

"You searched my personal things?" Kate watched Roman rummage through a framed, black backpack beside the ladder. "Answer me, damn it. You went through my belongings?"

Roman pulled a plastic-wrapped block out of the bag along with some wires, duct tape and a little black box. He shoved the duct tape into his pants pocket.

"Doc, there wasn't much to go through. A dead cell phone, a wallet, keys, a flashlight, some tissue and a condom." He started back up the ladder but not before he shot her a hard look. "Remind me to ask you about *that* later."

Kate ignored him and watched, fascinated, while he removed what looked to be a couple of pounds of a claylike substance from its wrapper. Carefully, he placed it on the door and the walls on either side.

"I know all your belongings are back at your apartment," he said while he continued to work. "Except your car, which is at the bottom of the ravine."

Even without her background and her work with the government, Kate had seen enough espionage movies to recognize the substance as a plastic explosive. In the muted light she couldn't be sure, but guessed it was C-4, a favorite of the military. He stuck the fuse into the volatile material.

"You were looking for the formula." She made the statement, watching when he pulled a roll of duct tape from his front pocket and taped the box across the crevice of the doorway. Then a thought hit her, leaving her numb with realization. "You drugged me to look for the formula."

"No, I drugged you because you needed it." With a satisfied grunt, he slid down the sides of the ladders like a firefighter, landing directly in front of her. "I used the opportunity to look for the formula." In one fluid motion he threw the ladder to the ground. "On the off chance you might have copied it before you destroyed the records at the lab." He squatted once again in front of the backpack, shoving the tape inside before looking up. "Did you?"

"No." Suddenly Kate wanted to know what else was in that backpack. "Marcus told me not to." She shrugged. "I know the core equations. Enough to recreate my research."

"That could take a few months." A quiet understanding filtered through the statement. She said what he didn't.

"A few months for me because I'm familiar with the research. Many more months or even a few years for someone who got the equations from me but didn't have the experience of the experiments to fall back on."

It was her safeguard. If she fell into Threader's hands and, for whatever reason, gave him the basic formula, his people would have a hell of a struggle recreating her research.

"No one else will get the formula, Doc."

Kate shivered at the intensity behind Roman's statement because she heard the words *no matter what* echoing silently after. "I know." Her voice was quiet but defiant.

He tossed something to her, forcing her to catch it and breaking the unspoken words that lay between them.

It was a stick of camouflage grease.

"Put it on your legs, arms and face." He glanced at her dark-blue T-shirt and gray sweat shorts. "Smear some on your shorts, too."

Following orders, Kate used the substance liberally, trying not to feel self-conscious even though Roman turned away. After snagging Dempsey's gun from his waistband, he placed it in the pack and closed the flap. Then he hoisted the bag onto his back and walked to the far corner of the cave. It wasn't until he turned back around that she saw the rifle on his shoulder and the shirt in his hand.

"Here," he said, handing her the shirt. "It's going to get cold."

She took the dark-plaid hunting shirt, donning it quickly before tossing him back the grease. He deftly smeared it over his face, T-shirt and arms before sliding it into his pocket.

"Can I carry anything?"

"No," he said with a slight tug on the pack's strap to shorten the length. "You just need to keep up."

Snagging the green light stick, Roman grabbed her hand and pulled her along the tunnel.

Suddenly, an explosion rocked the ground, causing Kate to stagger.

"They blew the door off the cabin. Let's go."

He yanked sharply on her arm, and Kate didn't need any more prompting. She ran behind Roman, expecting the tunnel to explode at any time from the bomb he had set.

Kate estimated they had run the length of a couple of city blocks before Roman halted. She skidded to a stop and almost collided into his back.

Immediately she doubled over, out of breath. Twice weekly for over a year, she'd faithfully attended aerobic classes, paying a small fortune for the privilege. So why was it she couldn't run a quarter mile without wanting to heave up her toes?

It took a few moments to regain some control over her oxygen intake, but she managed, barely, before straightening again.

A glow of light, cast from the fluorescent green, flooded the end of the tunnel, showing the outside opening. At first, it appeared too slim for even her body to squeeze through, but as they approached Kate realized the outlet was deceptive.

"Clever," she said, and meant it. The opening curved in such a fashion that on first inspection it appeared to be only a small crevice, but in truth was wide enough to accommodate Roman.

"Thanks," he murmured, intent on checking the gap.

"Your creation?" The words came out in short pants, her breathing almost back to normal.

"My idea," he said, running his hand over the edges of the crevice. "But your brother's creation."

Before she could reply, he dropped to his knees directly in front of her.

"There's no sign the opening has been breached, so we're safe." Quickly he buried the green stick, once again surrounding them in darkness.

The sun must have set because no glimmer of light broke through the crevice. For the first time in her life, Kate was glad she was acrophobic and not claustrophobic.

"So, how long has my brother been a government agent?" she asked with the same feigned casualness she tended to use at her parents' dinner parties. Since her parents held many, Kate had the manner down to an art. He didn't seem surprised at her question but amused. It was the amusement that got to her. What did he expect? It didn't take a genius to put together the bulletproof glass with the escape tunnel and come up with "Spy Central."

Roman dragged her through the entrance. She winced as her knee scraped against the sharp edge of the rock.

"We're called field operatives." He stopped, tense and—she knew—totally aware of their surroundings. Instinct told her to keep quiet.

After a few moments he continued. "Your brother has been at it as long as I have."

"And that's been—"

"Since the Naval Academy." He continued the climb up the slight incline, cannily avoiding treacherous holes and rocks.

"I see."

Roman pulled her up a few feet to a huge rock that protruded from the side of the mountain, making a natural ledge. Darkness or not, she instinctively backed away.

"Do you really see, Doc?" Slipping off the backpack, he retrieved a small pair of night goggles. "I doubt it." He lay down on the edge of rock and surveyed the area.

She let the comment pass, not sure if she agreed with him or not. Instead she watched him. Recognizing the infrared binoculars for what they were, Kate asked, "Are they following?"

"No. But I'm betting they're going to find our escape route anytime now."

"You placed enough explosive around the trap door to wipe out half the cabin."

"No, I placed enough to take out one hundred percent of the cabin." He glanced back and his eyes raked her from head to toe. "You know I never do anything half-measure, Doc."

Heat licked its way up from her toes, setting her blood

on fire. She cleared her throat. "It will bring attention to us from the state police."

"It will bring attention to the bad guys. So much that they won't have time to find where the tunnel plays out." He looked through the binoculars again. "And it'll give us a little more of a lead."

Just as Roman prophesied, a few seconds later a tremendous explosion tore through the air, and the ground trembled beneath Kate's feet. She gripped a nearby rock.

"Is it gone?"

Roman paused. Another explosion shattered the night.

"Yes." Roman continued to peer through the eyeglasses.

"What the C-4 didn't destroy, the propane tanks did." He glanced up from his surveillance with a grim acceptance. "Hopefully it took a few of them with it."

"Cain loved that cabin," she said, knowing the words sounded inane. God, she'd never sounded inane in her life, but the talk of killing men, even evil ones made her sick.

"He's not going to be happy."

"Wrong, Doc." He slipped the pack once again over his shoulders and pulled off the goggles leaving them dangling around his neck. "Cain is going to be very happy."

He caught her to him when she would have stepped away. Her nerves snapped like live wires at the contact.

"Why?"

"Because he always has a backup plan. And this time it saved your life." Roman rested his forehead against hers for a moment and closed his eyes. "Mine, too."

"Did it, Cerberus?" Her voice sounded breathless to her ears. "Or did it just delay the inevitable?"

He brushed a soft kiss over her lips. "It saved us." Then he released her with a suddenness that almost sent her stumbling. "And I don't believe in the inevitable."

She'd barely recovered when he grabbed her hand, his night lenses back in place. She sensed the tightly controlled Cerberus was back.

"Stop tugging on me." She dug her heels in. "At least until you tell me where we're going."

"Hiking." He yanked hard, punctuating his answer. In the moonlight she saw the sharp angles of his face deepen and knew her choice was either walk or suffer a disjointed shoulder. Kate happened to have a very low threshold for pain and a particular fondness for her shoulder. She gave in immediately, allowing him to pull her up the rough terrain. "Just telling me we're hiking doesn't answer my question."

"No, it doesn't."

They'd only gone a few steps when he suddenly stopped midstride.

"Doc. One more thing." His gaze locked somewhere in the gloom above them, his voice drifted back, soft but arresting. "Don't call me Cerberus."

Not waiting for an answer, he resumed their trek up the mountain.

For the first time that night, Kate was glad that she was behind him. If Roman saw her defiant expression, she'd be in deeper trouble than she already was.

QUAMAR STEPPED off the subterranean elevator, his nostrils flaring against the odor that hung in the air. The antiseptic smell reminded him of the makeshift hospitals that were set up during the war. A war in which he'd seen many of his friends die. Here there were no wounded or dying lining the walls, only expensive art, but the scent always succeeded in bringing the painful memories forward. It was the scent of evil.

A glance in both directions of the white hallway assured him everything was secure, and he started toward the observatory, his Italian loafers soundless against the tiled floor.

The powerful rumblings of the computerized environmental control units vibrated around him, causing him to curl his lip in disgust. He'd never adapt to the Westerner's belief that artificial intelligence was worth more than the intelligence that Allah had given to Man.

The money Threader used to create his massive underground laboratory could have meant the difference between existence and extinction in many small tribes in his country. Tribes that had lasted thousands of years were no more because of this same type of devotion to technology.

The passageway ran the perimeter of the laboratory, which was huge by even most Western standards, covering several acres of space behind Threader's villa. It had taken Nigel Threader years to build the research facility, and although Quamar didn't care for what it represented, he could still appreciate the masterpiece of it. The fact its existence remained a secret to the outside world was impressive in itself.

He reached the secure door to the observatory and typed in his twelve-digit security code. After waiting a few seconds before the keypad light flashed green, he stepped to the retina scanner, allowing the thin green line to pass across his cornea with quiet precision. Once verified, he stepped back, smiling slightly at the feminine computerized voice when it welcomed him by name and released the door's lock.

Some aspects of technology he could accept.

NIGEL HEARD the door open but didn't bother turning around. Instead he continued to gaze through the wall of glass that overlooked the main laboratory.

His laboratory.

He enjoyed overseeing the progress, sometimes standing there for hours, observing the people below while they worked toward his goal. Reminiscent of Caesar overlooking Rome.

A drugging sense of power filled him.

Quamar's reflection appeared in the glass beside Nigel, ruining the moment.

"Move," he commanded sharply, and immediately the image disappeared. Almost as quickly, the irritation faded, replaced by an easy feeling of benevolence.

"I have sad news, Quamar." He watched the stream of white coats move steadily toward the door. Eleven o' clock. It was the end of the evening shift.

"Russia has suffered a tragic loss," he continued as he withdrew a cigar from the inside pocket of his suit then rolled it between his thumb and fingertip. "Their most prized ballerina, Marina Alexandrov, died early this morning." Changing his mind, Nigel placed the cigar back into his pocket, knowing he could smoke in the room if he chose, but decided against breaking the rule just yet.

"Her private plane crashed in the ocean shortly after taking off from New York, leaving no survivors." He smiled faintly. "We must send our condolences to Marina's parents." He thought a moment. "A card, perhaps with some flowers. You decide."

"As you wish." The words, spoken obediently from behind, triggered a rush of pleasure through Nigel.

"Have we heard from Alcott?"

"Alcott is dead."

Nigel's eyes tightened into slits, making the keloid scar near his right eye pulse, as he remained focused on the room below. "How?"

"An explosion." Quamar responded. "Cerberus booby-trapped the cabin."

Nigel forced himself to relax. Too bad. He'd been looking forward to taking care of Alcott himself. "That is interesting but not altogether surprising. Go on."

"Dempsey and Jackson are also dead."

"Well, well." Now Nigel *was* surprised. He'd figured one would eventually eliminate the other, but he hadn't anticipated them both dying. He glanced back at his servant. "In the explosion?"

"No," Quamar hesitated, a frown formed a deep crevice in the normally smooth brow. "Dempsey was shot, but I cannot be sure about Jackson. His body was severely mangled in the blast, making it difficult to determine the exact cause of death."

Nigel nodded in understanding before continuing his vigil. The two men were among his best, but certainly not *the* best. "Dr. MacAlister?"

"On the run with Cerberus somewhere in the mountains."

Running with her ex-lover. Anger coiled within. "You will find them, Quamar." He snapped the order before he could stop himself. Immediately he forced his voice into a more civilized tone. "Bring them to me. Alive."

"As you wish."

Nigel allowed the anger to ease before tilting his head to the side with speculation. "Phoenix has reported that the brother is back from his overseas trip." He tapped his forefinger against his lips. "It will take him less than a day to be informed and on their trail." He turned, his look pinning Quamar's. "Bring him to me, also. I'm sure the elusive Prometheus would want to attend his sister's wedding."

Not waiting for a reply, he swung back and waved his hand in dismissal, suddenly in need of solitude.

A few moments later the soft click of the door echoed behind him while he studied the empty room below.

Nigel linked his hands behind his back. Cain MacAlister wasn't as familiar with Prometheus as he was with Cerberus, he was aware of the man's lethal reputation.

He'd already requested the rest of the Prometheus file from Phoenix. With the information, he could work Prometheus's appearance to his advantage.

Growing up on the streets of London, Nigel formed a knack for thinking on his feet. Running illegal scams on the docks was no different from controlling an empire. Both required intelligence, finesse and a certain degree of ruthlessness.

A thought started to take form, and he smiled. As the idea grew so did the smile, until it had him laughing aloud.

Chapter Seven

"We'll stop here for the night."

Kate would've laughed at the curt words if she hadn't been on the verge of collapse. Any effort to show her amusement would have sent her over the precarious edge she'd been clinging to.

They'd been walking for hours—in silence—and she didn't need a watch to tell her the night was more than half over.

"Are we safe?" she asked quietly.

It was the first time she'd talked since the explosion. Even though other questions raged in her head demanding answers, she didn't voice them. Instead she had used all her concentration to maneuver through the jagged terrain in the darkness, knowing questions would have slowed their progress.

"For now," he said, sliding off the goggles.

"Is there somewhere I can sit?" Her voice was rough with fatigue, enough to make Roman take a second look at her before dropping the backpack and rifle on the ground. Her legs trembled, threatening to collapse now that they stood immobile. Kate locked her knees in an effort to stave off the inevitable.

Suddenly Roman's hand was there steadying her, keeping her from falling on her face.

"Over here." He half lifted, half dragged her to a tree.

The moonlight weaved its way through the canopy of branches, allowing Kate to see the flat rock balanced between its forked roots.

Sitting, she drew up her legs, clamping them tightly to her chest to keep them from shaking, and rested her forehead against her knees. Instead of going directly over the peaks as she'd expected, Roman had led her mostly around the mountain, sometimes backtracking, sometimes descending, only to abruptly start climbing again. After a few hours the adrenaline from the escape had worn off. That combined with lack of food left her body weak from exertion.

"Here," Roman murmured before he crouched in front of her and prodded her shoulder. "Drink this."

The muscles in her neck screamed in protest when she lifted her head and took a few shallow sips. The coolness of the water soothed the dryness in her throat.

Far too soon he pulled the bottle away, ignoring her involuntary cry of protest.

"You'll get more later. Right now, you need to eat."

He snagged the pack, dragging it across the ground. After replacing the water bottle, he grabbed a package from the side pocket and ripped it open.

"A protein bar?" she asked, taking the food with some reluctance.

Roman smiled. "It might not have a taste but it will give you back some strength."

Kate's stomach growled. Considering she hadn't eaten anything except some vegetable soup in the past twenty-four hours, this would have to do.

She took a bite and grimaced. The texture was similar to cardboard and sawdust. Roman was wrong, it did have a distinct flavor. "This tastes like my meat loaf."

He chuckled softly. "It tastes better than your meat loaf."

Instead of being insulted, she swallowed and smiled, already feeling better. Her culinary skills—or lack of—made her the brunt of many jokes in her family. Everyone knew her forte was Bunsen burners, not stove burners.

"Why did they recruit you?" Now that she felt better, she couldn't contain the questions any longer.

"Do you mean originally or to find you?"

Roman moved silently in the darkness, careful not to disturb the natural surroundings while he gathered pine branches, laying them in a large cleft between two boulders. She assumed it would be their bed for the next few hours.

"Originally," she said, taking another bite of the bar. Kate already understood why they'd sent him for her.

"Because of my background." He knelt down and started to rearrange the branches. "My father was an important diplomat over in Italy."

He stared off into space for a moment. "One day when I was about eight years old, my parents decided to take a boat trip to an island off Sicily. A short romantic holiday of sorts."

Abruptly he broke a branch over his knee and tossed it down away from the rocks. "My father had been working hard for months trying to expose a terrorist faction that had infiltrated the military. Once in, they had access to sophisticated weapons. Weapons they could use to kill innocent people in order to emphasize their warped political views."

He walked back to her, grabbed another protein bar from the backpack and opened it.

"I remember he'd been in a good mood that day, light on his feet, laughing the whole time they were getting ready to leave. He grabbed me in a bear hug, telling me to be good for my *bambinaia*." He glanced up from the bar in his hands. "My nanny."

"I know," Kate said softly, not wanting to disturb the moment. Never before had she heard such a loving tone come from Roman. Not even at their most intimate moments together. A dull ache spread under her heart at the realization that Roman might have shared this part of himself only with Amanda Salinas.

He sat down a few feet away and leaned his back against a tree. "I found out later that the reason my father was in such a good mood was because the warrant for the terrorist leader's arrest had been dispatched." He let his head rest against the trunk before continuing. "It was the last time I saw them."

She watched him take a bite, chewing only a few times before swallowing, hard. Kate had to swallow hard herself, trying to dissolve the lump of emotion that gathered in her throat.

"What happened?" The question hung between them with Kate hardly aware she'd asked it until she became conscious of the fact she was holding her breath.

When Roman answered, his husky tones became distant. "Someone in the embassy betrayed my father, revealing his plans to the terrorists. They retaliated by placing a bomb on the boat. A few hours after they'd set sail my parents were dead."

Kate didn't know what to say. In her mind she could see the little boy he'd been. Suddenly alone and not understanding the reason why. She couldn't imagine a loss like that at such a young age. No one could, unless they'd lived through it. She finished off the rest of her dinner, deliberately not pushing him for further information.

For a distraction she took off her shoes and began rubbing her feet, paying special attention to the areas where the shoes had left her bare skin raw.

"How are they?"

"Understandably sore," she said, the soft concern in his question making it hard for her to respond.

"Do I need to look at them?"

She shook her head, grateful the darkness masked the stilted movement. "They're fine." She replaced her shoes, not really wanting to think about anything but this moment of closeness.

"I'll check them in the morning to be sure," he decided.

When they'd been together, Roman had mentioned both his parents were deceased, but he'd never given the details. Only that they'd died in a boating accident when he'd been too young to really remember them. In retrospect she realized he did that with most of his past, telling her enough to appease any curiosity, but not enough to reveal any hints of the true person.

The brush rustled somewhere close. Instantly alert, Roman tapped his finger to his lip. Kate watched in silence as he slipped into the darkness, pistol in hand. A rising wind whistled through the aspen trees, sending a flurry of goose bumps across her skin. Mentally she ticked off the seconds while focusing on the fact that the government had trained Roman well.

Minutes later he reappeared, his gun tucked back in his waistband.

"A coyote didn't take too kindly to our company," he said, then hesitated. "You okay?"

"I will be in a minute." Kate let the breath ease from her

chest. "Why don't you tell me how the government re-cruited you."

"At the time of his death, my father had many friends and even more connections." Roman's voice was sharp, cutting through the night air and startling Kate.

"Connections that were easily extended to the son of one of their most trusted." He shrugged with an air of cyn-icism. "Naturally our government kept track of me. Hop-ing to use my legacy to their advantage. My chosen careers, first with the Navy, then in computers, cemented their interest, so when the time was right they made their offer."

He raked his fingers through his hair. "You know the rest, Doc. Shortly after my parents' funeral, I came back to the States to live with Uncle Joe, my father's brother."

Although Kate had only met Joe D'Amato once, she'd loved him on sight. In his late sixties, bald but still trim, the ex-military man had welcomed her with a big hug.

As far as she knew, the former Green Beret was Roman's only living relative. Retired from the military, he owned a small bar in the heart of Little Italy in New York City.

"How is he?" she asked, her voice reflecting her affection.

"Fine." Roman responded gruffly. "Still complaining about how tough it is to own a business these days and threatening to retire." Roman shot her a sideways glance. "He asks about you. If I didn't know better, I would think he has a thing for you—"

Roman bit off the sentence. If she hadn't known better, she would've sworn he'd almost said "also."

Neither, for a long while, moved nor spoke.

"Time for bed, Doc."

At first the firmness of his words didn't penetrate. She blinked, struggling to connect with Roman's swift change in attitude. No, not Roman, she corrected, focusing on the hard set of his mouth. Cerberus.

Kate stood using the tree for balance. Other than some stiffness in her one knee, both limbs did their job holding her upright. "I need some privacy," she said coolly, trying not to let the hurt from his rejection show.

"Right there," he answered with a tone the same temperature as hers nodding toward some scrub bushes behind the tree.

It took Kate only a few minutes to relieve the pressure in her bladder, all the while, trying not to think of the empty void that seemed to overtake her.

When she returned, she discovered Roman hadn't moved.

"Hell, Doc, I—" He lifted his hand as if to touch her face but stopped in midair. "I didn't mean to tell you all of that."

She didn't want to hear what he had to say. "You mean you didn't want to reveal one of your secrets," she replied in a low, tormented voice. By sheer willpower, she swallowed her emotions.

"How did you get the scar on your hand?" The hand in question dropped back to his side. Sensing, rather than seeing, Roman's hesitation, she forced a brittle laugh. "Don't tell me, a paring knife slipped while you were peeling potatoes."

"It's just a scar, Doc." He massaged the back of his neck. "It doesn't matter how it got there."

"It matters to me," she said, quietly.

He stared at her for a full minute, the dark orbs of his eyes glowing in the darkness, ordering her to back down. She crossed her arms and waited.

Annoyance made his movements jerky as he picked up the rifle and, in doing so, broke the contact. "A knife fight in Mexico."

"A knife fight," she repeated unnecessarily, and placed her hands on her hips. Feeling a sudden thrill of victory, she nodded toward his chest. "And your shoulder?"

"A grappling hook from an unhappy poacher in the Arctic."

The gruesome image flashed through her mind, almost causing her to balk.

Determined, she clenched her jaw. "The broken ribs?"

With an impatient sigh, he answered. "I fell from a ledge while chasing a Mossad agent over the rooftops of Paris."

He balanced the rifle barrel on his shoulder, grasping the butt with his hand. "Look, Doc. Injuries go with the territory." He tilted his head. "What do you want to hear about next? My dislocated shoulder when a drug lord decided to use me for a hood ornament, or the bullet scar on my thigh?"

"You were shot?" Kate couldn't control her horrified intake of breath. "By whom?"

"A bad guy, babe," he said. "Only bad guys shoot me." He let his head fall backward as if asking the stars for patience. "Are we finished?"

"Not yet." There was still one more secret. "But we will be after you tell me about your broken nose."

He jerked his head back toward her with surprise. "Not bad, Doc. You've got a good eye."

She stifled the smile that threatened. No use getting a big head over one compliment. She'd caught a glimpse of the ridge before he kissed her in the kitchen, but the minute imperfection didn't register until she started listing his other injuries.

Whoever worked on Roman was a master. Her mother, Christel, was one of the leading plastic surgeons in the country. Kate knew the amount of skill required for results of this caliber.

"Noticing details is part of my profession," she said drolly, emphasizing the intellectual slant in her voice. "So?"

"So what?"

"So," she went on relentlessly, "how did it happen?" Roman grabbed the pack and headed toward the pine branches, tossing the answer over his shoulder. "Playing racquetball."

She followed, curving her lips into a saccharine-sweet smile at the obvious lie. "Don't tell me—your partner mistook your face for the ball."

"Something like that."

"More like a fist in the face, I'll bet." Something her own hand was itching to do.

It was his turn to smile as if he could read her thoughts, before he pulled a thin roll from the bag and snapped it open to reveal a thermal blanket. "More like an Uzi to the face, I'll bet," he said, mimicking her voice.

She refused to let him see the truth—that she couldn't stand the thought of him suffering the least pain. "Ouch, that must've hurt."

The lack of sincerity in her response made him laugh outright and shake his head.

"Only after I regained consciousness."

She studied his profile in the darkness while he placed the backpack into the crevice. "They did a good job repairing it." The words came out unwillingly.

"She."

"She?" Kate asked, not understanding his meaning.

"*She* did a good job." He maneuvered himself onto the branches until he was leaning against the pack in a half-reclined position, the rifle propped beside him.

"The surgeon was a woman." His hand snaked out and pulled her down on top of him. Kate landed with an unladylike thud against his chest. "A very beautiful woman."

Her mouth made an *O* before she snapped it shut.

"Now I understand." The jealousy hit Kate unexpectedly, keeping her from stopping the hurt that laced her words. She squirmed, intentionally using her elbow to work into a more comfortable position. The sting of jealousy eased a bit when she heard his grunt of pain.

He smiled against her forehead as he adjusted her to fit the length of him. "No, you don't understand," he said, and wrapped his arms around her, successfully spoiling her attempt to move again and locking her head under his chin.

"But because I want some sleep, I'll clear it up for you. What you're looking at is some of your mom's handiwork."

That stopped her. "Mom?"

"She wouldn't have had it any other way," he said with a chuckle. "Didn't trust anyone else to do the job."

That sounded like Chris MacAlister. She supposed her mother had no reason *not* to operate on Roman. After all, she'd never discussed their breakup with her, not that her mom hadn't given Kate the opportunity. Kate just didn't want to put her mother in the middle. Chris was fiercely protective of all her children, which had included Roman for some time now.

Besides, her mom *was* the best. Chris MacAlister specialized in reconstructive surgery, mostly with children born with deformities or ones that had suffered from catastrophic injuries. Kate grudgingly admitted to herself she wouldn't have allowed anyone except her mother to touch Roman.

"Does Mom know?"

Roman grunted. "No. She believes the racquetball story."

But Kate knew her mom. It took quite a lot to fool Christel MacAlister. "I wouldn't be too sure," she murmured.

"Go to sleep, Doc. We've got a long day ahead of us," he ordered, and draped one of his legs over both hers before covering her with the blanket.

Hiking, along with the quilted lining of the hunting shirt, had kept her from noticing the chill in the air until now. She shivered as the warmth from his body seeped into hers.

"Cerberus?"

"What?"

A slight smile curved her lips over the irritation in his voice. Kate relaxed against his body, absorbing his strength, enjoying the feeling of security before giving in to the fatigue. "I want to thank you for all you've done." She let out a sigh and shifted, moving her head into the curve of his chest. "Believe it or not, I am grateful."

"I don't want gratitude." A sound that hovered between irritation and laughter rumbled under her ear. "But a little obedience wouldn't hurt."

Within minutes, comforted by the rhythm of the heart-beat under her cheek, the warmth of the body under hers and the gentle rocking of the man who held her close, Kate finally obeyed Roman and eased into a deep sleep.

Chapter Eight

The humidity washed over him in slippery waves. Roman drew a shallow breath, fighting against the thick, oppressive mass threatening to liquefy what little air he had left in his lungs.

It had taken him hours to get into position. Hours of crawling through the mud and stagnant water slime, through the insect- and snake-infested brush. Hours of listening to agonizing screams that eventually turned into guttural lamentations reverberating through the jungle. Like tiny splinters, they pierced into the marrow of his bone, generating sharp jabs of pain with every movement that drew him closer to Amanda.

As team leader, it had been his decision to send the other three, including his spotter, back to the rendezvous point. It meant he had to get closer than usual for his shot, but he refused to involve anyone else in his plans.

Once in position, he waited, not feeling the oozing earth against his skin or the tickle of the creatures that found the gaps in his clothes. He only felt the burden of his decision. The screams ceased, which meant her tormentors had backed off, not wanting her to lose consciousness. By now, he knew the routine. A little respite, then a lot of suffering.

He tucked the butt of the high-powered rifle into his shoulder, wrapping the strap tight around his forearm. She loomed unobstructed within his crosshairs.

With every shot, the heat of the barrel threw off the weapon's accuracy. The need for retaliation raked against his gut, but he couldn't take the chance of wasting the first bullet on the enemy. He owed Amanda that, he thought as he ground his teeth. Afterward he'd send them all to hell.

Roman blinked the sweat from his eyes, allowing a few precious seconds for the salt sting to fade. Her face, clear through the scope, was severely battered and caked with congealed blood, her hair matted. Tension griped his gut while his finger tightened on the trigger. He held his breath, choosing not to struggle against the weight in his chest.

She looked up then, directly into the scope. Almost as if she saw him several hundred yards away, hidden in the brush. He forced himself to look into her eyes, begging silently for her forgiveness. But the eyes were no longer the dark color of rich, Columbian coffee. Instead, they were light, resembling the stormy sky he'd witnessed many times over the Atlantic Ocean, swirling with torment. Bile thickened on his tongue.

Amanda was no longer the woman strung up in the compound, broken and battered. It was Kate.

"Do it," she whispered, her swollen and bloody lips forming the words clearly in his sights, her red-rimmed eyes pleading with unshed tears. "Please."

Even as his heart screamed in denial, Roman couldn't fight what made him who he was. Duty before all else. A sob escaped his throat and he squeezed the trigger.

The explosion startled him awake. With an effort he let out the air that clogged his lungs, but it didn't relieve the pressure in his chest. How could he do it? How could he kill Kate? The heaviness became unbearable, and he jerked his hand down in a desperate attempt to alleviate the weight, only to find Kate sprawled across him. Living, breathing, beautiful.

Unaware of the tension that held him in its clutches, Kate continued to sleep. Roman forced his muscles to relax, but he was unable to stop the reflexive shudder that passed through his body. Her face was soft with slumber. Not restless as he expected but serene and peaceful, like the first time they'd met.

He felt a strong tug at his guts, the same pull he'd experience years before and many times since. The indiscernible thread of destiny.

It had been the weekend of the Army-Navy game. For most, the Super Bowl was the football event of the season. For the MacAlisters, it was when the Navy faced off against the Army. Roman had agreed to join the festivities once he'd discovered from Cain that Kate wouldn't be there. Up to that weekend, he'd made it a point to be unavailable with business at the times she visited, not wanting to meet the woman whose pictures littered the MacAlisters' Connecticut home and haunted his dreams.

But Kate rearranged her schedule and took an overnight flight into Bridgeport, surprising her family and Roman. He walked into the living room and saw her sleeping on the couch. With that one look came a sharp yank on his soul—like a line anchoring—and in that moment he'd lost all will to fight fate.

At least for a while.

A few months later a car bomb meant for Cain killed Cain's girlfriend instead, and Roman walked away from Kate, not willing to risk her life because of his choices.

Running his hand over his eyes, he blocked out the

memory, vowing to leave her again once he saved her from Threader. Hell, he'd do it a hundred times if it meant she'd be safe.

Roman inhaled deeply, expecting the thick air of his dreams to fill his lungs. Instead, he tasted the clear crispness of the mountain's evergreens and wildflowers. He glanced up, taking in their surroundings. The dawn sun glinted through the pines and aspens, providing plenty of light for him to see. All was quiet, except his unsteady breaths.

Threader's men were already on the move, Roman was sure, but he hesitated before waking Kate, finding comfort from his nightmare in her body's warmth. Then she shifted, moving closer into the curve of his arm, causing his muscles to tighten with desire. For the first time, he realized his palm rested against the soft slope of her thigh, just under her bottom. He could almost feel the silk lines of her underwear that lay a few inches from his fingertips. It was insane, he knew, but it didn't stop him from slipping his hand under the cuff of her shorts.

The caress elicited a mewling sound from the back of her throat that sent his blood racing. Ignoring its trembling, he slid his other palm under her shirt, up the smooth curve of her back until he reached her shoulder blade. Applying gentle pressure, he molded her closer, taking pleasure in the soft lines fitting against him. It was what he had wanted to do that first day on the couch. And again the other night when he'd carried her up to the cabin's loft. What he'd wanted to do every day, every moment, between the two.

His gaze lowered to her lips and locked on their fullness. Unable to stop himself, he swept down and slowly devoured them. Savoring the sweetness. Feeding on it.

But their texture and tang left him craving more.

He groaned against her mouth as he moved. Keeping his hand under her, he nudged Kate onto her side, giving him the freedom he required. He traced a path over the skin of her abdomen, all the while damning himself as he made his way up to the lacy cup of her bra before pushing it aside. Her nipples firmed instantly under his touch. He checked his desire with another groan, even knowing as he did the attempt came too late. While he teetered on the brink, Kate let out a whimper, her eyes opening briefly with awareness. The passion Roman had suppressed over the years broke free, and he stepped into its backlash, allowing it to carry him over the edge.

With a silent acceptance of a drowning man, he dipped his head. He whispered a kiss across her nipple, then he caressed the rosy peak with his unshaven jaw until it hardened into a tight bud. His body tightened and his muscles strained. Unable to wait any longer, he took the tip into his mouth, slowly circling the hardness with his tongue, before flicking hungrily over it.

Kate awoke under a deluge of yearning, then moaned when his mouth left hers, only to gasp when the moistness touched her bare breast. Delicious shivers ran down her spine. Instinctively she leaned back and allowed him more access. He skimmed his hand down her body, over her thighs before returning to cup her breast. Her whole body seemed to be balanced on a precipice of need—until she felt it—the heat of Roman's body, separated by mere inches.

Suddenly, it wasn't enough for Kate. A sense of urgency drove her as she turned toward him, arching her body into his, straining to feel every inch of hardness. In response, he grabbed her hips and pressed his groin tightly against hers. If he'd been in her, the feeling couldn't have been more carnal.

She writhed beneath him, while her arms slid up his throat and curved around the back of his neck. Fisting her hands into his hair, she jerked him back up to her, wanting to feel the rough caress of his tongue on hers. She felt on the verge of violence in order to fulfill a need. It scared her, exhilarated her. And when Roman complied with an urgency that matched her own, their mouths meeting in a frantic, passion-driven kiss, it overwhelmed her.

"Babe, tell me no."

Kate didn't recognize at first the person that rasped the plea against her cheek. It wasn't Roman. She slid her mouth under his jaw, using her tongue to explore its strong lines, relishing the coarse texture of his whiskers against her lips. Their lovemaking had always been tender but restrained, at least on his part. This man shuddered in her arms with the intensity of someone close to losing control.

Suddenly Kate wanted to see it happen. She wanted him to lose control. She ran her hand down the front of his body and felt the muscles clench as she neared the clasp of his pants. Her breath came in short gasps. His mouth grazed her earlobe before nipping at the tender flesh just underneath. Jolts of desire ran along her nerve endings.

"Tell me to stop," he demanded as he blazed a trail down to her collarbone. She responded by unsnapping his pants, and his breath hissed over a curse.

"Tell me not to," she whispered against his ear, her mouth moist against its outline, her hand poised over the zipper. "Please, Cerberus."

Roman stiffened and then his arms became bands of steel that wrapped around her, crushing her to him. "Damn you."

The amber in his eyes blazed. Kate blinked, trying to focus.

"Damn us both," he muttered as his mouth clamped over hers.

Meant to punish, the kiss forced her lips apart, while his hold prevented her escape. There was something savage, almost cruel in the way his mouth took hers, bruising and unbending. Instead of being frightened, it made Kate hot—and angry. Fiercely angry. She shoved against his shoulders, trying to fight his hold. Finally he let go when her fist hit his temple. She scrambled away from him, her body shaking with fury.

"How dare you." She wanted to rant and rave, but instead her voice came out low, aroused. In one fluid motion he was on his feet. He took an intimidating step toward her. She held her ground. "You think you can use fear to punish me?" He halted at her words, his face set in rigid cuts like the mountain walls that surrounded them.

"You should be scared of me, Doc—of Cerberus." He spat out the name contemptuously. "If you know what's good for you."

The warning chafed her temper. Its flare reflected in her tone. "Let me tell you something." The arrogance of her statement gave her momentum. "I've lived with fear my whole life, battled it alone. Every time I step down a stairway, every time I look out a window. And, trust me, that is much more paralyzing for me than any kiss you could inflict."

Unwilling to think about how much she'd wanted the kiss, she fed the rage. "If you think to keep me in place, you'd better think again. Like it or not, you are Cerberus as much as you're Roman D'Amato. And neither of you frightens me. You confuse me, yes. Anger me, definitely. But you don't frighten me."

Roman went still, his body defined in clear, tense lines. "What the hell are you talking about?"

In the dark, it was easy to ignore the environment around her but her fear wouldn't be as simple to control while hiking during the day. He needed to know.

"I'm acrophobic." She glared, daring him to say something, anything. She didn't take the character flaw lightly.

"For the love of—" He bit off the words, blowing the air out of his lungs in a long, angry breath. The effort didn't diminish the frown on his face. "When were you going to share your little secret? *On the top of a damn mountain while you're in the middle of an anxiety attack?*"

Kate regarded him, her stance militant as she let the question go unanswered. Why should she bother explaining herself? He didn't understand, no one could unless they lived it.

"The question is what are we going to do about it?" She yanked the tie from her hair.

"We are not going to do anything. You're going to take care of business behind that bush—" he pointed to a cluster of nearby brush "—while I break camp." His gaze swept down. "I'll come up with a plan while I check the damage to your feet. Threader's men haven't wasted any time getting on our trail." Without waiting for an answer, he swung around and headed for the boulders. "We can't, either. You've got two minutes."

Irked at the dismissal, Kate observed him for a moment while he scattered the branches. The only thing that held her tongue was the fact she knew he was right. Heading for privacy, her eyes searched the trees for possible danger.

"Doc." The name shot to her from behind, forceful enough to halt Kate but not enough to make her turn around.

"Any more secrets I should know about?"

"No." *Except maybe I'm falling in love with you again.* The statement whispered through her mind, catching her off guard. The terrain shifted beneath her feet. Intuitively she knew the words were true. *Dear God, no.*

"What?"

She jerked at the sound of his voice, realizing she'd spoken the last statement aloud. Quickly she cleared the emotion from her throat. "No secrets." She swung around to face him. "You?"

Perched with one foot on a rock, his arms crossed over the knee, Roman studied her. When the sunlight glinted across the crown of his hair, her heart turned over in response.

"Funny," he said, before dropping his foot from the rock. "Go take care of business."

With her unanswered question hanging between them, she walked away, her cloth hair tie clutched in her hand.

BY THE TIME Kate returned a few minutes later, her hair braided, Roman had finished breaking camp and was kneeling beside a rock with a small first-aid kit open beside him.

"I can take care of my feet."

He leaned back on his heels, giving her room to sit on the stone. "I know you can, but I'll be quicker." He lifted her foot, resting it on the top of his thigh. "I don't want any injuries slowing us down."

The briskness in his voice stopped her from arguing. That and the way his palm cupped the backs of her ankles when he removed her shoes.

Kate watched in fascination as he carefully examined her feet. Both big toes had taken a beating, their sides rubbed raw, along with the back of her heels and the tips of her small toes.

"Where did you get the shoes from?"

"Cain's closet," she responded vaguely, her attention riveted to his hands.

His thumb absently rubbed a polished toenail. The familiar caress had Kate biting her lip to keep from groaning aloud.

"They must be your mother's."

"Or a girlfriend's."

He placed her foot at the top of his thigh while he opened the first-aid wipes. "Cain doesn't take women to the cabin."

Before she could ask for an explanation, his muscles flexed under the pad of her foot. Little shocks of electricity shot up her calf, forcing Kate to control the urge to slide her toes up and down in a feline caress.

"Tell me about the formula." The words broke into her thoughts just as he raised her foot from his leg. She grimaced at the sting of the antiseptic wipe.

"Looks like I may have found a way to slow down the process of annihilation between antimatter and matter particles."

He worked efficiently, cleaning and bandaging the chafed skin. Any blisters had broken long before, leaving sores. The featherlight brushes of his fingertips, as he applied the medicated cream, soothed the small injuries.

Kate relaxed under his ministrations, enjoying the touch of his hands. They moved over her toes, across the arch of her foot and up her calf to the back of her knee.

"What are you doing?" She snatched her leg away. "I'm pretty sure there are no blisters behind my knee."

He sighed. "You have a cut," he explained in a tone an adult used on an ill-mannered child.

Startled, Kate looked down and, for the first time, noticed that blood and dirt covered her left knee.

Roman pulled out a pair of tweezers from the kit. "I see some pieces of grit, but don't worry," The smile that crossed his face was too innocent for her to trust. "I'll be gentle."

Automatically Kate started to brush off some of the blood, but he pushed her hand aside.

"Leave it." Not waiting for a response, he bent over his work. "Why didn't you mention this cut last night?"

"I didn't realize." She shrugged. "I remember scraping it against the opening of the tunnel, but it didn't bother me." Quickly she bent the knee back and forth to prove her point.

He waved the tweezers. "Why don't you finish your explanation while I finish this."

Kate frowned.

"The formula, Doc."

Determined to watch, she leaned her head next to his, ignoring the protest of her stiff muscles. "As I said, I may have found a way to slow down the process of annihilation between antimatter and matter particles. Controlled, the explosion or annihilation creates a productive, viable energy source."

With her head next to his, her female scent mixed with the soft breeze, brushing against his cheek and creating havoc with his desires. He set his teeth and tried to concentrate on his task.

"Think of it. An energy so pure, so powerful, it could provide unlimited potential for space exploration—or environmental conservation."

Kate's hair brushed his arm, making him jerk in reaction. "Ow!" She started to pull back, but Roman was faster. He gripped her calf, planting her foot back on his thigh.

"Hold still," he snapped, angry for allowing her closeness to affect him enough to make him jumpy. "And quit crowding me."

"I wasn't," she snapped right back until she caught his glaring response, then she hastily twisted her head away.

"We would be better off if you watched the perimeter while I worked." The logic in his suggestion must have appealed to her, or maybe self-preservation instincts took over, because soon her gaze skimmed the trees and brush.

"How much energy are we talking, assuming your theory is correct?" Satisfied the cut was clean, he wiped the tweezers down and tossed them back into the kit.

"A shoebox full could light up Las Vegas until our grandchildren collected social security," she responded dryly. "Many don't believe it's possible." Academic arrogance infused her next words. "I refuse to believe otherwise."

"But there are problems with the development."

Kate hesitated a moment, and Roman glanced up. He saw a brief flicker of indecision, or so he thought. It happened so quickly, he couldn't be sure.

"Other than supply and money, you mean?" she admitted with a laugh. "Time. Up till now, researchers have only been able to slow down the annihilation to a fraction of a second. With our new process, I've been able to increase the time to twenty-four hours before it destabilizes and explodes."

"Not long enough for an energy source, but long enough to make a good bomb." He applied the bandage, his clipped words sounding like an accusation.

But it didn't stop her from agreeing. "If made portable, sure, several grams could wipe out all of Texas—plus some." A low buzz rustled the leaves surrounding them. Roman's gaze snapped to the skies as dozens of birds took flight.

"Let's go!" he barked before shoving the first-aid kit into the backpack and snagging the rifle. Quickly Kate grabbed her shoes and they scrambled for denser foliage.

Within seconds an aircraft came within sight. A tilt rotor, Roman thought grimly.

"What is it?" Kate whispered, her breath tickling his ear. He pulled her snug against his crouched body.

"A combat assault plane with hover and vertical landing capabilities. One that carries more men." Roman watched the aircraft disappear over the treetops behind them. "Threader's getting impatient and upping the stakes." After she put her shoes on, he tugged her hand. "Time to move. We'll eat later."

Before he could stop her, Kate grabbed the rifle from beside him. He recognized the stubborn expression on her face. "Give it to me, Doc."

"I can carry it," she answered, slipping the strap over her shoulder.

"It's a wasted effort for you to tote something you don't know how to use." He could tell his cool, aloof answer irked her, but he didn't care. "Besides being dangerous."

"I know how to respect a weapon, Cerberus."

He quirked his eyebrow at that remark. God, she was sassy. Mentally he stomped on the urge to kiss her, irritated with himself. "That's not the point."

"Then let me carry the backpack," she challenged, her chin stubborn and tilted.

"It's fifty pounds. The idea is to outdistance Threader's men, not slow down so they can catch us." His response held a note of impatience. "Give me the rifle."

"No. I'm tired of not sharing in the responsibility here." She crossed her arms over the strap. "Do you want to stand around and argue or get a move on?"

Roman held his frustration in check and didn't say anything. After all, how could he tell her that he didn't want her carrying the rifle because he didn't like the look of her with a weapon on her back. Or how her image reminded him of a choice he might have to make.

"Okay, have it your way." After a glance at the rifle assured him the safety was on, he adjusted the pack and started through the trees. If she was pleased with herself, he didn't want to see it. Deciding against a direct angle upward, Roman veered to the left, keeping their path relatively horizontal.

"Does anyone have a duplication of your research?"

Kate fell into step behind him. "No. There have been no hard copies made in weeks, except my personal notes. The breakthrough occurred only a couple of months ago. I destroyed everything, including the computer files."

"I've been meaning to ask you about that." He didn't try to cover the impatience in his voice.

"You want to know how I got around your security system to destroy my files." Her response was full of confidence, her lips curling slightly.

The minx. She was enjoying this.

He decided to let her gloat. "Even with your IQ, I know it would have taken more than a few hours for you to crack my system. And I'm aware that's all you had between Marcus Boyd's phone call and the time you left."

"Actually, it was little less than an hour." Her answer came quietly, losing the humor. The subtle difference in tone should've prepared him, but it didn't. Her next question caught Roman off guard.

"Is it true that Marcus is dead?"

"Yes." He stepped over a large root, then paused, making sure Kate cleared it, also, before continuing. "My associates found the body." If she asked him how Boyd died, he didn't know what his answer would be—if he could answer at all.

"Marcus changed his mind, you know. He said as much when he warned me. It wasn't his words that scared me and made me run, it was the terror in his voice."

Roman stopped, wanting to see her expression. "What did he tell you, Doc?"

What he saw impaled him. The fear, the sadness. Both overshadowing her beautiful features like a haunted mask.

"Not to trust anyone. That Threader had eyes everywhere. To destroy it all and disappear. Forever, if possible."

Satisfied that his theory had been right, but still bothered by her troubled expression, he nodded and continued up a small slope. The trail was denser than most, the trees almost sitting on top of one another, not allowing any view of the canyon beside them. The route was a good way to test her acrophobia and to keep hidden from any additional aircraft that might come along.

"So how did you destroy my program?" he asked, knowing the importance of keeping her mind occupied while they hiked.

"They didn't tell you?"

He heard the smile in her voice, the superiority. His lips twitched with amusement.

"I found the backdoor into your system and gave it a virus. One I developed to specifically fit your program."

Kate knew the instant her statement registered on Roman. When his shoulders tightened, she regained some of her pride.

"How did you figure out the backdoor?"

"Most computer experts leave backdoors into their systems with a password only known by them. I assumed you did also."

She waited for a response and got none, so she continued. "After months of trying different words, I remembered the framed photograph in your bedroom. It was the one of you as a little boy, standing with your parents in front of the ship, the *Bella Rosa*." A picture, Kate now realized, that had been taken shortly before his parents died.

"You worked at this project for months?"

"It was therapy." The words grew sweeter as she spoke. "I couldn't take my anger out on you after you left, so I took it out on your work. When I would get frustrated with my research or life in general, I worked on the program. I never planned to use it, of course. But the process became addicting. Similar to solving a complicated jigsaw puzzle. I completed project CREEP—" she cleared her throat "—the virus six months ago and just kept the disk in my drawer."

He glanced back. "Creep?"

She didn't hold back the grin then. "It worked for me."

He stopped, and Kate almost bumped into him. For the first time, she noticed they were on an incline. Automatically she turned to look, but Roman grabbed her arms, stopping the movement.

"Don't."

Her pulse quickened, but this time she was sure it was Roman's touch and not the acrophobia. She'd expected to see his features shaped in anger, but instead she saw only regret.

"I never wanted to hurt you." Solemnly, his gaze locked onto her face. "You have to believe that."

A sound echoed off the canyon wall, surrounding them and cutting off whatever she was going to say. A sound that had Kate's scalp prickling and her Celtic blood humming.

It was the sound of dogs barking.

And it was coming closer.

Chapter Nine

Roman grabbed Kate's wrist, dragging her beside him, this time up a slope.

"Don't look down, Doc. Not even at your feet."

They were running now, as well as anyone could run up the side of a mountain. The branches scratched at her legs but she barely felt them. She stared at the ground a few yards ahead of her, praying that Roman wouldn't let go of her hand. Panic welled at the base of her back, and she wrestled to keep it from flooding her body.

"It could be hikers with dogs." She puffed out the sentence, struggling to maintain her balance.

"Could be, but I'm not willing to chance it," he replied and yanked her toward a wall of boulders before stopping abruptly.

Kate swung around, trying to take in her surroundings. The trail dead-ended in a wide crevice, flanked on either side by walls of sheer rock. Huge boulders stood directly in their path, effectively cutting off their only means of escape. Before she could question Roman, he grabbed the binoculars from his backpack and edged back to the opening.

Kate leaned against a large rock and waited, her deep breaths sounding ridiculously loud in the narrow space.

After a few moments Roman returned and shoved the binoculars into his bag before crouching in front of her.

"We're going over, so shut your eyes," he ordered, then hoisted her onto a boulder. With her eyes shut tightly enough to see spots, she grabbed hold of the top, feeling the rough edges digging into her knees. She sensed rather than felt Roman scramble up behind her and over, his motions fluid, almost silent. Before she knew it, he was in front of her, dragging her up over the boulder to the other side.

"You can open them now, babe." His tone was urgent and harsh. As if realizing it, he brushed a kiss across her lips, the gesture dulling the sharpness of his next words.

"Keep looking at me while I explain this." She couldn't tear her gaze away if she wanted to. His eyes were aggressive, the gold flecks burning with a dangerous fire. Before her once again was Cerberus. Her protector.

"I couldn't locate them with the lenses. But if Threader's men got ahold of some tracking hounds, they could've picked up our scents from your car and the SUV. Going over the rockslide bought us time, but the animals will find the trail quickly. Once they do, the men will bring the dogs over the boulders."

She nodded, gulping a large amount of oxygen. "What do we have to do?"

"Behind me there's a sharp incline. No, don't look." He grabbed her chin as she started to glance beyond his shoulder. Anxiety pinched her spine, making her knees go weak. She clutched his shirt.

"I've been hiking here before with Cain. There are few trees to block your view. The slope leads to the river, which is about a quarter mile away. I've been avoiding it up till now because I know they've been keeping an eye on the bank, hoping to catch us while we refilled our water supply." He leaned his forehead against hers, his hands clasping the sides of her face, his breath coming in ragged pants. "You have to trust me, Doc. We have no other choice. It's either take our chances in the river and lose our scent or be run into the ground."

As if something just occurred to him, he grabbed her arms, forcing her away, his eyes pinning hers. "You're not afraid of water, are you?"

"No." She attempted a smile, to cover up the alarm gripping her, hoping she was successful. "I'm a regular fish."

"Good." His mouth tilted, reassuringly. "Here's what we're going to do. Close your eyes when I turn around. When I say it's okay, open them again."

Kate followed the order, forcing her hands to ease their clench on his waist.

"Okay, babe. Open your eyes but keep them glued to my backpack. I'll lead us down. Whatever you do, don't look away. Do you trust me?"

"Yes." Her voice trembled, but she focused her gaze on the stitches of thread in the black canvas. It occurred to her that she was blindly following Roman into hell. Her hell.

Somehow she'd never felt safer. After all, she thought grimly, who would know hell better than its appointed protector?

"Let's go," he said.

"HOLD ON, DOC."

Kate slid on the loose gravel and gritted her teeth. As *if* she was going to let go, she thought, her panic festering just under the surface. Even if she wanted to, it would take an act of God to pry her cramped fingers from his waist. Her temper flared, urging her to voice that very opinion, but the words stalled in her throat, blocked by the fright already there. Instead she chose to concentrate on his voice, allowing it to filter through her. The low, soothing timbre kept her from snapping.

"I can see the river from here." His words of encouragement floated fuzzily past her head. "You're doing great, babe."

She didn't feel great. She felt sick. Nausea bubbled in her stomach from the anxiety and heat. Shifting her shoulders, she tried to ease the pinch of the rifle strap against her skin. The afternoon sun hammered her back, making the plaid shirt stifling and the space between them oppressive.

But when she skidded again, the air's suffocating effect didn't stop her from edging closer to Roman, nor did the screaming muscles in her neck keep her from putting her nose mere inches from the pack.

The odor of the musty canvas tickled her nostrils, and Kate sniffed, loudly, fighting the urge to rub the itch away.

"Are you okay?"

Kate tensed at the concern lacing Roman's words. But there was no hesitation in his step, no hitch in his pace. Just as well, Kate thought. She was too close to the edge and a little sympathy would push her over. The sooner they were off the incline, the better for her.

"I'm fine." Her throat croaked out the words, muffled by the backpack. Not once had he lost his footing on the loose terrain, his body swinging in a graceful gait while hers jerked with uncertainty.

Although her arms ached with the effort, she found her balance using Roman as a crutch.

It had taken them a good half an hour to make it this far down the slope. She'd lived three lifetimes in that span, Sweat flowed, making her already-clammy skin dank with moisture. Her injured toes, crammed against the inside of her shoe from the sharp incline, burned in protest. Her legs were rubbery and sluggish. Every fiber in her being screamed at her to concede, but she didn't dare.

"A few more steps, Doc, and we're home free."

Home free. From the slope maybe. But they still had the river to contend with. Kate grimaced as a cramp shot through the arch of her foot making her stumble once again. Quickly flexing her toes for relief, she figured the river would seem like a stroll in the park after this.

A sudden step and they hit the flat trail, abruptly enough to make her lurch into Roman. She barely let out a shaky sigh before he roughly wrapped her in his arms.

"You were perfect." The whisper of reassurance flicked across her ear.

Funny, she didn't feel perfect. Especially when her relief quaked to the surface, causing her limbs to shake uncontrollably and her knees to buckle. Not like the man holding her. Roman scarcely had broken a sweat, his breathing even and steady. His muscles, unlike hers, were relaxed and reassuring. When the arms increased their pressure, she settled in, allowing them to take her weight.

No, she felt far from perfect, but she did feel safe.

"Promise me we won't have to do that again," she said, burying her face.

The muscles of his chest hardened beneath his shirt in response, and she drew back to see his expression. The angles and planes, blade sharp against the sunlight, remained unreadable. Uneasiness caused her to produce a quavering laugh. "Lie if you have to."

"We're wasting time," he responded grimly, levering her away.

Having no choice, she let go of his waist, but not before she noticed the wet handprints that saturated the wrinkled material of his shirt. Shaking her fingers to regain some circulation, she swung around, trying to sooth the throbbing stiffness in her joints, trying to soothe the pain of his abruptness.

Roman grabbed one of her hands and pulled her back toward him. He slowly massaged the palm he held captive. Once his soothing strokes eased the discomfort, he switched hands and repeated the process. A different heat spread through Kate. A heat fierce enough to make the sun sweat.

Suddenly tired of riding hot-and-cold emotions, she yanked her hand from his grasp and held both of them behind her back. Ignoring the rise of his eyebrows, she took a step back.

"I...I'm okay." Hating herself for stuttering, she concentrated on their surroundings. "Don't you think we should get moving?" She looked pointedly past his shoulder. *Before I curl up inside you and never come out.*

"If you're ready." Understanding coated his response, mixed with an emotion she couldn't quite identify.

"I am." The stiffness in her voice sounded harsh, even to her own ears.

"Then, after you," he said, before waving his hand and bowing at the waist, his sardonic expression lost when his brow lowered in mock obedience.

Kate resisted the urge to smack him across the top of his head as she marched past.

But as she approached the river, her annoyance disappeared. The scent of the water mixed with the damp, moldy odor of decaying brush hit her full in the face. Her nostrils flared as the smell tugged at her memory, reminding her of the old graveyards of Scotland she'd once visited in her childhood.

But it wasn't the scent, unpleasant though it was, that made her eyes widen. It was the river beyond.

No more than fifty feet wide, it lived at the base of the jagged walls of rusty granite, roaring in rage against its confinement. The white, foaming mass writhed, battering and punishing the plague of rocks in its path.

Her stomach churned, matching the agitation of the rushing water. She fisted her hand against her belly to ease the tension.

The wind kicked up then, gusting around them, drying the film of perspiration that coated her skin. Kate shivered and instinctively took a step back.

"It's a monster, hence its name, Demon." Roman came up behind her, his voice raised over the thunder of the crashing waves. "During the runoff season, it's one of the most difficult rivers in the country to raft."

She glanced at him, hugging her arms to her chest, until the lure of the jetting water pulled her gaze back. The pulsating rhythm hypnotized her, stirring conflicting emotions within her and leaving an edginess she didn't quite understand.

A nudge made her jump. She swung around to find Roman had taken the canteen from the side of the pack and now was offering it to her. She didn't want the drink, but knowing a refusal would only bring trouble—or worse a lecture—Kate took a small sip before handing it back.

"We're past the runoff, but additional mountain rains have the Demon running high and moving fast." He pointed across the water and up the canyon where stone jutted out of the rock face thousands of feet high.

"Just beyond the overhang, about a quarter mile upstream, is a place where we can cross with relative safety." After tilting the canteen up, he took a long, deep swig. Kate watched the way the corded muscles in his throat contracted. Despite their dangerous situation, a coil of desire uncurled within her, turning her apprehension into something more tangible, dangerous. She found herself fighting an overwhelming need to be close to him.

As if sensing her battle, he brought the bottle down slowly, his eyes locked with hers, their smoldering flame striking a vibrant thread within.

Afterward, she would never be able to remember who moved first, but when his lips slid over hers, shaping and fitting the soft contours of her mouth to his, she went beyond caring. She grabbed hold of his shirt and hung on, opening herself up.

He imprisoned her mouth, caressing her more than kissing her, his tongue stroking and soothing. It was a familiar kiss that sparked memories of the past. A kiss that her tired soul could melt into.

Warm and willing, she sank in.

It wasn't until his lips brushed the tip of nose, then her eyes and finally moved lightly across her brow that Kate surfaced again.

"This is a mistake," he murmured huskily, his lips softly exploring her cheek. Her lids fluttered open.

"Yes." The word shot through her, causing her to stiffen. "I mean, no." Her voice sounded strange, distant—turbulent. She sighed, stretching her neck away from the warmth of his mouth. "I'm not quite sure."

He touched his lips to hers before stepping away. After snagging the canteen from the ground where it had fallen, he placed it back into the pack.

"I am." He moved toward the edge of the water, and the sucking sound of mud brought her back to reality.

"We're going to have to go at least deep enough to lose

the scent but close enough to land to make a quick run for it if we're spotted."

She heard him, understood the logic of his reasoning; but hesitated to follow him. The embankment was not only mucky but slick from the high water. Her legs, already weary, trembled at the thought of carrying her further. Kate started to shake her head. God, she couldn't do this right now. Her body was a knot of emotions. Her mind wanted time to assess and assimilate. She was a scientist for crying out loud, not an eco-extremist!

Ready to defend her position, she glanced up to find Roman surveying the area, knee-deep in the swirling water. There had to be another way to lose their scent.

"Come on, Doc."

It was an order. One she wasn't sure she could obey. Not this time. Maybe not anytime. She would beg him if she had to. Then Roman looked back at her, his stare urging her to hurry, his hand raised to help her.

It was the hand that did it. The words of refusal died in her mouth. He hadn't asked for this, hadn't wanted anything to do with her, she was sure. Still, he was risking his life to save hers and didn't deserve to deal with a coward.

"You can do it, babe." Softening perceptively, Roman's gaze remained on hers. "I'm not going to lie. This brute is as dangerous as it looks. The water is shallow enough but unbelievably swift if we get too far from the bank." It was almost as if he'd read her thoughts. "I promise to pick the safest route. You'll be fine. Keep your footing solid and hang on to the waist strap of the backpack."

Kate flexed her fingers. They were still stiff and sore and lacking their earlier strength, but wrapping them around the strap would give her extra stability.

Come hell or high water. The absurd saying crossed her

mind as she wiped her damp palms on her shirt and picked her way through the scrub of bushes toward Roman. Who knew it would be both?

Kate stepped into the river and immediately felt the slap of cold against her heated body. The shock caused her to gasp in surprise, the sound drowning in the thunder of the rapids. Before she could recover, however, the current pushed against her knees, and drove her backward as if it was testing her resolve. Its heaviness caused her to stagger and she grabbed for Roman just as he caught her.

"Careful." The command was sharp. "I don't care how good a swimmer you are. Nothing is going to save us if we're swept downstream."

Kate believed him. The iciness actually felt good against her feet now, replacing the burning pain with numb relief. Still, the hesitation was there when she stepped. The rocks, worn smooth by years of gushing water, made the footing treacherous. Even more dangerous, she realized, was the waist-deep water. The depth and violent push of the river made their progress difficult, almost as if they were wading through three feet of sludge. She grasped the backpack strap, clutching it tight.

Instinctively she didn't speak, but kept her eyes peeled for Threader's men. She couldn't hear the dogs' barking over the din, but she strained her hearing nonetheless. They were out there.

Roman took his time, giving instructions, pointing out places to step, and soon confidence replaced the tightness in her chest. He held his gun in one hand, its movement constant and alert while the other lagged in the water for balance.

Kate was in awe as she followed in his path. Even as he struggled upstream, there were no jerky movements, no motions wasted. An aura surrounded him. One of power and predatory instinct. Her protector was on the prowl, and for now she was secure.

It wasn't until they rounded the curve and Roman pointed up the river toward the opposite bank, that the terror crept back.

Broken trees, upended by their roots, lay snagged amongst a group of huge, serrated rocks. The water pooled around the debris, deceptively calm with only a hint of the turmoil underneath. What frightened Kate was the rapids that stood between them.

"We'll wade past the rapids on this side a few hundred yards, cross over, then work our way back to the pool." Roman used the back of his gun hand to wipe the moisture from his forehead. "They won't expect us to backtrack. I'm hoping they'll ignore the eddy knowing the rapids are impossible to traverse."

She squinted against the glare of the sun, her gaze traveling up the river. The distance seemed almost insurmountable to Kate, but she also knew there was little choice. "If you're sure——"

The rest of the statement turned into a cry of alarm when a lancing heat hit her left calf and the tendons behind her knee. With one hand, she automatically grabbed at the pain, attempting in vain to stop it. Her leg collapsed underneath her, unable to support her weight against the cramp that now seized her entire limb. Frantically, Kate tried to hang on to Roman. Her anchored hand, already weakened from hours of straining, clawed uselessly at the belt, trying to maintain a grip.

The hard yank nearly toppled Roman. He scrambled to recover by leaning into the current, realizing at the same time his actions jerked him away from Kate who was down and struggling to keep her hold on the pack. Turning, he dropped the gun and made a desperate grab for her wrist, catching her fingertips. But his hold couldn't stop her slick skin from sliding through his palm and out of his grasp.

She catapulted down the river, her body bobbing up and down, her head coming perilously close to the rocks that swarmed in front of her.

Roman threw off the backpack and plunged after her.

Water clogged his throat while he struggled against the river's punishing weight. It forced him down toward the buried rocks only to shoot him into the air, slamming him against the boulders above. Recognizing the fact that he faced a deadly enemy, Roman fought with all his will, his mind's eye hearing Kate's screams of terror.

Lighter than him, she would move more swiftly in the turbulence, far out of his grasp. Fire burned in his lungs and Roman used his arms to shoot upward. He bobbed, attempting to swim, needing the extra momentum to reach her. The rapids showed no remorse, allowing him only precious seconds to suck air before pounding him back into the river bed.

Terror seized his body. He knew this river, its beauty and its treachery. Bear Falls lay a mile downstream, a waterfall that poured out fifty feet to a rocky patch beneath. Even if he could reach Kate, the chances of them both having enough strength to fight the current and reach safety would be slim.

Then he spotted her and assessed the situation in the flash of a second. She lay in the rapids, no more than fifteen feet from the bank. Wedged between the rocks, the rifle held Kate with its strap, one of her arms tangled inside. As he drew closer, he caught a glimpse of hundreds of pounds of water hitting her face and pushing her under the surface. Soon the deluge would break the strap or pound her into unconsciousness, leaving her hanging there to drown.

Just then her head broke the surface, her mouth gulping in air before the water pressed her back down. Her strength wouldn't last much longer.

His muscles burned while he fought the undertow, spinning with the current and adjusting his body, legs first. The only way to reach her would be to smash into the rocks, cushioning the blow with his feet and praying he wouldn't break any bones in the process. A gush of white foam hit, rolling him over a rock bed of shale, their edges catching him in the ribs. Scorching heat shot down his side, causing him to clench his jaw to keep from swallowing more river water.

He struggled to regain his position, barely managing before he slammed into the boulders that held Kate. A jarring pain reverberated through his body. Blindly he grappled for a dead tree limb. His head banged a rock. Sharp, painful stars exploded in his skull, but he didn't dare loosen his hold on the branch. Even this close to the bank, the water was too deep for him to touch bottom. Swinging around the roots, he grabbed for the rocks and using his upper body strength maneuvered toward Kate.

Water spewed around him making it hard for him to see, difficult to keep his grip. When he reached her, his heart skipped a beat. Her arm, twisted in the strap, was the only part of her not submerged in the water. For how long, Roman wasn't sure.

"No!" He heaved her up by the waist of her pants, dragging her limp body across his chest. The rifle, coming unjammed in the process, dangled from her arm only a moment before slipping into the stream.

Adrenaline surged through him, setting his blood pumping wildly. "Wake up, MacAlister!" He shouted the words into her face but she didn't respond, her skin deathly pale. Realizing he was wasting precious time, he hauled her over his shoulder and worked his way to the bank, his actions like that of a madman. Fire seared the places where the debris ripped at his skin but he ignored it, half walking and half crawling to the embankment with Kate across his shoulder.

Once they reached the ground, he rolled her onto the dirt and dropped down beside her. He smoothed away the wet, matted hair from her face, her lips and skin now tinged a faint gray.

Damn you, Kate.

"Damn you, Kate. Breathe." Clasping his mouth over hers, he blew air into her lungs, trying to force life into her limp body. He pulled back repeatedly, desperate to see a rise in her chest. Costly seconds flew by and he got no response.

"Please, baby." Using the heels of his hands, he pushed against her diaphragm, his spirit willing hers to purge the water. "Don't do this. Don't give up." He whispered the words, ignoring the rivulets of water that stung his eyes. "*Please.*" Roman had never begged in his life, but he was begging now. Begging her, begging God.

But neither worked. She lay on the ground, a rag doll. Her once-translucent skin bluing. Rage like he'd never known overwhelmed him. There wasn't justice in the world. No justice for Kate, for Amanda, none for his parents.

"Damn it, Kate! Wake up!" He clutched her shoulders, shaking her. "You aren't going to haunt me, too. Understand?"

A sudden gush of liquid spurted from Kate's mouth, causing her to choke. He bent her over, slapping her back as she expelled river water. The choking soon turned to coughing and Roman grabbed her to his chest, rocking her against him until finally she took a heavy breath.

"You're okay, babe." Her eyes fluttered in response. "You're okay." He murmured against her temple, holding her as the color returned to her face. Closing his eyes briefly, he swallowed hard against the knot of fear that refused to dislodge itself from his throat.

"Cerberus." Her voice was hoarse, and shivers racked her body, but her heart beat steadily against him. He shuddered in relief. "You called me Kate." Then she smiled weakly. "It's about time."

His laugh grated the air like a rusty file. "Yeah, it's about time." He rubbed his chin across the top of her head, taking comfort in its silken texture. "It's about damn time."

Chapter Ten

"I'm so cold."

Kate's head lolled against his shoulder, muffling the words against his neck. He felt her teeth chattering before she spoke again. "I can't seem to stop shaking."

In one deft movement Roman removed both the hunting shirt and her T-shirt before tugging off his own. The temperature was in the nineties, but her skin pressed to his with an icy clamminess.

The sharing of their body warmth wouldn't help much, but the knowledge didn't stop him from cradling her on his lap. It was obvious Kate was suffering from shock over the near drowning. What she needed was warm clothes and some time to rest. Hell, he needed time to rest. But with Threader's men breathing down their necks, time wasn't available.

She tilted her head against his shoulder, passing out from sheer exhaustion. Her hair, having come undone during their trip down the river, lay loose around her face. Gently he brushed the tangled tendrils off her flushed skin. His gaze lingered, his body still feeling the echoes of fear from minutes before. She'd been as good as dead, and he'd been helpless.

God, he'd been so helpless.

The agony he'd suffered following her down the river compounded with the fear when she'd stopped breathing had taken him beyond his sanity. Yet neither compared to the anguish he felt now, holding her close to his heart, knowing no matter how much he loved her, he could never keep her. If the past half hour did nothing else, it cemented his resolve to get Kate home safe to her family.

A twig snapped in the distance somewhere behind them, breaking into Roman's thoughts. His tired muscles tightened with alertness. Slowly he slid Kate onto the damp clothes beside him and at the same time ran his hand over his boot. His fingertips touched the cool ivory of his knife handle.

"Manos arriba!" Hands up!

He saw Kate's eyes fly open in fright. Her body tensed against his. Pretending to consider the guttural order, Roman sent her a sharp look and shook his head slightly. He didn't expect her to understand his silent message. But within a space of a breath, she went still, her eyes shutting once again.

His gut told him there was only one man. He hoped fervently his instincts were right. A brief thought about the rifle and pistol lying at the bottom of the river flickered through his mind before he palmed the blade.

"Hands up! Now!" The soldier, switching to English, emphasized the order with the clicking mechanism of his assault rifle.

Knowing the man would punctuate his third warning with a spray of bullets, Roman whirled around, maintaining his crouched position. It only took a fraction of a second. A fraction in which he let the knife fly.

Roman heard the static of the radio, saw the man press the transmitter button. "I've got them…"

The soldier's words faded as his eyes fell to the knife handle protruding from his chest. A deep, crimson spot began to spread across his shirt. He dropped both the machine gun and radio to grasp the handle of the knife. With one tug, he pulled the weapon free even as he slumped to his knees.

When the soldier fell forward, Roman heard rather than saw. Still in the attack position, his eyes were searching the brush, for signs of the man's compadres.

Satisfied they were alone, Roman stepped toward the dead man.

"*¿Juan, los encontro?" Did you find them?*

The words crackled over the discarded walkie-talkie. Roman didn't hesitate. He grabbed it and punched the button with his thumb.

"Yes," he said, deliberately sounding out of breath as he responded in Spanish. "I'm just above the falls. They're across the river, on the east side. Too far to reach from my position. They're heading southeast into the mountains. Out."

"Copy that, amigo. Good work. I'll notify the others. After we capture them, we'll rendezvous on the ridge for a victory tequila, no?"

"I'm buying." Roman laughed thickly and then signed off. *In hell maybe.* With that thought, he chucked the radio into the river. No sense taking a chance that it contained a homing device. Giving the man false directions just bought him and Doc some time. They could stay on this side of the river and head north, missing most of Threader's men.

He leaned over the dead man. "*Muchas gracias, amigo,*" he whispered.

As soon as the words left his mouth, he felt Kate's presence behind him.

"Do you need help?"

Roman glanced up at the quietly spoken question. Kate stood there, her pale body shuddering in the light breeze. So frail, Roman knew that if the wind picked up any, it would bowl her over. Stunned disbelief etched her face, her skin once again a sickly gray as she stared at the corpse on the ground. The fact she stood in the open, dressed in nothing more than a bra and shorts, told Roman her state of mind.

"Go sit down, Kate, before you fall down."

When she started to argue, he cut her off.

"You need to conserve what little strength you have. If you can't walk, I'll be forced to carry you, and I would rather have my hands free in case some of this guy's friends are around."

He expected an argument in answer to his terse words— or at the very least a hurt expression. What he didn't expect was the soundless compliance as she walked, almost trancelike, to the clothes on the bank and sat down. Her demeanor almost did him in, but the stakes were too high for him to back down. He returned to the job, knowing if he didn't, she'd be in his arms in a heartbeat and to hell with the risks.

Threader's man was small in stature, dressed in camouflage pants and shirt. Roman flipped him over, retrieved his knife and wiped it on the blood-soaked shirt before returning it to his boot. Quickly, he liberated the man of his daypack, canteen and guns before searching the bag. There he found a day's supply of food— mainly canned meat and crackers—a couple of cigars, some water tablets and much-needed ammo to match the Uzi and pistol.

After placing the pistol, a 9 mm SIG-Saur, in the back of his waistband, he stripped the body of its boots, socks and pants.

He slung the soldier over his shoulder and grabbed the

discarded boots. The body's sour smell of death and sweat permeated Roman's senses. It was a familiar smell. One that his mind processed, then disregarded. Wading into the river, he tossed the body far enough to allow the current to catch it. The boots followed. For an instant, Roman thought the dead man would snag on the protruding rock, but the force of the river quickly carried him downstream. With luck the current would take the body over the falls, delaying its discovery and giving them more time.

While Roman worked Kate sat on the embankment with her arms wrapped around her knees, her eyes staring off into space. She managed to drag some oxygen into her lungs, trying to concentrate on the logic of Roman's actions and not the face of the dead man. It didn't work. Every time she shut her eyes, she saw the disbelief on the soldier's face, so she kept them open and focused on something that did comfort her—Roman.

He made his way to the embankment, the alert line of his body telling her they were far from safe.

She swung around, checking the movement when dizziness assailed her. Forced to fight off the assault, Kate rested her forehead against her knees. It reminded her of the time, as a child, she had ridden a merry-go-round. She hadn't liked the feeling then, either.

Roman tugged at her wrists, pulling her to her feet. Her knees buckled, but the hands refused to let her collapse back onto the ground and instead circled her waist for support.

"What happened?" The words sounded foreign to her ears, muted and rough. "The last thing I remember was trying to catch my balance." She frowned.

"You took a dip in the river."

Memories followed his words in a rush—the fear as she

fell, her choking screams for help, the smothering heaviness of the water.

"You saved me." Her words held a certain awe that she couldn't have stopped even if she'd wanted to. "You could've been killed."

Roman frowned and ran his hands over her body, clinically checking for injuries. "Actually, you saved yourself. If you hadn't been so insistent on carrying the rifle, we would both be river fodder by now."

She searched his face for the answers. It was then she noticed a gash in his forehead. With trembling fingers, she touched it, impulsively trying to soothe the hurt away. Tears formed in her eyes. "I'm so sorry."

And then she cried.

She cried for her, and him, and even for the dead soldier who tried to kill them. She cried for Marcus and the millions of people she unwittingly put in jeopardy. She cried because it seemed, for the moment, the only thing her body was capable of doing.

Roman cradled her in his arms, comforting her with soft words. As the tears dried, he reached for her hand, unhurriedly bringing it to his mouth before placing a light kiss against the palm. His eyes flashed with emotion, and this time Kate read it plainly. It might not be love, but it didn't matter anymore. As she pressed her palm against his mouth, she closed her eyes and opened her heart. No matter what the consequences, she would love this man until she took her last breath. Whether that was tomorrow or a lifetime from now.

"Doc, we have to go."

Kate's eyes opened slowly, only to go wide when she saw the danger lurking in the depths of his. Reluctant to move away, she waited for him to take the first step. When he did, she stifled the need to draw him to her again.

"I'm fine. Shaky, but fine," she responded to the unspoken concern that creased his face. It was true, she realized as Roman retrieved the soldier's clothes from the ground and walked them to her. The crying had helped.

"I'll rinse these out in the stream," he said briskly, then walked past her to the river, a pair of white socks in his hand. "Put the pants on."

Her stomach pitched at the thought of wearing a dead man's clothes, but she fought against it, clinging to the fact that Roman was safe. If he hadn't killed the man, Roman would be dead.

The thought sickened Kate even more.

Turning her back, she stripped off the shorts and used them to wipe the mud from her skin. Shivering in her underwear, she donned the T-shirt then the pants. She cinched the belt tight and rolled up the cuffs. When she'd finished, she faced Roman and noted the backpack in one hand and the socks in the other.

"They're wet, but clean." He handed her the socks. "And they'll protect your feet."

Roman's gaze followed her eyes to the daypack. "I tossed ours when I followed you down the river. Our food supply now consists of unidentifiable meat and crackers."

Kate gave a brief nod and tied her T-shirt above the pants before donning the shoes and socks. Kate grimaced against the sogginess that cocooned her feet but didn't allow herself to dwell on her discomfort. After tearing a strip of cloth from her shorts, she quickly finger-combed her hair and tied it back in a ponytail.

"Ready." She puffed out the words, her arms trembling from the exertion.

Roman shot her a penetrating glare. "Not quite. Eat these."

He handed her some of the meat and crackers. Resisting the urge to sniff the brown lump of food, she placed some in her mouth and chewed.

"Are you up to walking, or do you want me to carry you?"

She looked up at the flat trail before swallowing. "I can manage." But she didn't offer to carry anything as Roman stuffed her damp clothes into the pack. Something she was sure didn't escape his notice.

She knew better than to complain about the fare, but the food sat heavy in her stomach while she waited for Roman to cover their tracks. When he finished, he pulled his shirt on and slung the daypack over his shoulder. "Let's go."

It wasn't until later that Kate realized two things. She hadn't heard any dogs, and she hadn't experienced a panic attack by the river.

Things were definitely looking up.

PHOENIX DESPISED WAITING. That's why, when she had climbed from the helicopter to the yacht and was told to remain in the salon until Nigel had completed his massage session, she'd ignored the servant and made her way to the exterior circular staircase that led to the forward deck.

When Nigel had first propositioned her about working for him, she'd jumped at the chance. Weeks of research had left her with information compiled of rumor and unconfirmed reports on Nigel Threader, but she'd been left with one indisputable fact. The money was real. The man was richer than Midas—and more diverse. Phoenix smiled. Her boss could give the Rockefellers a lesson or two in financing a empire.

As she approached the swimming pool, her stiletto heels clicked against the deck with the reverberation of an automatic weapon. The pool, shaped like an open scroll, wasn't nearly as impressive as the opulence surrounding it. The yacht, over four hundred feet in length, was like stepping into a Greek bath.

She glanced around, spotting Nigel almost immediately on the far side, fully exposed to the sun. Classical Greek columns draped in ivy surrounded the vicinity. After stepping around a brocade chaise lounge, Phoenix made her way among the statues that decorated the deck.

Many were nudes with missing limbs, but some depicted woman draped in togas playing lyres or holding grapes. Phoenix's gaze skimmed over the potted palm trees and huge, painted urns only to halt at the center of the pool. Set in its curve stood a fountain of nymphs. Water flowed from their hands, lips and vases into the pool.

To the side, Nigel lay prone on a massage table while a servant stood above fanning him.

"Where are you holding them, Nigel?"

With a sigh, Nigel swung himself off the table. His lean, well-muscled body, clad in white trunks, moved with the easy grace of a lion. Her mouth twisted, well aware of the awe he inspired in the peasants as El León.

"And how are you, my dear?" He settled himself onto a deck lounger and reached for his drink.

She ignored the pleasantry and stepped closer, allowing her shadow to fall across his legs. "Are they in the torture room?"

She knew Nigel sometimes entertained undesirable guests in the boat's gymnasium. The screams tended to carry over the water, but none of the villagers could hear them with the ship offshore five miles.

He hesitated over the tea, the glass rim scarcely touching his bottom lip. "Have a seat, Phoenix, you're blocking my light," he said with a deceptively soft tone. Immediately the shadow disappeared, allowing the sun to touch his dark legs.

Biting back the retort that wavered on her tongue and discreetly sliding into a nearby lounger, she caught the palm waver's eye and gestured toward the bar. "I'll have a martini. Straight up. No olives."

The servant deferred to Threader, waiting for an affirming nod before complying.

Her lips tightened with annoyance. "Where is Cerberus?"

"Still grappling amongst the trees, I imagine," he said calmly.

"You haven't captured them yet?"

"I won't be questioned, Phoenix. Things are going as planned, that's all you need to know."

The weather had been unusually warm this year and at eleven o'clock, the temperature had reached well into the nineties. What little breeze the ocean provided barely stirred the heavy weight of her hair. Impatiently Phoenix snatched up the caramel tresses and draped them over the back of her lounger.

Setting his drink on the table, Threader eyed the unnaturally coarse streaks of blond striping the thick mane. "Nice look." His gaze flickered over her features. "It compliments the surgeon's work."

Not waiting for an answer, he continued. "I told Miguel to take you into the salon where you'd be more comfortable. I don't like to be disobeyed." His dark, Armani glasses made it impossible for Phoenix to read his eyes.

"I have an appointment with our Cuban friends in a few hours. They're excited about the new merchandise we've promised. I didn't want to keep them waiting." She accepted her drink from the servant.

"The Cubans will wait if I tell them to."

Phoenix didn't bother to argue. Silk clung to her back as she shifted. If she perspired much more, the delicate, sleeveless Bob Mackey blouse would be ruined. It didn't matter that she could buy fifty of the damn things. She hadn't brought a change of clothes, intending to leave the ship as soon as possible. She paused over the first button.

"Do you mind, doll?"

With a wave of Nigel's hand, she undid the buttons. After shrugging the shirt off, she hung it from the back of the chair. "Much better." With a wry smile, Phoenix noticed that the servant didn't even falter at the sight of her nakedness.

At Nigel's raised eyebrow, her smile increased to a laugh. "It's too hot to wear an overabundance of clothing."

To emphasize her point, she also removed her black miniskirt and reclined on the lounger, wearing only her black thong and designer sunglasses.

"What information do you have for me today, my dear?" Nigel leaned back once again, a faint smile lingering on his otherwise serene face.

"Cain, against orders, is in the mountains searching for D'Amato and the sister. Mercer wasn't happy with him, but the old man knows better than to argue too much. As I told you before, he's grooming Cain for the head position at Labyrinth."

"Yes, you commented on that some time ago."

Phoenix contained a smirk. "My sources say after an argument with Mercer, he walked out the door. Said he was going on personal leave." She turned her head toward the sun and closed her eyes. "And no one's heard from him since."

"You're certain Cain's on their trail?"

The question irritated her. "My sources don't fail me."

"No, they don't. They only repeat their information."

At her indignant intake of breath, he continued. "This is old news, Phoenix. We already assumed Cain would go after his sister once returned from his mission. In fact, I'd anticipated it."

"Did you anticipate Ian MacAlister joining him?" As Phoenix watched her boss from over the rim of her sunglasses, she didn't stop the impudence from rolling out with the information.

Nigel's head jerked in her direction. "You're sure?"

"Yes," she snapped, not liking the disbelief in his voice. "It seems the SEAL has taken an emergency leave of absence. You put it together?"

"Sounds like Prometheus pulled in some favors." Nigel leaned back, his hands steepled on his chest, his brow wrinkled thoughtfully. "They're making this almost too easy for me, aren't they?"

"Their deaths will certainly weaken the inner structure of Labyrinth."

He snorted derisively. "Oh, I'm not going to kill them."

Phoenix sat up. "What the hell do you mean? That was our agreement."

With a sweep of his hand, Nigel removed his own sunglasses, his blue eyes turning glacial. The crescent shaped scar pulled at his eye, making his anger seem more demonic. Realizing she'd just made a tactical error, Phoenix forced herself to relax against the cushions.

Nodding at her obvious compliance, Nigel continued. "Cerberus is the only one who will die. Not because of some promise I made to you—" the tip of his forefinger flicked over the disfigurement "—but because of a promise I made to myself."

Phoenix's gaze rested on the scar once again. She knew Nigel's disfigurement had something to do with Cerberus. How, she didn't know, nor did she care. Just as long as Cerberus died.

Nigel settled himself and closed his eyes. "My fiancée would be extremely vexed if I killed her brothers, especially with our wedding imminent."

"Your fiancée?"

Nigel ignored her question, obviously lost in thought. "More importantly, it doesn't suit my purposes. Who better to have as a brother-in-law than the leader of the most elite covert unit in the country? And from what you say about young Ian, the boy will be a general someday. Then there's MacAlister Industries to consider." He tapped his teeth with his fingertips. "No, it's much more beneficial to become part of this family."

"Quentin MacAlister is a powerful man. You're insane to think he will bend to you."

Before Phoenix could react, Nigel had grabbed her arm, forcing the elbow backward against the side of the lounge chair. Sharp blades of pain sliced up to her shoulder. All he had to do was apply a little more pressure and her elbow would snap.

"I must caution you, my dear." He tugged on her arm, eliciting a small gasp of pain. "To choose your next words wisely."

Nigel's unblinking stare met hers for a long moment before he loosened his grip and slowly ran his palm up her arm almost as if he regretted marring her skin.

Forcing herself to remain calm, she said casually, "What I meant, doll—is that having the sister wouldn't necessarily guarantee the family's obedience."

He placed his Armani glasses back over his eyes as the corners of his mouth lifted into an evil smile. "Then we'll have to persuade them otherwise. Won't we?"

Chapter Eleven

"Wake up, Doc."

A hand shook her shoulder, and Kate automatically turned away. The scent of damp earth filled her nostrils. With an effort she fought off the heavy stupor of sleep and forced her eyes to focus.

"I thought you might prefer a shower before we eat."

Sitting took two attempts. Every muscle in her body seemed to scream in protest. She tried stretching out the soreness while she took in her surroundings. Where was she?

"It's an abandoned mining tunnel." His answer startled her. She hadn't realized she'd spoken the question aloud. But her reaction went unnoticed as Roman crouched to tend a small fire.

Even though they were several feet from the entrance, Kate could tell the sun hadn't quite set. The wind howled against the aged wooden beams and the air was thick with moisture. She strained her ears until she heard a faint pattering. "Rain."

Roman gave a quick nod. "Just started. I got a good look at the clouds while I was gathering wood. Within an hour it'll be quite a rain storm. But no signs of lightning, so we should be safe."

Kate understood. Lightning and old mining tunnels didn't mix well. A shiver danced down her back, so she scooted closer to the fire.

"About four hours." He shot her a brief glance, probably to ascertain she was okay, before skewering a small carcass with a whittled stick. "You fell asleep against me when we stopped to rest. Initially, I was looking for a cave or a crevice." He double-checked the meat to make sure it was secure. "But this will do."

He must have carried her. The act shouldn't surprise her, but it did. She took a long look at Roman. The words *earthy* and *rugged* tugged at her. When a piece of hair fell against his forehead, she had to fight the urge to brush it back.

"Thank you," she said, knowing she'd put them both at risk. Carrying her had not allowed him to keep his hands free.

"Don't thank me yet. You haven't seen the trail we're taking out of here. I might have to blindfold you."

Kate shuddered inwardly at the thought, but said, "It doesn't matter. What you did—what you're doing, I appreciate it."

The lifting of his shoulder told her he considered the gesture unimportant, as if he'd just escorted her across a street. All in a day's work for a hero.

She let it go. "Is that dinner?"

"Yeah." He placed the meat across the fire. "I came across a rabbit scurrying for cover from the rain. I got lucky with my knife."

Kate doubted if luck had anything to with it. Still the idea of something warm and filling in her stomach started her mouth watering. An overwhelming feeling of homesickness seized her.

"Where are we, Cerberus?" Irritation at her weakness tainted her voice.

He smiled and for the first time didn't take offense at the name. "We're about a half-day hike from Cedar. A town northwest of here."

Kate knew of the town through several of her father's business acquaintances. Smaller than the elite Vail or Aspen, Cedar still received its fair share of summer tourists. With the Rushing Fork River only a few miles away, the town was an offbeat location for rafting enthusiasts and mountain climbers. Those who weren't into outdoor recreation still enjoyed the ambiance of the small mountain town with its little shops all whitewashed and rustic.

"They have a small airport there where we can appropriate a plane and get you the hell away to somewhere secure."

She didn't ask him to define the term *appropriate*. Instead, she stood, taking a moment to adjust her none-too-steady footing. If what he said was true, she should be safe by tomorrow night.

And he would be gone.

Rocking on her heels, she tested her balance. Relief flooded her as the strength poured back into her legs. She lifted her hands high above her head and arched her back, hoping to loosen the last of her kinked muscles.

Roman, once assured she was safe, would go after Threader. Avenging her. No, not her. Amanda. Slowly she brought her arms down. The possibility of him not coming back alive loomed before her.

"So how 'bout it? Do you want to bathe before we eat?"

"Very much," she responded with a smile, allowing the thought of being clean to push her worries away—for the present.

"I found hidden treasure." He tossed her a package from the backpack.

"Soap." Kate almost squealed with delight, clasping the small bar tightly in her hands. The rough texture told her it was handmade, but Kate didn't care. As far as she was concerned, in her hands lay a little piece of heaven.

She looked up to thank Roman and instantly saw the flare of awareness in his eyes. After a few moments Kate remembered to exhale.

"It's raining hard enough to cause water to gush from a crevice not too far from the mine's opening." His slow drawl sent a low thrum racing in her blood. "It's like taking a shower."

She pictured him nearby while she bathed and desire hit her with the impact of a nuclear blast.

Obviously misreading her facial expressions, he assured her, "You'll be safe, Doc. I'll keep watch."

She felt a blush of mortification rise in her face. But he'd already swung around to tend the fire, saving her from further embarrassment.

"Strip down to your T-shirt and underwear. That way you will have the pants and hunting shirt to keep you warm when you're finished."

Closing her eyes briefly, she prayed for control before she answered. Still, she couldn't dismiss the picture of him watching her bathe.

"All right." She spoke the words softly, but her voice, raspy as dried leaves, gave her thoughts away.

Roman glanced up. Thick tension swarmed between them, crackling like a live power line.

Kate cleared her throat, hoping the action would relieve the terrible ache in her chest. It didn't.

"I'll only be a second." She needed air and space. Roman didn't move, his body unnaturally still. She could feel his gaze follow her as she tossed the soap onto the pack and walked to the back of the tunnel to kick off her pants, shoes and bra, before going to the crevice to shower.

"It might be better if you turn around, Cerberus."

"No, Doc. That wouldn't be better at all." She froze at the rough tone. "I'll wait for you outside."

Damn the man. When he said things like that, it sent her desire into full tilt. Her hands shook, forcing her to take several uneven breaths before reaching for her pants zipper. It was almost as if they were playing a game—except she didn't know the rules.

Frustration shot through her, causing her to jerk the zipper. A cry escaped her lips as the metal teeth caught the tip of her finger. Damn! Damn! Damn! She shook her hand and spun around in a full circle. Stomping her foot when the pain didn't subside.

"What the hell happened?" Suddenly Roman was there, trying to grab the hand. She jerked it away.

"Don't touch me!" Fury welled up in her, then gushed from every pore. "Don't touch me again unless you mean it!"

Roman scowled. "Is that statement supposed to make sense to me?" He made another grab for her hand, but she slapped him away.

"Damn it. You're bleeding."

"I don't care." In deference to her statement, she sucked on the finger, almost gagging at the metallic taste of blood. Roman planted his hands on his hips and lifted his eyes to the ceiling. "I'm not even going to ask what this is about." Then his head dropped with an exasperated sigh. "But if you're finished, I suggest you take that cold shower."

His words fed her already-seething temper. She wasn't finished yet, not nearly. "Go to hell." She turned her back and yanked the pants off, kicking them across the ground for good measure. The action didn't soothe the fury, only inflamed it. She swung around. "Better yet, run away before I change the game rules." Reaching under her shirt, she unsnapped her bra before tugging the straps out her sleeves.

"Now what are you talking about?" His eyes narrowed, but she didn't care. She threw the bra onto the ground and got in his face.

"I'm talking about how you seduced me, lied to me and left me." She jabbed her hurt finger into his chest. "But most of all you made me love you. I hated you for that." The tears she hadn't realized she'd been holding in check ran.

The events of the past few days had left her too tired to control her emotions. Annoyed, she dashed the tears away. "You want to know why I had a condom in my purse?" She folded her arms tightly across her chest. "I carried that damn condom around for months because of you. I thought you'd come back and sweep me into your arms, then beg for my forgiveness." A bitter laugh escaped her. "God, I was so naïve."

She waited for a response, but Roman's face was set in cement. The lack of emotion didn't surprise her.

"Eventually, I smartened up and realized you weren't coming back. That you probably found someone else." *Amanda.* Her chin shot out. "I decided to use that condom for a one-night stand. To prove to myself I was still desirable."

A violent stream of Italian curses followed her words. She smiled derisively, only to have it drop away with his next comment.

"Of all the——"

"Don't say it." She snapped back, putting her fist up. "Don't you dare call me stupid." Grudgingly she added, "I couldn't do it, anyway, but even if I did, you would have no right to be upset about my actions."

He let out a disgusted sigh. "I can't believe you even considered it."

"*You* can't believe—" Dumbfounded by his self-righteous disappointment, she sputtered for the right words. "God, you...are...*unbelievable*. You leave me because you decide you don't want me, but the fact I might sleep with someone else makes you angry."

Suddenly the fight went out of Kate, and she let her fist drop to her side. "You not only broke my heart, you hurt my pride. One of the few things that gave me strength."

Cool fingertips slid under her chin, raising her head until her gaze met his. The tenderness reflected in the brown depths became blurry as tears flooded her eyes. She blinked them away.

With a gentle hand Roman cupped her cheek, his thumb skimming over the wetness. "If you'd decided against a one-night stand, why was the condom still in your purse?"

She closed her eyes against the love that welled up at the simple touch. She knew he expected her to resist answering, but instead she turned her face into his palm. "As a reminder never to put my heart at risk again."

But she had, despite her desperate fight not to. And she had risked it on the man who had shattered it the first time.

She opened her eyes in time to see his jaw clench.

"I guess I deserve that," he responded.

She shook her head. The pressure in her chest increased, forcing her to take a deep breath. It didn't matter that he couldn't love her. Not anymore. She loved him and that was enough. Slowly, she reached around his neck and buried her fingers in his hair, drawing his face to hers.

"Doc," Roman pleaded while his hand gripped her forearm to pull away.

"Shhh," she whispered, fear of refusal causing her to place her injured finger over his mouth. "I need this." The pad rubbed his lips. "I need you." "Please, she silently pleaded.

His lips moved lightly over the cut, sending shock waves down to her toes.

Then she was kissing him, opening her mouth, allowing him full access to the depths that waited. Her tongue met his as their bodies swayed together, lingering as thigh touched thigh, chest brushed chest. Kate's heart beat wildly, thundering in her ears.

With a groan Roman broke away and buried his face in the soft folds of her hair. His body convulsed against hers as he struggled for control. Something she didn't want. She tugged at his hair, wanting his mouth on hers again. This time he pulled her hand back, locking it between their bodies.

"It's not going to happen. I'm sorry." His arms fell and he stepped away. "I don't expect you to understand my decision, but I hope one day you'll accept it." He picked up the discarded Uzi. "I'm here to protect you, nothing more."

After he turned away, Kate slumped to her knees. Partly from disbelief, mostly from anger at herself. She only had herself to blame. She'd taken the risk and lost.

He walked to the entrance, his body rigid, his demeanor once again that of Cerberus. Kate clenched her hands in her lap to help fight her frustration. Why couldn't he be both lover and protector?

Kate blinked, stunned at the thought. Her mind raced back over the past few days. Every time they moved emotionally closer, he drew back behind the wall of protector. Roman's sense of right would allow nothing less.

A faint smile curved her lips and she whispered, "Ah, Kate, you used to be such a clever girl."

"We don't have all day, Doc."

The impatient order snapped her to her feet while a thought heaved against her heart. *But we have all night and it might be our last.* More determined than ever she grabbed the soap and headed toward the crevice.

THE POSSIBILITY OF TORTURE had never concerned Roman. When he'd become an operative, he'd known the risks involved. He'd been taught by the best and understood that at any given time, the enemy could capture him. But not once through his training did any of his superiors mention the purest form of torture would be observing Dr. Katherine MacAlister take a bath under a mountain waterfall in a downpour.

Nerves tense, he had watched her step under the torrent of water falling from the mountain crevice, grateful she'd meant to keep the T-shirt on. The less enticement the better, he had thought, turning to eye the leaden sky.

"Hurry up, Doc." He had swung back around to give the warning and felt the full impact of his mistake. Soap bar in hand, she had just reached underneath the shirt to scrub her body.

She stopped, hand hovering over her stomach, the wet underwear doing little to conceal her from his gaze. "I'll just be a few more minutes." The words came out hesitant and husky as she moved the soap in languid circles over her breasts and torso before sliding it down each limb with fanatical deliberation.

His heart quickened, a high vibration strumming through his veins, matching the tension of the tempest overhead. A nerve in his cheek twitched, and he gripped the Uzi tighter before redirecting his gaze back to the terrain.

The spattering drops soon turned to pelting rain soaking Roman. But the cold mountain storm did nothing to douse the heat building in Roman's body. Clenching his jaw, he fought down his hormones.

A muffled groan from behind snapped Roman back around before he realized it was the sound of pure satisfaction rather than of alarm.

. With her head thrown back, Kate washed her hair, using her hands to work through the glistening tresses. Unable to control the impulse, his gaze dropped to her shoulders then to her breasts, defined clearly as they pressed forward against the wet T-shirt. His groin tightened, growing into a full, heavy arousal.

Then she rinsed.

He watched with hooded eyes as she lifted her T-shirt and allowed the water to cascade over her body. The suds slid leisurely down the long length of her before dropping, almost unwillingly, to the ground.

She took exactly thirteen minutes. And during those thirteen minutes, Roman lived in hell.

Frustration edged his order to end it—which she did with a slight smile that lasted through dinner. A smile that set his teeth on edge and drove him to the opening of the tunnel for air.

"Make love to me."

Roman's nostrils flared at the softly spoken words.

"Go to sleep, Doc." He didn't turn to her or step back into the tunnel. The storm served as a distraction to what waited for him by the fire. "I thought we settled this. Don't do something you'll regret later."

"The only thing I regret is that I didn't try harder before."

He heard the rasp of her pants' zipper, then the faint brush of cloth against skin. If he turned around, she'd be standing there in nothing but that damned hunting shirt and a wisp of lace. Roman swallowed audibly, feeling the hold on his control grow more tenuous with each moment.

"It won't change anything, Doc. I'm still the same guy who left you two years ago."

"You might be. But it doesn't matter."

Roman's eyes searched the night, almost hoping one of Threader's men would make an appearance. Useless, he knew. The weather made it too dangerous for anyone to traverse the mountainside.

Like a cornered animal he got mean.

"Do you want me to use you and leave you like I did before? Because that's what I'll do." Snarling, he swung around to face her. Unblinkingly she met his glare, her silver eyes clashed against his.

"I'll take my chances," she said simply.

Disbelieving the quiet determination in her voice, Roman grunted.

She reached for the collar of her shirt. His heart jolted.

"What the hell are you doing?"

"I'm unbuttoning my shirt."

Damn. Desire slammed into his loins, almost bringing Roman to his knees. He tightened his jaw against the searing flash of heat. "Doc." The plea slipped out of his mouth before he could stop it. He tried to recover. "Don't be stupid, we have no protection." Out of shear desperation, he threw out his last bluff. "If you get pregnant I'll still leave you."

That stopped her. He could feel her hesitation. But it lasted only a few seconds before she laughed. The pure feline satisfaction in the tone caused Roman's blood to thicken and his body to throb. He watched, spellbound, while she finished slipping the last button free. Slowly she allowed the material to slide over her shoulders.

A hiss escaped from between her teeth.

She draped the shirt down her arms, then let it drop to the floor. "I'm beginning to realize I'm tougher than I look." Another laugh, this time deeper, more confident. "Maybe even tougher than you, Cerberus."

The truth of her words set off alarms in his head. Right now she *was* stronger. And he was growing weaker by the moment.

The muted hues of the firelight surrounded her, genting her features until she became an exotic creature of the night. The shadows danced across her body, camouflaging the bruises and casting her skin with a warm, golden glow.

A cold sweat slicked his skin.

She stepped closer.

Desperate to do the right thing, he reached up and grabbed the entrance of the tunnel with both hands, white knuckling the wood beam. But the bite of the pine did nothing to soothe his urge to bury his hands in the thick, mass of hair that flowed over her shoulders and down her breasts. The dusky pink of her nipples peeked through the dark tresses, their crested peaks tempting him to taste.

She turned away and he sucked air, grateful for the reprieve.

"Damn it, Kate, I don't want you." If she walked away now, he'd pull through.

The stiffening of her shoulders told him she'd heard. Against his will, his eyes sought her body, following the gentle arc of her hips, hanging for a brief second on the small indentation of her back.

"You're lying." She frowned over her shoulder before hooking her thumbs on the miniscule strings of fabric that draped her hips. "But even that won't stop me." She snapped the bands against her hips and Roman felt the reverberations through his groin.

"Are you watching?" She wiggled her bottom.

Are you wanting? were the words he heard. A growl rumbled deep from inside him, like an untamed beast fighting for a morsel of food. He didn't watch, he devoured. Unable to stop himself—not wanting to stop himself—his gaze locked on the soft roundness of her bottom as she bent over, slowly slipping the material down the slopes of her thighs. He flexed his hands against the beams, imagining the feel of the supple skin beneath his palm. The lace slid easily over the backs of her knees then down the slender arch of each calf. With a short flick of her ankle, Kate left the cloth lying on the ground.

Gnashing his teeth, Roman fought the tightening of his muscles.

She wasn't finished.

In the next millisecond she swung around to face him. Leisurely, she reached down and ran her hands back up her legs to her torso, pausing from time to time to tantalize.

Roman swore, viciously. The battle raged within him.

A battle he couldn't win.

"Do you like what you see Cerberus?" she whispered, the husky words unknowingly putting an end to the war. His fists came down from the ceiling to lay clenched against his sides. He shoved the guilt back into the recesses of his mind. Nothing was going to stop him. Not now.

Then he closed the distance, his eyes narrowing on his prey. "You've got two seconds to say no before it's too late." Even as he gave the warning, Roman wasn't sure he could afford two seconds.

"Don't you understand?" she murmured. "It's already

too late." Her eyes, luminous in the firelight, filled with emotion. "I love you."

A jab of intense pleasure hit him. On its heels came extreme pain. He didn't deserve her love or even want it. But the fact the he had it, if only for tonight, humbled him. With a growl he yanked her to his chest and tangled his hands in her hair, relishing the silken texture against his fingertips. God, how had he gone so long without her? He tugged her head back and exposed the tender flesh of her neck. How had he gone so long without *this*? "I can't love you back." He rasped the words against her throat before licking the area underneath the slope of her jaw.

"I know that, too," she acknowledged, trying not to let the truth of the words hurt.

She wound her arms around his neck and arched her body closer to his, suddenly the fear of him rejecting her again too much for her to bear. Then his body shuddered, swamping her with relief. This time he wasn't going to turn her away. He wasn't going to hide behind his duty.

His hands cupped the slope of her backside and lifted, fitting her tightly against the length of his arousal. Heat swirled in her belly, sending liquid fire sweeping down her thighs as she wrapped her legs around his waist.

"*Cerberus.*"

Roman swung her around and pinned her against the wall. She nearly cried out from the hard lines of his body rippling against the soft contours of hers.

His hand seared a path across her belly and dipped into the triangle of curls. He swallowed her gasp of sweet agony as his stroking fingers sent jolts of electricity through her body.

Fully aroused, Kate matched his urgency with her own unsated needs. She tugged at his shirt, whipping the offensive barrier over his head, before returning to the kiss with reckless abandon. She rubbed her breasts against his chest, trying desperately to ease their throbbing ache against the rough hair.

Roman released a tormented groan against her mouth and shifted her slightly down his hips, his muscles bunching under her hands with the effort. It was a heady invitation. Without breaking the contact of their lips, Kate reached down and unsnapped his pants. Freeing her mouth from his, she demanded, "Now, Cerberus."

His smoldering gaze seared her, the amber flecks in his eyes glinting liquid gold. "Try again, babe," he ordered, his hardness probing her soft entrance.

"Please."

A low, ragged laugh erupted by her ear in response to her entreaty.

"Don't ask me nice, just tell me correctly." He rocked against her seductively.

She couldn't control her shriek of frustration. She knew what he wanted her to say, but fear stopped her from giving in. He was asking her to sever her last lifeline, the last barrier between them. It was too much.

But then he pushed again, farther, only to pull back one more time. The feel of his hard body, the taste of his mouth, the fresh, damp smell of his skin and hair—all of it flooded her senses. Her thoughts fragmented as his hand and lips continued their hungry exploration. As her body began to vibrate, any need for self-preservation vanished.

"Now, Roman!"

Then he was in her, filling her just as he'd promised. It was an act of raw possession, of domination and control. One that sent her soaring, shattering into a million particles.

Chapter Twelve

A thunderous roar crashed against the mountain walls, shaking the timber of the mine and jolting Kate awake. A scream caught in her chest as the noise became deafening.

Roman gathered her close, shielding her for what seemed to be an eternity.

"Stay here," he ordered when the noise finally faded. He slipped on his pants, not bothering to zip them and stepped to the mine entrance, gun in hand.

Tufts of dirt fell from overhead and Kate looked toward the ceiling. Peering at the shadows left by the fire's flickering light, she searched the beams for any signs of weakness.

"A rock slide," Roman commented as he returned to their makeshift bed of clothes. Quickly he disposed of his pants and settled beside her. "We'll have a few rocks to climb tomorrow, but we're safe for now," he said, pulling the hunting shirt across her like a blanket.

Kate wasn't as confident as she laid her head back down. The mine had lasted more than one hundred years—she hoped fervently it lasted one more night. A cool, moist breeze danced across the dirt floor, sending shivers rippling over her skin. Squirming her backside into his body, she took comfort in the heat that radiated from his chest and thighs. He wrapped his arms tighter around her torso.

A sharp jab at Kate's hipbone elicited a small yelp of pain.

"What's the matter?" Roman tensed. Swiping her hand underneath the clothes, Kate realized the object was in Roman pants pocket.

An instant later it lay in her palm.

"Your lighter?" She handed it him.

"It's more than a lighter," he said, giving the object a quick once-over before setting it on the ground by their heads.

"Really?" Curious, she rolled onto her stomach and snagged it again. "Is it a flamethrower?" After turning it over several times in her hand, she studied the beat-up disposable lighter in the firelight.

"The bottom contains a small homing device."

Kate sat up, using Roman as a backboard, and looked at the base, still unable to see anything out of the ordinary. "Are you saying we're being tracked?"

Roman sighed, obviously realizing Kate's curiosity came before sleep. He unfolded himself and stood.

"Cain has the receiver. Another one of his backup plans." He reached over her shoulder and released a false bottom on the lighter to show a minuscule electronic chip. "It was designed by MacAlister Security."

After a moment he closed it again. "He can track us up to fifty miles away." Handing the device back to Kate, he walked over to the fire.

In the light, Roman's skin glistened. He had the body of a predator with an alertness defined in the sinew and muscle of his lean form. The sudden flash of him pinning her to the cave wall awakened a response deep within Kate.

"Cain has the only other device in existence. Unfortunately, I lost my receiver during our trip down the river."

She forced herself to look away as Roman fed the fire and draped the plaid shirt around her shoulders. "Otherwise, we would have known if he was close."

"It doesn't matter," she said and listened to the crackling of the fire, trying to ignore the uncertainty that wound through her heart. "Cain will come. The question is when."

"Soon. When I left, he was due back from another mission. The timing depends on his return." He snagged the canteen and took a swallow before handing it to her. "We'll be in Cedar by tomorrow. I expect he'll catch up there."

"Once you have me safe, what are you going to do about Threader? Kill him?"

"No. I don't want him dead." His eyes turned cold. "Dead is too easy. I want him to suffer."

Kate hesitated, taking a sip of the water. She chose her next words carefully. "Even at the risk of becoming like him?"

But Roman took no offense at her question. Instead he lay next her and pulled her close.

"From what our intelligence gathered, Threader was born poor, on the streets of London. His mother was a heroine-addicted whore, and he never knew his father. As a boy, he was extremely intelligent. He could match you IQ-to-IQ, Doc. By the age of eight, he ran petty scams and built a relatively small fortune. As a teenager he broke into the big-time with drug trafficking, arms dealing and white slavery. You name it, the man has his fingers in it. Somewhere along the line, he gained a fondness for inflicting pain."

He dropped a kiss by her ear. "Make no mistake, Threader is pure evil without a trace of humanity. There's no risk of becoming like him."

Kate heard the certainty in his tone but wasn't reassured. Somehow, she felt that if Roman brought Threader down as planned, he would lose part of his own humanity.

"Rumor had it," Roman continued, oblivious to her thoughts. "Threader was trying to turn legitimate. Now I'm not so sure. All our information is pointing to the fact that if he gets possession of your formula, he'll start destroying countries one by one until he is given what he wants."

"Which is?" she whispered.

"Power. But this, like most of the information we have on him, is unconfirmed."

"So he's ransoming mankind."

"Yes, it's possible but not plausible. World domination would be closer. I've been studying him for years trying to nail him. Came close once, but had the operation blow up in my face."

"Amanda?" She rested her face on his arm, savoring the feel of the crisp hair against her cheek.

"Yes, Amanda. Whenever we tried to plant an operative into Threader's operation, he'd find out almost immediately. We lost several. Amanda Salinas was the first woman who tried to infiltrate."

Roman caressed her shoulder. An odd twinge of jealousy passed through her at the admiration in his voice.

"Threader has a weakness for beautiful woman—and a reputation for maiming them if they displease him. She knew this and was willing to take the risk."

"Tell me about her," Kate asked. Maybe knowing more would alleviate the envy she felt for the dead woman.

He rolled onto his back pulling her with him until she ended up sprawled across his chest. When she laid her head in the crook of his shoulder, he pulled the hunting shirt back over both of them. Then he moved his hand to the base of her scalp and began to massage the area, a tendency from the past she took mistakenly as affection. Now she realized it was nothing more than a habit.

"Periodically, field operatives are assigned new recruits. A year or so back the director assigned Amanda to me. She impressed me from the start."

A quiet laughter rumbled in his chest. "And that's not easy to do. Her Puerto Rican–French heritage made her exotic and unusual. And yet that was only window dressing." His hand stopped. "Some people are born savvy. Amanda was one of them."

Gently, he brushed the hair from her cheek, his words growing distant. "And tough. Some of the women who come to work at the Agency put up a front, trying to be one of the men. Amanda didn't have to, she had a spine of steel."

He shifted and slid Kate back onto the clothes, then looked into her face. "I liked her from the beginning, Doc. The more missions we worked, the more I admired her. She followed procedures, never questioned field orders and caught on quickly. So quickly I ended up showing her a few things about computer intelligence. The technology fascinated her. She said it was the key to the future."

"I agree," Kate said softly.

"Not her future. Not anymore." Lightning flashed and the air around them crackled with electricity. With the flicker of light, Kate caught the lines of his face, somber and brooding.

"We set up the meeting at a casino in Monte Carlo. Dressed Amanda up sleek and cool. She'd studied Threader's profile until she had his personality down pat, then adapted."

He brought Kate deeper into his arms, obviously lost in

thought. "That was Amanda's talent you know, understanding the enemy. She could slip into their shoes and become them."

When he paused, she could feel his jaw clench, his throat muscles contract. "Threader fell into the trap. He was fascinated with Amanda and took her back to his Mexican island. For the next several months, she could come and go as she pleased. Always under his watchful eye, of course. Her job was to access Threader's computer and retrieve his business records. He had some powerful people on the take and we needed those records to bring them down."

Suddenly his voice changed, the tone becoming laced with frustration. "But after several weeks we were running out of time. Threader was becoming bored with Amanda, so I ordered her to pull out."

Kate could feel the tension in him build.

"She protested of course, but I wouldn't risk her life. Ultimately we decided on a secondary plan. Threader had arranged a nuclear warhead shipment for a terrorist group known as the Brotherhood, a vicious bunch of renegades who wanted nothing more than to kill for notoriety. Amanda was going to damage the shipment then disappear."

"They'd want Threader's blood."

"Exactly. We're talking a hundred million dollars in nuclear. His other customers would get nervous, leaving the door open for us to get to him another way." He heaved a sigh. "Everything was a go. She'd set small charges to damage the merchandise. Then we rendezvoused in a cove by the fishing village."

"If you had suspicions, why not—"

"Send in the troops?" he said derisively. "Because we only had suspicions. No hard evidence. Threader has too many international connections for us to lead with our chin and come up empty. It could be disastrous for the United States diplomatically."

"You sound like this was your only chance."

"It was our best chance. We'd come close once before in Morocco, but lost a warehouse full of contraband when a few stray bullets ignited some stored explosives," he said. "That left us with Amanda's plan."

"But something went wrong." Instinctively she knew Roman needed to say the next words aloud.

He nodded. "The day of the pickup, she broke his security code but didn't have time to download it."

Kate understood. "She went back for the information."

"She couldn't without my go-ahead. I gave it to her. We needed that information."

"What happened?"

"I don't know exactly. Somehow Threader must have discovered she'd set the charges. Within a few hours of her return to the villa, he had her strung up in the courtyard, beaten and bloody. When he got tired of the game, he let his men have her while he watched."

Roman touched the side of her face, then slid his fingers down her cheek before letting his hand drop away.

In a heartbeat his voice turned to steel and his eyes became flat and hard.

"I sent the rest of the team back to the rendezvous point. It took me eight hours to get in sniper position." He closed his eyes briefly, remembering. "Eight hours of hearing her scream like a wounded animal, until her vocal cords broke. Then I took her out at four hundred meters."

Sensing his torment, Kate tried to comfort him. "You had no choice, Roman. She had information that could've gotten you all killed."

"I operated strictly on a need-to-know basis. Any information she possessed was directly related to the mission." A muscle worked spasmodically in Roman's jaw as he searched her gaze for understanding. "He tortured Amanda in ways you'd only see in a concentration camp. Even if we could've penetrated Threader's defense and rescued her, she was so badly injured we couldn't have saved her."

He showed Kate the scar on the back of his hand, his fist clenched tight. "I ran into a couple soldiers with knives on my way back to the team and got this as a reminder. One I'll carry for the rest of my life."

The unquestionable pain in Roman's eyes caused an intense ache under Kate's heart. "You must have loved her very much."

Roman sat up, untangling himself from Kate. "Is that what you think?"

"Yes." She slipped her arms into the sleeves of the hunting shirt, then hugged it tight, trying to stave off the cold that suddenly seeped into her bones.

"I cared for her, sure. I never loved her. She worked for me, she was one of my team and my responsibility. Her death was a direct result of my order. I got greedy and made a bad call."

He drew in a long breath. "After the doctors released me, I decided to use my own time to bring Threader down by myself."

Kate understood what he didn't say. His pain, his revenge, his way. The thought had barely registered when another followed. A thought that had lingered in her mind for some time.

"Roman, back in the cabin when Dempsey held me with the gun, you told him your orders were to keep the formula out of Threader's hands. I assumed that meant either by bringing me back safe or by taking me out of the equation."

"When in danger, bluff. That's exactly what I was doing, Doc. I had to make sure he didn't pull that trigger."

"You weren't bluffing. You and I both know that if Threader gets hold of me, I could end up like Amanda, strung up in the courtyard." A needle of fear pricked her spine, but she continued. "I work with equations every day of my life, some more difficult to comprehend than others. This one is simple. If you take me out of it, Threader has nothing to deal with."

"You're missing one key element." His voice was calm, his gaze steady. "You see, I'll already be dead. Because the only way Threader is getting to you is through me, and the only way he's getting through me is over my dead body."

Kate nodded, hearing the statement for what it was—a call of duty.

"Ridiculous as it sounds, I thought you left me for Amanda. I know now I was wrong."

"She was my responsibility, nothing more." There was a tense pause. "You were a good time."

Stunned and sickened, she could only repeat the words. "A good time." She stiffened and her defiance rose. "Was that before or after we went to bed together?"

When she started to stand, he grabbed her arm and tugged her back onto the makeshift bed. "Things changed. The more time we spent together, the more important you became to me."

"And you couldn't allow that," she snapped, pulling against his grip.

"My job is my top the priority—will *always* be my priority. You'd always be secondary." He let her arm go, his glare daring her to get up again. "Hell, we both know you were raised in an environment where family comes first. Could you accept that?"

Kate couldn't argue the truth of his statement. The love and closeness she had experienced growing up were something she'd always hoped to pass on to her children.

"Not to mention the secrets. My line of work doesn't permit the typical end-of-the-day discussion between couples. The fact that you know I'm a government operative only makes the circumstances worse. Think of it, Kate. You'd never know where to reach me. If I was in danger or not. Or even dead."

He thrust his fingers through his hair. "It's no way to live. Eventually the stress would eat at the relationship until we hated each other."

"I see." She saw the conviction etched his face, telling her he would never consider retiring—would never love her as much as he loved his job. "So you terminated the relationship, quickly and efficiently."

"I thought it best."

He had decided with no consideration to her thoughts or feelings. She didn't realize until that moment that she still held out hope. Hope that Roman loved her. Hope that one day they would be together...

She took a huge, ragged breath before finally letting that hope die. "So what do we do now?"

He gathered her stiff body close and lay back on the ground. "We sleep until the rain stops. Then we hike to Cedar."

THE MUTED SHADES OF DAWN touched the tunnel entrance when Roman woke. Silence surrounded them, interrupted only by Kate's rhythmic breathing. Sometime during the night, she'd crawled on top of him. The shirt lay open, leaving her bare against his chest with her hair splayed across his throat and shoulders. He touched the sleek tresses with the tip of his fingers.

He'd hurt her last night, intentionally, with half truths. But he couldn't let her waste love on him. His hand slipped under the shirt and traced the line of her spine until it reached the soft indentation of her bottom. Still, the knowledge he'd done the right thing didn't alleviate the guilt.

"Wake up, babe," he said roughly, masking the feelings inside him. Kate squirmed until she settled herself deeper into the apex between his thighs. Her soft triangle of curls brushed against him, making him instantly hard. With a groan, Roman rolled over, then levered himself above her. Precious inches of air separated them, giving Roman little space to control his urges. He wanted nothing more than to lose himself again in her warm willing body, but he refused to let his hormones distract him from the danger they were in.

"Time to go. Now."

Kate's eyes fluttered open and she looked up, trying to see if any of the earlier emotions from last night remained on his face. Not surprised, she saw nothing but the inherent strength of the man beneath.

Rising from her, Roman extinguished the fire and carefully buried the coals while she dressed in silence. Once she was clothed, he handed her some rations. "That's all. It'll have to last until we reach Cedar." Then he reached into his pocket and pulled out the lighter. "Take this."

When she didn't immediately do as he said, he grabbed her front pocket and shoved the lighter in.

"Keep it on you at all times. If we're separated or something happens to me, find the deepest, darkest ditch you can and stay there. Don't come out, not even to relieve yourself." The dark eyebrows slanted. "Cain will find you."

Realizing arguing was futile, she forced a smile. "Okay."

They stepped out into the glare of the morning sun, and for the first time Kate had the opportunity to take in their surroundings. The mine was built on a flat wide ledge of the mountainside, crumbling from years of erosion. Roman had carried her up to the rim of the timberline. A glance above revealed the jagged and unscalable walls of the mountain. Anxiety jabbed at her as Roman walked to the edge.

She stepped back, not able to bring herself to follow him. For distraction, she searched for the side trail they'd taken to the waterfall. Foreboding brushed her nerve endings and started them tingling. No more than a few feet away, where the trail used to be, lay a high wall of rock and mud.

Suddenly Roman was by her side, studying the wall of debris. "It looks like we're doing this the hard way."

She swallowed and tried to laugh. Her breath came out in a puff. "What else is new?"

"The rock slide was worse than I thought. It goes at least several thousand feet down and it took a good portion of the mountain with it."

If he noted her hesitancy, he ignored it. Cerberus was firmly in place. He dropped the backpack to the ground. "We can't climb over the slide here. With the degree of the slope and the sodden ground, those rocks could give anytime." Grabbing Kate's ragged shorts from the bag, he said. "We'll scoot down on our butts, you behind me like before. We're going to have to use our hands and feet for balance." He ripped the shorts into wide strips. "Give me your hands."

Quickly, Roman wrapped the cloth around her palms before securing them with a knot. "This will protect your skin. When we reach a safer point, where the terrain is more level, we'll scale the rocks and climb back up to the trail."

Kate found herself glancing uneasily over his shoulder. "It's going to be okay, Kate. You're not doing this alone."

"I know." When she tried to speak, her voice wavered. She cleared her throat before trying again. "Just promise me the next time we have to run from a psychotic arms dealer, that we do it where there's nothing but flat land, okay?"

Amusement flickered in the eyes that met hers. "I promise."

The descent was surprisingly simple once Kate got the hang of it. Planting her feet and hands wide, she slid over the gravel and mud. Deliberately she kept her gaze focused on the back of Roman's head and ignored the pinches of anxiety that plagued her. The route he'd picked kept them parallel with—but at a safe distance from—the slide. Once, when speed almost caused her to lose control, his back was there to halt her momentum. After a few hundred yards, he stopped. Kate took a shaky breath in an attempt to slow her racing heart.

"Here's a good place. The slopes are less drastic and the rocks more stable."

She glanced up to the side, following his gaze. The barricade of debris reminded her of a rock pile she'd once seen in an old prison movie. Approximately six feet high, it hardly looked stable.

Not trusting her limbs, she locked her arms around her bent knees to stop the trembling and waited while Roman took a closer look.

Within minutes he was back and pulled her to her feet. "It's secure enough. Take your time, find the larger rocks and use them as steps. If it feels unstable choose another and wait until you're balanced. I'll be right behind you."

Still wary, Kate picked her way over. At the crown of the wall, Roman snagged her pants. "Turn around and face me. It'll be easier to keep your balance."

Following orders, Kate shifted her feet until she faced the rocks, gripping Roman's shoulders for balance.

"Take it slow."

She smiled at his warning and started her descent. Rocks crumbled all around her, but he urged her on. "Only a few more feet and we're home free."

She stepped down, instinctively feeling for the ground underneath her feet. She settled her weight and breathed a sigh of relief. "I did it."

Kate heard the sharp snap of boards just as Roman screamed, "Move!" Time slowed as the earth gave way underneath her feet. Suddenly Roman shoved her hard, sending her flying. A horrendous crash echoed around her, mixing with her own scream of terror as she slammed into the ground.

Chapter Thirteen

"You didn't have to shove me so hard. I was moving." Kate laid her cheek against the dirt, struggling to get air back into her lungs. When no reply came, she rolled over and sat up. "Roman?" She scrambled back up a few feet. "Roman!"

A hole about four feet in diameter lay where she'd been a few moments before. From the look of the broken boards, it appeared to be part of an old mining shaft.

She took a step closer, trembling. "Roman! Damn it, answer me!" She waited, but there was no response.

"He's okay, Kate. He's okay." She chanted the words under her breath as she dropped first to her knees, then her belly. Impatiently she tore the cloth from her hands. *He's okay.* She gripped a ragged board that rimmed the opening and pulled herself to the edge. Closing her eyes, she eased her head and shoulders over the lip.

"Open your eyes, Kate. It's just a hole," she told herself. She blinked once, then a second time, before forcing her eyes to stay open.

Below lay nothing but a black void.

"Roman, please answer me." She reached into her pocket for the lighter, praying that it actually worked.

Shakily, she lowered the flickering light, bracing her arm across the hole for support. Fear washed over her, drenching her with perspiration. The hole was several feet deep, disclosing a wide tunnel below. The earth tilted and a sudden need to retch cramped her insides. She closed her eyes for a brief moment and took another deep breath.

"Roman!"

No response. She opened her eyes and then saw him lying on his back, his arm distended awkwardly. Fighting her panic, she scooted back, clasped her knees to her chest and began rocking.

Best-case scenario, he was unconscious with a broken arm or shoulder. Worst case, he had internal injuries.

Kate stared at the hole. God, he might be dying and she couldn't even look at him without falling apart. Desperately she took in her surroundings, seeing nothing to help her save Roman.

What would *he* do? Probably weave a rope out of leaves or something. She looked at her clothes, instantly dismissing the idea to use them for a rope as ludicrous.

Think, Kate! Furious with her helplessness, she hit her fist against her head, only to swear when the corner of the lighter jabbed her forehead.

Slowly, she opened her hand and stared at the lighter. Her thoughts snapped into focus. She had two options. She could stay put, see if he came around and take the chance his injuries weren't life threatening. Or she could find help.

Kate studied the mountain. Roman had said Cedar was a half-day walk northwest of here. Did half a day mean five hours? Or six? In five hours he could be dead.

Of course, that was avoiding roads and people. Maybe if she found a well-used trail, she'd find help. It was a risk—one that put her in danger of running across Threader's men. Still, it was a risk she had to take.

For the first time, she understood Cain's need to always have a backup plan. She hugged the lighter to her chest. "Find him, Cain, please, for me. Don't let him die."

Without hesitation, she dropped the lighter into the hole and quickly covered the opening with loose branches. Then bit by bit, she picked her way west across the mountain.

WHITE-HOT FIRE seared Roman's shoulder. He jerked away. Bone ground against bone, eliciting a grunt as he struggled to focus past the onslaught of dizziness. In his mind, he saw the ground give out from under Kate and his shove to keep her safe.

He raised his head. "Doc?"

Razor-sharp stars glanced off the inside of his skull and bile rose in his throat. Roman let his head drop back to the ground. Fending off another explosion of stars, he forced his muscles to relax and took inventory.

He'd dislocated his shoulder. Having accomplished the same feat several times over the past few years, he was familiar with the jarring pain. The head injury was another matter.

Using his good arm, he probed the back of his scalp until he felt the warm, sticky blood. A hindrance certainly, but not critical.

He moved the rest of his limbs cautiously, each stiff and sore from the fall but otherwise undamaged.

"Kate?" Gritting his teeth, Roman sat up, only to suck in air as his right arm dragged up against his body, useless. He counted to ten slowly, then scooted against the wall.

He willed his eyes to adjust to the darkness. Another slug of pain hit him, but he ignored it and slid off the backpack. When his hand closed around the flashlight, he thumbed the switch.

The beam glanced over the area. Splintered pieces of wood lay at his feet. He flashed the light over the ceiling. The hole, toothed with more broken boards and covered with debris, was several feet above his head. An old ventilation shaft. From the smell of the stale air, it must've remained hidden for years until the rockslide weakened the already rotting wood.

"Kate!"

No answer. Except this time Roman didn't expect one. She was gone. Instinctively he knew it. The tension inside him tightened, threatening to snap.

After tucking the flashlight in his waistband, he struggled to his feet, using his good hand to claw the wall for support.

She had screamed just before he'd fallen through the hole. If near, Threader's men would've heard it, too. He shoved away from the wall and grabbed the light. Time was running out.

With an effort that left his body damp, Roman searched the passageway only to find that the hole above him was his only means of escape. He bit out a string of curses. Even if he had a rope—which he didn't—the dislocation prevented him from climbing.

His gaze settled on the pine support beam half buried in the dirt wall. The possibility of another cave-in loomed over Roman as he gave the beam a couple of hard shoves, testing its strength. Satisfied the wood wouldn't budge, he placed his shoulder against the pine.

He pulled back, preparing to use every ounce of power to try to reset his shoulder, when a faint rustle of branches drifted from the opening. He froze and within moments a flash of light bounced through the tunnel.

The soft twittering of a bird whistled.

Cain.

Thank God. Kate was safe.

"Here." Roman called and slid to the floor. Another wave of dizziness hit him, underscoring the throbbing in his skull.

"Your mama was worried," came the warm, welcoming response from above. Roman smiled grimly at the code words. In normal circumstances Cain's voice was never warm or welcoming.

"My mama loves me," he replied.

Any other response, and Cain would've known that Roman had undesirable company in the tunnel. A rope dropped from the hole.

"How's Kate?" Roman shouted, unable to wait until his partner joined him.

"She's not with you?" A sudden, thin chill hung on the question as Cain, dressed in full military gear, rappelled, hitting the ground only a few feet away. He unclipped his harness and crossed to Roman.

In the dimness, the similarities between brother and sister appeared stronger. The black hair. The aristocratic features. Usually Cain's gray eyes remained passive under hooded lids, but now they glittered with the hue of tempered steel.

"What the hell do you mean? Didn't you track the lighter?" Anger singed the corners of Roman's control as comprehension dawned. Cain had tracked the lighter—to the tunnel.

Cain flashed the high-beam light across Roman before sending it over the floor. Within moments he stopped on an object lying by the opposite wall.

"You mean this?" Cain asked before picking up the lighter.

Swearing, Roman turned on Cain. "Your sister is the most reckless—"

Cain held up his hand, cutting off Roman's tirade. He touched a small transmitter on his ear. "Repeat that."

Roman raised an eyebrow. "Ian?"

With a nod of affirmation, Cain answered. "Everything's secure. Copy that. I'm going to need your help. Roman dislocated his shoulder."

This time, Roman interrupted. "Tell him to stay put. There's no way out of here except up."

"Disregard that order. Roman says we're sitting ducks down here. Watch our backs and I'll let you know when I need help."

Cain hesitated, his features impassive. "Kate's not here. Scope the area and see if you can pick up anything. I want to know if she had company or if she went looking for help."

There was a long pause. Cain's voice burned with emotion when he spoke again. "Affirmative. We'll each take a turn beating her when we find her."

Roman's lips tightened in understanding. Neither brother nor Roman would ever hurt Kate, but the thought was somehow comforting nevertheless. "What time is it?"

Cain dropped his gear to the ground. "Ten hundred hours."

He'd been unconscious for two hours, then. Roman leaned against the wall, wincing when he bumped his scalp wound. "Kate's got about a three-hour start on us."

Alerted by Roman's pained expression, Cain crouched, then held the light to Roman's head. "Do you know where she's gone?"

He probed the wound. Roman's jaw tightened. "Cedar."

"We'll catch up," he said, before examining Roman's shoulder. "Any other injuries?"

"No."

Cain stepped away and flashed the light against the hole. "You'll survive." He brought the beam back to Roman, his voice cool and clear like ice water. "It's probably a good thing you hit your head first. Anything else would've killed you."

Roman knew when his partner was making a joke. The man had a sense of humor drier than the Sahara. "Yeah, tell me that again, after you snap my shoulder back into place."

Dropping the flashlight, Cain grabbed Roman's arm in a viselike grip and placed his foot snug against the indent of the injured shoulder. Roman steeled himself for what was to come.

"Ready?"

Before Roman could respond, Cain gave a vicious yank. Bone slid and snapped. Roman let out an agonizing roar. "Damn, it never gets any easier." Taking in a few puffs of air, he waited while the burning dissipated into a dull ache. Then he tested his arm.

Not much strength, but at least it was mobile. What he needed was a sling, but it would let their enemies know of the injury and give them an advantage.

Taking his good hand, Cain pulled Roman to his feet and helped him with the backpack before donning his own equipment. "Let's find my sister."

A few minutes later Roman, Cain and Ian stood on the ground by the hole.

"I found the trail." Ian, also outfitted in fatigues and gear, pointed west. "She was alone and not running from anyone." Different in looks from his siblings, Ian had cobalt-blue eyes and the chestnut hair of his father, cropped military short. "The tracks are practically invisible up to a hundred yards away. She did a hell of a job hiding them."

"She's been watching me for the past few days." Watching and learning, Roman thought. *Let's hope it saves your life, Doc.*

Aloud, he issued orders. "Take point, Ian. You're the better tracker. Cain and I will bring up the rear."

Cain nodded his agreement before adding, "Let's move. My little voice is telling me we're running out of time."

Roman had learned to respect that voice over the years. It had saved his and Cain's lives so many times he'd lost count.

He glanced at his partner when Ian jogged ahead. Forged from an innate sense of caution, precision and justice, Prometheus was one of the best in their field.

"When this is over," Cain said, interrupting Roman's thoughts. "You can tell me what the hell you did to my cabin."

Roman smiled. "I blew it to pieces." Then his lips turned grim. "But you have a bigger problem, chief. Labyrinth has a mole."

KATE HIKED THROUGH the trees that hugged the paved road, loosening her back muscles now and then, trying to ease the ache between her shoulder blades. Had she done the right thing? she wondered for the hundredth time, her eyes searching the deserted road. Surely help would come soon.

Pinpricks swept up her spine and over her scalp. Braced to run, she watched as a rabbit hopped from a nearby bush. When it paused, its nose twitching in the air, Kate smiled, light-headed with relief.

"Don't worry, bunny. I don't have a knife. Even if I did, I'm a lousy aim."

"Perhaps all you need is a little practice, Dr. MacAlister."

Kate's heart jumped at the softly spoken words. Before she could move, a huge, bald-headed man dressed in camouflage stepped from the trees.

"Allow me to introduce myself," the man continued, his tone thick with a Mediterranean accent. "I am Quamar Bazan." He salaamed. "I work for Nigel Threader."

Suddenly a half-dozen men surrounded her, all pointing machine guns. Each was dressed in army fatigues, unshaven and drenched in sweat. One in particular smiled at Kate, his oily face gleaming with pleasure. Kate suppressed the urge to gag.

She'd failed. A heaviness settled in her chest. She'd failed all those innocent people. And she'd failed Roman. No doubt if she didn't get these men out of the area soon they'd eventually locate Roman. She couldn't let that happen.

When in danger; bluff. Kate stiffened when Roman's words jarred her thoughts. Her mind reacted quickly.

"It's about time." She addressed Quamar as if she were an assistant. "I want to see Threader."

When surprise registered in the man's face, Kate contained a bleak smile. Somehow, she'd bet the giant didn't surprise easily.

"Forgive me if I don't believe your enthusiasm." Quamar looked at Oily Face. "Search the area. I want Cerberus found."

"You're wasting your time," she interrupted. "He's dead."

"I have time."

"I don't. I wish to see Threader now." Quamar's lips twitched slightly at her words, so slightly Kate almost missed it.

"Pardon me, Doctor, but once again, I do not believe you." She lifted her shoulder negligently, and the ache in the center of her back grew worse with her nervousness. "We lost our footing in the river and ended up tangled in debris. Cerberus got trapped underneath and drowned."

"How is it, then, you were last sighted across the river?"

"You mean by Juan? You'll find his body downstream also. Cerberus killed him before we tried crossing the river. It was Cerberus who told your men we were heading southeast."

Quamar studied her for a minute, the opaque eyes boring into her. "And now you wish to see Threader."

"Yes. Do you think I'm wandering around alone in this godforsaken place for my health?"

"I don't know, but you've managed to wander far and in the opposite direction from where Cerberus sent my men."

Kate let out an impatient sigh, then looked down her nose at the man. A difficult task considering he towered over her by almost a foot.

The giant ignored the look. "I'm curious, Doctor. You've been running for two days. Why the sudden change of heart now?"

"I'll discuss my reasons only with Threader."

Quamar's thoughtful gaze rested on her a moment, then, speaking brisk Spanish, he nodded toward a man near Kate. "Eduardo, you and your men will escort Dr. MacAlister to Isla El León. You will treat her with respect." His eyes narrowed on the men. "If she is harmed in any way, you will suffer. Am I understood?"

"*Sí, Señor Quamar,*" answered the man called Eduardo, his voice tight with apprehension.

A strong sense of relief swept through Kate making her knees weak. With Roman's life at stake everything depended on Bazan's calling off the search for him. She bit the inside of her lower lip. *Please, God, let him be alive.*

"After the tilt rotor drops you off at the airstrip," Quamar continued, "have the pilot refuel and return. By then I will be ready." Quamar smiled at Kate, a full steely smile. "In the meantime I will look for Cerberus."

"I told you, he drowned," she warned.

"Doctor, I am the best," Quamar replied in English. "And you were convincing up to a point. But you—how do you say—underestimate me." He paused as the men flanked her. "I do not believe you had any intention of seeing Threader. And I do not believe Cerberus is dead." His gaze skirted over the area. "Injured maybe, but not dead." The black eyes danced with anticipated pleasure. "You see, I have known Cerberus for many years."

Kate felt the blood drain from her face at the cold familiarity in the man's words.

"To drown in a river is an easy death." He ran his tongue over his teeth. "And the Cerberus I know would not die so easy."

Chapter Fourteen

Roman had to admit Kate possessed a good sense of direction. They'd been tracking her for a couple of hours, and all the signs indicated she was headed straight for Cedar.

"You're right. She's going for help." Cain voiced Roman's thoughts. Something that happened often between the partners.

"She should have stayed put."

"I agree." Cain whistled and immediately got a response. Ian was still ahead, scouting.

While hiking, Roman told Cain about the past few days. Everything, that is, except the more intimate details.

"The mole could be anyone. All it takes is knowledge of the computer-access codes. Hell, there could be more than one person," Cain concluded.

Roman glanced at his friend, noticing for the first time the lines of fatigue etched in his face. He knew better than to mention it. "I realized that, too. That's why I didn't call in for reinforcement and attempted to extract Kate myself."

Cain scanned the area, his brows drawn together, his expression set. "Mercer would've given you the order to eliminate her if you couldn't save her."

Roman was aware of the emotions his partner held in

check—he'd been battling them since Mercer's phone call several days earlier. "It never became necessary. But I have to tell you, that damn Scottish attitude of hers almost drove me to it."

Cain's lips curved slightly, then he turned serious once more. "If you had to make the choice of either eliminating Kate——"

"It would never reach that point. We'd both be dead first," Roman interrupted, his tone harsh with emotion. Cain nodded his understanding and stepped through the bushes.

A deep voice spoke from behind. "But as I have said before, Cerberus, you are a man who will not die easily."

Cain and Roman swung around in unison, hitting the ground in opposite directions before coming up crouched and armed. The giant had no gun, just Ian, who was unconscious and casually slung over the man's shoulder.

Roman let the tension flow from his body and pointed his weapon down. "Damn it, Quamar, you almost got yourself shot."

The giant laughed and slowly lowered Ian to the ground.

"Did you hurt him?" Roman asked, concerned over the stillness of his friend.

"He better not have." Cain's growl rumbled through the trees, his eyes searching for additional company.

"He's a friend, Cain," Roman inserted, raking his fingers through his hair. "I'm sure Ian is all right."

Quamar nudged Ian gently with his foot. "He will be fine. I cut off his oxygen, but he should be unconscious for only a few more minutes." Then the big man laughed. "As a soldier he is good, but I am better. Somehow he heard me." Quamar shrugged. "I incapacitated him before he sent out a warning. In a few more years, he will make an excellent adversary."

Sensing Cain's rising anger, Roman decided to defuse the situation. "Cain, this is Quamar Bazan."

The lines of suspicion deepened on Cain's face at the mention of Quamar's name.

"I'm aware of who he is." Cain's voice flattened into a deadly edge as he stepped from his brother and tilted his gun up. "An ex-Mossad operative, one of their best before he turned renegade. Trained also with the old KBG. Now a soldier for hire with a reputation for walking both sides of the law."

Quamar shrugged his indifference at the insult. "The law is to the people. I choose to follow the laws of *my* people."

Roman cut in before the situation got any hotter.

"He didn't turn renegade. He's a contract agent. I trust Quamar with my life, Cain."

That stopped Cain. His partner grudgingly lowered his gun.

Quamar removed a handkerchief from his pocket and rubbed the sweat from his bald head, ignoring Cain's suppressed hostility. "What Cerberus failed to mention is that on a mission, an Arab rebel unit targeted my tribe. He saved my people and now has my loyalty."

Roman, uncomfortable with the praise, interrupted. "After Amanda's death, Quamar used his contacts for an introduction to Threader."

Quamar tucked the cloth in his back pocket and watched as Cain crouched by Ian. "Threader prefers gore and it is easy for me to give him what he desires most." Then the big man sighed. "So far my victims have been undesirables. But I have not been able to prevent Threader from taking innocent lives, either."

Ian's eyes fluttered open and Quamar grunted when the

SEAL's pupils focused. He glanced at Cain. "Your brother, he is fine."

A groan cut across the air as Ian sat up taking the friendly scene in at a glance. Quamar slapped his shoulder goodnaturedly, ignoring how Ian's fists rose defensively.

"I would stand beside you in battle."

"Am I missing something here?" Ian asked, his eyes wary.

"We're wasting time," Cain bit out. He grasped Ian's hand and hauled him to his feet. "Kate's still missing."

"She is on her way to Threader's island," Quamar responded.

"You couldn't stop it?" Ian demanded.

"I ordered it. There were too many men around when I discovered her. I could not rescue her safely." Nodding to Roman, he added, "Dr. MacAlister is a brave woman. She told me you had drowned, then demanded to see Threader."

Roman frowned. The woman was determined to protect him, even if it meant her own life.

"The only thing she fears is heights," Quamar said. "Because of this, I ordered them to blindfold her."

"Damn it!" Roman cursed as the image his friend painted flashed through his mind.

"They know Kate's an acrophobic?" Cain snarled. "From what you've told me, Threader will use it to his advantage."

Roman snapped around at Cain's comment. "You knew—?"

"That she was afraid of heights? Of course. You can't keep something like that from family."

"We've kept up appearances for Kate's sake," Ian inserted, echoing Cain's attitude. "Although it hasn't been easy. She didn't want her secret known. Probably considered it a weakness. We decided a long time ago to humor her. Figured that was one of the problems of being so smart—she couldn't accept any flaw in herself." He glanced at Roman with only a hint of a grin. "I take it you didn't know."

The men waited for Roman's confirmation. He gave it bluntly. "Not until yesterday morning."

"There are too many hours between us," Cain said, steel blades edging his tone. "He'll have plenty of time with Kate to play his sick games."

"Possibly, but I don't think he will harm her," Quamar responded, thoughtful. "I think he intends to marry her."

"The hell you say!" Ian spat at the ground. "She'd kill him first. I'll kill him first!"

Roman ignored Ian's outburst, a deadly calm settled over him. "How do you know? Did he tell you his plans?"

Quamar sighed. "No, he shares his thoughts with only one person, a woman named Phoenix. My opinion is based on my orders to bring in Prometheus to enjoy his sister's wedding."

"If what you say is true, I'll be there." Cain stepped up, bringing the two men chest-to-chest, his face set in stone. "Can you guarantee she'll remain unharmed?"

Quamar shook his head. "That is impossible. The man is insane. More so each day."

"I've a plan that will guarantee it," Roman countered. The idea of Threader touching Kate incited his fury and his fear. "We just have to give him a way to control her other than using pain." He locked his gaze on Cain. "Do you trust me?"

Cain met the stare, his feet still firmly planted in front of Quamar. "If it will save Kate, I would trust Satan."

"No, not Satan," Roman said grimly. "Just Satan's protector."

"It's decided." Quamar glanced at the sky and stepped

back from Cain. "I have the tilt rotor waiting for us. When we reach the aircraft, we will dispose of the pilot. Then I will give thanks to Allah and ask him to watch over us before we fly to Isla El León."

Quamar turned to Roman. "On the way, you can explain your plan," he said. "And I will give you information regarding the woman named Phoenix. It is very possible she is your mole."

THE SWELTERING HEAT of the island slapped Kate in the face like a wet rag as she stepped from the twin-engine plane with her escort. Considering her docile, Eduardo had accompanied her with the help of only one other man, leaving the rest to follow in a separate cargo plane. They'd treated her with a cool politeness. And both were careful not to touch her.

A white limousine crossed the tarmac and stopped a few feet from Kate. Eduardo opened the passenger door.

"Please join me, Dr. MacAlister," an elegant voice insisted.

Kate hesitated, wanting to ignore the request until she felt the soft prod of Eduardo's gun. When she slid onto the cool leather seat, Eduardo closed the door. The lock clicked.

Her first look at Nigel Threader's profile surprised her. Handsome, like an Adonis, he was younger than she expected. Not much over forty, he was the perfect male specimen with his blond hair, blue eyes and gray Armani suit. Nevertheless, a slickness ran underneath the elegant persona, which made Kate's skin crawl.

Then he turned to face her. She barely stopped the sharp intake of breath as her gaze locked on the right side of his face. A crescent scar, larger than a silver dollar, half circled his eye, puckering the skin and pulling grotesquely on the eyelid.

"Welcome to Isla de El León. I trust you had a good trip."

Recovering, Kate's attention turned from the deformity. When she didn't answer, he shrugged. "No matter. I expected obstinacy at first. You haven't disappointed me." He poured her champagne. "Yet."

Kate recognized the Waterford pattern. The man had expensive taste. After handing her a glass, he raised his champagne in a mock toast and drank. Kate continued to hold hers, unwilling to participate in the charade.

His mouth tightened but his voice remained silky. "I would introduce myself, but I'm sure it's unnecessary." Threader's eyes caught hers, the blue turning laser. "And knowing Cerberus, he has told you what I am capable of. Didn't he, Katherine?"

He lifted an eyebrow when she stiffened over her name. "You don't mind me calling you by your given name do you?"

"Yes, but not as much as I mind being in your company."

His lips thinned against his teeth. "Well, it will be your responsibility to adjust. You'll find that I do as I please and you'll learn to accept it." He set his glass on the small cherry wood table in front of their seat.

Kate cleared her throat, determined to keep her voice even. "Let me be direct, then." She set her glass beside his with only a faint tremor. "You want the formula. I have it. And I'm willing to negotiate."

His amused gaze slid over her face, down her body.

He leaned back and crossed his legs. "Very well, my dear, let us negotiate.

"My equations for the formula are instrumental in—"

"You misunderstand," Threader interrupted. "The formula is only a part of the negotiations." He waved his hand. "A bonus."

Kate couldn't hide the confusion that crossed her face.

"What we are bargaining for," he said, drawing out the words until they slithered through the car, "is the life of your brother Cain and your lover, Roman D'Amato."

Kate froze. "I don't understand."

Threader clucked his tongue. "Yes, you do."

Kate willed herself to ignore the dread that gripped her.

"I'm sure this comes as quite a shock, but I received a call as you taxied in. I believe you have met my employee, Quamar?"

Kate could only nod.

"It seems he's captured your brothers and Roman. He's bringing them to me."

"From your expression, I'm assuming you had no idea Ian accompanied Cain on his rescue mission." Nigel waited a few moments. "Unfortunately, Ian died trying to escape and fell out of the helicopter."

"You're lying!" she cried. She would've felt Ian's death, known it. Not wanting to hear any more, she stared out the window, shaking.

The limousine halted in front of a large gate. But when the wrought iron slid open to allow them through, Kate hardly noticed.

"You realize, of course, what's at stake here."

Kate glared at Threader, refusing to give him the satisfaction of seeing her grief. "Are you willing to trade the formula for Cain's and Roman's lives?"

"No, but I am willing to trade their lives for your loyalty." He ran his finger down her jaw. "And obedience."

She wrenched her head back, and a predatory smile curved his lips. "As I said before, the formula is a bonus. We'll call it your wedding gift to me."

Wedding? Even if his words hadn't registered, his look left no doubt that the man was serious.

The limo stopped. Kate closed her eyes, wishing the nightmare would end but understanding it had just begun.

Chapter Fifteen

Kate rose from the rich blanket of bubbles and grabbed the thick bath sheet lying beside the Italian marbled tub. Any other time she would have enjoyed the bath. But her thoughts were on her upcoming meeting with Threader. She quickly patted herself dry and donned a sapphire silk robe the servant had laid out.

Three hours had passed since she'd been locked in. After the guard had closed the door, sobs had wracked her body. Once drained, her agony turned to anger. She spent the balance of time searching for weapons or a means of escape, only to come up empty-handed.

She walked into the adjoining bedroom, using the towel to rub the dampness from her hair. Her cell was crimson, the color of blood, with the finest furnishings. The brocade wallpaper, velvet bedspread and matching drapes—all dark red—were high quality. Even the mahogany furniture cost a small fortune. But everything collectively made the room appear vulgar somehow.

"Are you enjoying yourself, my dear?"

With a startled cry, Kate's gaze snapped to the balcony. She clasped the towel to her chest.

"Come, come. Modesty has no place here." Threader

chuckled, his body leaning against the French door frame. "In time you will get used to my seeing you naked and even start enjoying it, I imagine."

"You have a better imagination than I do, if you think that." She threw the towel onto the bed.

His smile turned icy. "I'm glad you finished your bath." He straightened but not before his gaze traveled over her. "I have something to show you before you dress for dinner. Outside."

Left with no choice, she followed him onto the balcony. The mosaic tile felt cool and solid under her feet, reassuring her until a gust of wind kicked up from the ocean and pushed at her, bringing with it the familiar panic. The rail of the balcony stood ten feet away with Threader leaning against it. To Kate the distance seemed like a mile. She focused on the horizon, now muted with the setting sun, and took another step forward.

Threader laughed, amused. "It is difficult for you." He walked toward her. "I thought the guards lied. My report on you never mentioned the phobia."

At his mocking tone, she lifted her chin and defiantly stood still.

Threader's anger erupted. He roughly grabbed her arm and brought her up to his face. His scar bulged, the purplish tissue pulsing in rage making him appear ghoulish in his anger.

"Just a few more steps, Katherine." The words sliced the air between them. "What I have to show you is over here."

He hauled her to the balcony's edge.

"Look down." When she turned her head away, he gripped her hair and forced her face toward the courtyard. "Look down, now!" Tears stung her eyes as his hold tightened. She glanced down to the courtyard, and what she saw sickened her.

Cain and Roman.

"No!" She gagged and dropped to her knees, ignoring the sharp tug on her scalp. Logically, she'd known Threader had captured them but until now, she hadn't truly believed him.

Threader hauled her up to face him.

"Your reaction is pleasing. It assures me we're getting closer to an agreement."

Again, he turned her toward the courtyard then nodded at Quamar. With a snap of the giant's fingers, two guards grabbed Roman, bringing him forward.

Roman's eyes, dark and dangerous, pierced the distance between them, until Quamar plowed his fist into Roman's stomach, sending him to his knees.

Kate bit her lip hard to keep from crying out. Already the guards had forced Roman back to his feet. When her gaze caught his once more, she clung to it.

"I'll do what you ask," she whispered, intentionally allowing the tears she'd held in check to spill. The man thrived on submissiveness. She'd use it to her advantage. "Just don't hurt them."

He swung her around and saw the tears. Pure satisfaction entered his eyes. "We understand each other then?"

Kate nodded and lowered her head, afraid if she didn't, she would claw his face.

"They're safe, for now. I've ordered Quamar to lock them up. No one will touch them unless I allow it." He paused, tilting her head up. "I hope you won't make that necessary."

He walked her into the bedroom where the maid had laid out an evening dress of black chiffon. One of many garments that stocked the closet. All in her size.

"I can trust you?" Kate kept her tone soft, obedient.

Threader caressed her chin. "Of course. We're to be married. If you can't trust me, who can you trust?"

With that, he walked toward the door, only to hesitate when he reached for the knob. "I'll wait for you in my study. There is one more thing to show you before we eat."

He swung the door wide and stepped into the hall. "You have ten minutes. Don't keep me waiting."

Nine minutes later a guard led her across the third floor to the opposite wing, pausing before two oak doors. When a brisk knock brought the awaited "Enter," he allowed Kate through.

"Prompt," Threader observed. He'd changed into a black evening suit that matched her attire perfectly. He handed her a glass of wine. "A trait I admire in a woman."

"I'll try to remember that," she murmured and forced her fingers to loosen their grip on the wineglass.

"You've done well." His gaze drifted from her loosely piled hair to the miniscule straps that left her shoulders exposed.

"Thank you," Kate said, mentally fighting down her revulsion for the role she was about to play. Slowly she pivoted, feeling the chiffon flare against her legs as she gave Threader the full view of the plunging back.

"You are stunning, my dear. A prize for any man to envy."

"I'm glad you think so." She flashed him a stiff smile.

He laughed. "Lying doesn't become you, Katherine."

Startled, she met his eyes.

"I know how you feel about me." He raised his glass in a mock salute. "I just haven't determined if it matters."

"Magnificent room," she commented, groping for a change in subject. A quick glimpse registered the closed circuit TVs.

"You won't see them on the monitors." Interrupting her

search for Roman and Cain, Threader came up behind her and took her glass, setting it down with his on a nearby table. "Trust me, your brother and his friend are quite safe. Until I decide otherwise." His breath skimmed the curve of her neck. "Quamar has escorted them to my yacht, where they won't be the underfoot." His gaze rested on her profile. "I'll be seeing them later tonight. Meanwhile, we will work on becoming more acquainted," he murmured, and teased a strand of her hair.

Kate moved, causing the hair to pull from his grasp.

He chuckled. "You are superb." His fingertips glided across the base of her spine.

She willed her muscles to function and turned directly into Threader. Finding an inner strength she'd never known she possessed, Kate fingered his lapel.

When he placed his hand over hers, his palm was surprisingly warm, not chilling as she expected for someone with no soul. "I possess the world's most exquisite treasures. But the moment I saw your photograph, nothing has compared or captivated me more."

Mentally she took a deep breath. "If I became…yours—"

You are mine! Understood?" His grip tightened, crushing her hand.

"Yes," Kate cried out.

"Good." Pleased with her response, Threader released her hand and took her elbow. "It's time to show you why you're here," he said cordially, all traces of rage gone.

A side door in his study revealed a steel elevator. After entering, she watched as Threader pressed the lower-level button.

"What you are about to see, my dear, is the future. A future you will be an intrinsic part of."

The doors parted, revealing a wide hallway. Artwork

lined the walls. One painting in particular the world believed had been destroyed during World War II. Threader's words floated through her mind. *I possess the world's most exquisite treasures.*

They stopped in front of a massive alloy door. Threader punched in a number sequence, then stepped up to a retina scanner. As they stepped into the observation room, Kate said nothing, immediately drawn to the area beyond a large glass wall.

The lab was fashioned from a science fiction movie—right down to the white tile and steel. With a chill, Kate recognized the technology. He'd replicated Las Mesas.

"This isn't possible," she murmured, and scrutinized the acres of antimatter equipment.

"Katherine, you disappoint me. Anything is possible if you have money." He walked over to a bank of TVs that monitored the entire facility. "Look beyond your own world and see the big picture." He paused. "My world."

She stared, unwilling to comprehend the ramifications of what she saw in the alternating screens. Threader's technology was more advanced than Las Mesas, including several government prototypes that were only in experimental stages elsewhere.

"We're already showing the signs of an energy shortage. In a few decades countries will be desperate for new technology."

"Control their energy source. Control the country," she responded, understanding.

"With our combined research, people will turn to me for salvation." He gestured toward the lab. "Fate brought you to me, Katherine. A woman who possesses not only beauty and breeding but also an intellect to rival my own."

Threader's expression flickered with thinly veiled insanity. "With you at my side, the possibilities are endless." World domination. With a wave of determination she realized she had to stop Threader. But how?

One of the monitors displayed a nearby workstation. The data, flashing rapidly across the computer screen, drew Kate's gaze. She leaned closer, her eyes widening with comprehension.

"You recognize the program." The statement drifted over her shoulder with a fiendish delight.

"It's the security system at Las Mesas Laboratories." *Roman's system.* A jolt of excitement ran through her.

"A gift from an associate." His emphasis on the word *gift* didn't escape Kate's notice. Roman's program was state-of-the-art. Very few could duplicate the technology.

"Quite a unique present, wouldn't you say?" Not waiting for her to agree, he added, "The fact that Cerberus designed the system made receiving it most gratifying."

"Why?" she asked, and studied the screen. Threader's people had added at least three more levels of security. The fact he hadn't mentioned the backdoor meant it might still exist.

"Surely you see the irony of Cerberus's system protecting my research. He and Prometheus are the best at what they do. Legends in their field," he remarked. Prometheus? Cain's code name, she decided. The champion of mankind. The name fit him just as much as Cerberus fit Roman.

"Of course, once implemented, I found the program lacking. Which I'm sure you're aware of, having disabled Las Mesas's." He pointed to several men. "My people improved upon the original system, making it impenetrable." Maybe or maybe not, Kate thought.

"Katherine, I can see your mind working furiously…but needlessly," he admonished. "Your virus would prove ineffective against the enhancements."

With a brief glance back in her direction, he continued. "I take pleasure in using his genius against him, you know. Especially since he is determined to avenge Amanda Salinas' death." At Kate's start, his smile twisted grotesquely.

"You're surprised. Why? I've known since the beginning, but he hasn't been able to—bring me down, as it were."

"You make it sound like a contest or a game of chess, when what you really want is them dead."

"It is a game. An intricate one that requires the strategic elements of chess. But one that doesn't necessarily have to end in death." He absently stroked his scar. "Killing them may prove necessary—but it isn't my first choice. They have connections I would find useful."

The words should have reassured her, but his polished tone only increased her unease.

"My campaign must not fail. Any interference will force me to destroy your brother and his friend." One tawny brow arched as he spared her a brief glance. "I would prefer otherwise. After all, if I'd wanted them eliminated, arrangements would've been made. Hiring an assassin is extremely easy these days."

"And you'd expect them to betray their country?" Kate couldn't stop her skepticism from tainting her voice.

"You forget, it will be *my* country soon enough." Threader actually chuckled as he, too, looked out over the lab. "Having you will guarantee their loyalty."

"There are other labs, other scientists developing antimatter possibilities," Kate stated, more fearful now than ever. "What about them?"

"They'll work for me or die." Threader lifted an indifferent shoulder. "An excellent case of supply and demand."

"Like Marcus Boyd?" she asked laconically.

"Boyd was a fool. He tried to pass your work off as his own, then lost his nerve. When I discovered the duplicity, he ran." Threader's voice held a vicious underlying tone. "You might take a lesson from that, my dear."

Then, like a chameleon, his demeanor changed. "Enough of this unpleasantness. It's time for dinner," he declared, the cultured veneer back in place.

"I hope you have an appetite, Katherine," he said, urging her toward the elevator, the touch of his fingers on her skin triggering a queasiness in the pit of her stomach. "My chef has prepared Filets du Lapin à la Sauce à l'Estragin. Filet of rabbit covered in a light tarragon sauce. A favorite of mine."

Chapter Sixteen

The gentle flapping of the balcony curtains awoke Kate with a vague sense of apprehension. After spending half the night pacing, she'd fallen asleep in the wing chair, still in her evening dress with her feet tucked up under her. Cautiously, she lowered her toes to the ground, curling them in the thick pile of carpet. Her gaze rested on the doors standing ajar in the moonlight. The same doors she'd locked just hours before. A warning played a quick staccato through her veins.

Sitting forward slightly, she eased off the chair only to shriek when a hand clamped over her mouth. Out of the corner of her eye, she caught sight of a guard's uniform, its rugged lines stark in the stream of moonlight.

Kate slammed her fist into the rock-hard stomach in front of her, happy when she heard a grunt of pain. Like a cornered alley cat, she scratched and struggled against the arm that encircled her and hauled her off the chair.

"Damn it, Doc, watch my shoulder." He flipped her around to one hip like a sack of potatoes. "And stop trying to break my ribs," he hissed when her elbow caught his side.

Recognizing the husky tone, she sagged against Roman with relief. With a familiar gentleness he released her mouth and gathered her close, pinning her body against his. He smelled of stale smoke and beer, which led her to believe the uniform had a previous owner. But after the past few days, Kate knew better than to question its origins.

"I should beat you senseless for what you've put me through," he whispered against her hair. She nodded her agreement, seeing the threat for what it was. Her cheek rubbed against the crisp hair of his chest, exposed beneath the half-unbuttoned shirt. The strong rhythmic tempo of his heart under her ear soothed her own heart's erratic beating. Roman was safe.

"If you ever pull a stupid stunt—"

"You looked so—" she said, swallowing against the unbending muscles in her throat, "and your arm, it was—"

"Dislocated. Cain popped it back into place, but my shoulder still hurts like a son—"

"Cain?" Startled, she drew back. "Is he—"

"He's fine. Ian, too."

"Ian?" Disbelief jabbed at her heart, jarring her to a complete stop. "He's alive?"

Without warning, he hugged her, placing her head against his shoulder. "It was a trick, Doc. Ian's fine, but I don't have time to tell you everything."

Ian and Cain had survived. And Roman, too. She slid her arms around his neck just as a sob escaped. Up until a few minutes ago, she'd thought she'd never be this close to him again.

"Hell." The muttered word swept fiercely across her ear and Kate's breath caught.

"Don't, baby." He kissed her temple first, then slid his lips over her cheek. Finally his mouth gently covered hers in a long, deep reassuring kiss.

"Time is slipping away, my friend."

Kate jerked, breaking contact with Roman at the softly spoken words. The unmistakable Mediterranean accent registered.

"Roman?" she asked, surprised at his lack of concern. Reluctantly he drew back.

"Don't worry, Quamar's a good guy," he said, placing his finger over her lips at her unspoken questions. Then with a deep breath, he shifted away, but Kate noted he didn't go far. He dropped a kiss on her nose. "He's also right, we don't have much time."

He grabbed her hand and pulled her into the stream of moonlight from the balcony. His gaze flickered over her. "Are you okay?"

"He hasn't touched me. Yet." Quickly Kate filled Roman in on Threader's plan. "What scares me, Roman, is that he could pull it off. All of it."

"Cain and I will stop him." The words were low and terse. Kate glanced toward the balcony. "Where is Cain?"

Roman snagged a flashlight from his waistband and thumbed the switch. Suddenly light pierced the surrounding darkness before resting on the closet. He pulled her toward it. "He and Ian are calling reinforcements."

His free hand cupped her face. "Right now, we need to get you dressed and to the cove."

Kate stepped back as her strength resurged. "Then what? We can't let Threader get away with his plans."

"He won't. Once you're safe, I'm coming back." His light flashed across a pair of dark pants and matching top. He tossed the clothes to her.

"So your plan is to dump me and go chase the bad guys." Riled, she stripped off the gown, ignoring the fact she had no bra, then yanked on the clothes.

He handed her a pair of flat shoes. "No, first I *place* you out of harm's way like I promised your brother I would. Then I go chase the bad guys."

He'd promised her brother. The words hurt and the hurt fed her frustration. She waved a shoe in his face. "What about the laboratory? He's duplicated Las Mesas, Roman. You need to get me into that lab. It's your security system protecting Threader's computer program. He's enhanced it with at least three additional levels. Your backdoor can bypass them. Once we're in, my virus will destroy the research."

He'd started shaking his head halfway through her explanation. "Tell me how to reconstruct the virus, and I'll take care of it once you're safe."

"It's in my head and too complicated for me to explain off the cuff." Impatiently Kate slipped on the shoes. "Obviously, Threader hasn't discovered your escape, so Quamar should still have access to the lab."

"No." The word was blunt enough to make her grimace. "You're not going anywhere near the lab. Hell, I'll just blow the damn thing if I have to."

"If you do that, you risk killing innocent people. Not everyone is here by choice. I won't let people die, if I can prevent it. And neither should you."

Kate watched the lines of Roman's face harden into granite and knew enough from the past few days that he'd made his decision and would no longer listen to her. Up to now, their argument had taken place in harsh whispers, but with his look, she had to curl her hands into fists in order to fight back the urge to scream in aggravation. Taking a deep breath instead, she tried not to forget that Threader's men stood outside the door.

"He could have it backed up somewhere off-site. He has dozens of residences throughout the world."

The critical note in Roman's tone set Kate's teeth on

edge. "Possibly," she hissed. "Although I think he's too arrogant to have worried about a contingency plan."

Roman studied her for a moment, his face unreadable. A terrible sense of bitterness assailed her. "For once you could let me decide my future."

The words hung between them for several seconds before Roman let out a heavy sigh. "I'm going to regret this."

A small spark of victory shot through her, and she almost squealed in triumph until he dropped his head and touched his ear. The sensation died instantly.

"Here." He glanced back up, his eyes locking with hers. The iridescent glow of their amber flecks flared in the dimness of the closet. "I've got her. She's fine."

Roman didn't have to tell her it was Cain. Kate's heart sank. It was hard enough to convince Roman to let her help him. Without Cain's agreement, the probability of Roman putting her at risk just dropped to zero. Frustrated, she turned away, her arms crossed tightly in front of her.

"Negative. There's been a change of plans."

She spun back around, not quite believing the softly spoken words.

"Your sister thinks she can sabotage Threader's lab. I agree." Roman's frown told her that Cain wasn't happy.

"There is no other solution. We take out the lab while you take care of the guard quarters."

Kate gaped, not quite understanding Roman's grim smile.

"It's done, chief. We've made our decision."

Then he paused. "I'll keep her safe." Once again Roman's face hardened. "Give us thirty minutes. And watch your back."

For several heartbeats silence filled the closet. Then she was in his arms, hugging him tight.

"You win, Doc." His voice was quiet. "But you better

do exactly as I say, or I scrub the mission." He pulled back. "Got it?"

"Yes." Her immediate agreement earned a disbelieving grunt from Roman before he led her from the closet.

"We're taking the lab out, Quamar. Cain and Ian will rendezvous with us for backup after they're done demolishing the guard quarters. We're not to wait."

Quamar's lack of reaction didn't surprise Kate as he slipped out onto the balcony. When a soft whistle floated through the open doors, Roman and Kate followed.

The moon carved shadows throughout the balcony, making it appear more treacherous than it had in the daylight. She stopped short. It was easier being brave in a closet than on the terrace.

Roman slid a comforting hand up her spine, acknowledging her hesitation. "We're going to have to use the balcony to remain undetected, Doc." Stepping away, he turned his back toward her. "Climb on piggyback, close your eyes and leave everything else to me."

Quamar, one leg over the railing, smiled at her. "Do not worry, Doctor. Allah protects us. You will be safe."

Hoping Quamar was correct, Kate smiled tentatively in his direction, then stepped behind Roman and wiggled into position.

She caught sight of the black nylon rope dangling from the railing just before she shut her eyes. "Ready."

Her heart hammered against the tight muscles of his back, and she pressed her cheek against the warmth of his shirt for reassurance. Roman eased over the side. "Here we go."

A harsh jolt slammed her teeth together and told her they'd hit ground.

"Allow me, Doctor." Before she could react, Quamar picked her off Roman and set her down. Resisting the urge to kiss the soft dirt beneath her feet, she took several moments to steady her shaking limbs.

"Thank you," she said hesitantly, still not quite sure how to react to Quamar.

Then suddenly he grinned. "My pleasure."

Before Kate could stop herself, she grinned back.

"One you won't have again," Roman growled. "Come on."

Kate didn't know the exact time, but the darkness of the sky and the placement of the fingernail moon told her it was the middle of the night. Noiselessly she followed Roman while Quamar trailed behind, protecting their back.

Even with avoiding Threader's surveillance equipment, gaining access to the lab was surprisingly easy. Quamar took them in through the personnel entrance. Located within an old blacksmith shed across the compound, the subterranean elevator was secured by only one of Threader's men. Within a fraction of a second, the giant rendered the surprised guard unconscious.

While she watched silently, Roman signaled for Quamar to boost him up to the security camera by the lab's door, allowing him to disable the apparatus with his knife. The easy precision with which the men worked left no doubt in Kate's mind that Roman's claim of friendship had been genuine.

The moments spent after, waiting while Quamar identified himself to the computer, were terror-filled. If Threader had discovered their deception, the security system would sound the alarm.

At the computer's softly spoken words of acceptance, she took a large, solid breath of relief. Their mission was hardly over with, but they'd passed the first hurdle successfully.

Just as she was about to step through the open doorway, Quamar caught her arm. "Remember, Doctor, the lab is monitored by camera and sound. We can talk, but we must keep our voices below the noise level of the equipment." She nodded her agreement and allowed the men to go first.

As they entered the lab, she automatically glanced around the empty room. Quickly they located a work-station—secluded by a portable half wall—and settled behind the desk.

Propping his Uzi beside him, Roman started to work. She watched in amazement as his fingers flew over the keys.

"You were wrong, Doc," he whispered as smug satisfaction settled across his face. "They constructed five new security levels, not three. Give me a minute to bypass the main menu and access the root file, then it's all yours."

Kate said nothing, noting the low current of excitement in the statement.

"Almost there, babe. Just let the commands slide into place." Roman's voice dipped to a husky timbre as he talked to the machine. As Kate watched, the screen went blank, leaving only a flashing cursor at the top.

Roman typed *Bella Rosa.*

Suddenly the computer screen flickered, filling with security data.

"Twelve minutes, Cerberus," Quamar whispered the words, but the warning came loud and clear.

Resisting the urge to tap her foot, Kate shifted, planting her feet firmly behind Roman. The man seemed to be taking forever to finish. She glanced at Quamar. Sensing the attention, the giant returned her look with an easy smile before continuing his surveillance of the empty facility.

Kate's gaze snapped back to the computer as Roman hit the enter button and leaned back in the chair. "Well, I'll be damned," he murmured. "This program controls all the systems on the island."

Kate peered over his shoulder. "What?"

"The perimeter alarm, the fire, even the power grid can be accessed through here."

"Is there a backup?" Not waiting for an answer, she started shoving Roman's shoulder. "Move, big guy. My turn."

She took the data in at a glance. The computer, knowing no different, gave her access to all of Threader's security and informational mainframes. Roman was right. There was no backup system. Threader had the island's network linked into the computer's mainframe. Damn, the man was arrogant, thinking his programs would never be compromised.

A surge of adrenaline shot through her. The virus would work like a charm on the system, not only destroying his files but also bringing the whole complex down in its crash. Unable to stop herself, she glanced at him and grinned.

"Don't take too long gloating, babe. The clock is ticking." But his tone of admiration belied his words. He understood. The exhilaration, the satisfaction. Her virus was going to work and bring Threader to his knees. For the first time in the past five days, she felt in total control.

Embracing her newfound strength, Kate swung back and started constructing the viral sequences. "First the bug deletes the files, then it triggers the meltdown."

It was Roman's turn to watch over Kate's shoulder. "Making it easy for Ian's team to infiltrate."

"Exactly."

The sound of the equipment pitched to a higher tone, and Kate paused. Some type of environmental system had just kicked in. "Hear it?"

The degree was subtle, but Roman had noticed. He glanced over the terminal, eyeing the room. "Speed it up."

Kate entered another sequence. "I only need a few

more minutes, then the virus will take over. We should be long gone before Threader detects a breach. By then it will be too late."

"We've got eight minutes before the guard house blows," Quamar inserted.

Kate nodded, concentrating on the abundance of data running before her on the screen. "Got it." Working quickly she continued programming. "We have to do more than just wipe out the information. We have to render the server useless. Otherwise, Threader can hire any half-decent computer expert to retrieve the deleted information." As quickly as possible, she inserted her commands.

"Six minutes," Roman urged, his hard body leaned further into hers, expelling its urgency. "You need to go faster, Doc."

"Almost there." She glanced up when his machine gun bumped her elbow. "Stop crowding me. I'm on your side remember?" she muttered, willing her hands to work quicker. To think she had actually worried about him when he'd been captured.

"You can use the time to tell me what Threader said to you out on the yacht."

Roman tensed behind her. "We never went to the yacht."

Startled, she looked up. The fine hair on the base of her neck buzzed with electricity as she recalled her earlier conversation with Threader. *Quamar has escorted them to my yacht where they won't be underfoot. I'll be meeting with them later tonight.*

Deafening alarms drowned out her warning to Roman, the loud horns mingling with the sound of the heavy steel lab doors slamming shut.

Roman spun around, his machine gun raised, and a stream of curses spilled from his mouth.

Desperately, Kate typed in the final sequences to her program and hit Enter. Roman glanced her way and she nodded. The file deletion had started.

"Good evening, gentlemen…Katherine. This is an unexpected pleasure."

The laboratory intercom amplified the deceptively friendly words. Kate glanced over the portable half wall to see Threader approach one of the observation windows not thirty feet away. Quickly she stood, hoping to draw attention to herself and away from the computer.

The harsh light of the observation room revealed the arms dealer vividly, compared to the dimness of the lab, his white suit adding a menacing simplicity to his manner. Kate could make out the smooth elegance of his features that covered the deadly anger she knew seethed beneath.

His hand brushed over the wall beside him, and the alarms stopped.

"Annoying noise, but necessary sometimes to gain one's attention," he said almost apologetically before his gaze moved to the threesome. "You realize your attempts are unrealistic. It will take far more time than you have available to break through my security."

"He hasn't discovered the breach, Roman," Kate whispered, keeping her face angled away from Threader's view. "Stall him." Perspiration dampened her shirt. It was only a matter of time before Threader's men converged on the lab.

"Stay put," Roman growled before he stepped away from the desk, putting himself in plain view of the observation room and Threader. His first thought was for Kate's safety and to hell with the mission. But they were far too close to succeeding, and the stakes were far too high for them to cut and run.

His radio had gone dead the moment they'd reached the

subterranean level, not allowing contact with Cain. They were on their own. Resigned to play the hand out, Roman sent a hard look to Quamar. The giant stepped to the other side of the workstation, flanking Kate.

"Isn't that brave." Threader's laugh came across the sound system low and menacing. "But there is no need for heroics. Not yet."

Roman's eyes narrowed as he took in Threader's disfigurement. The hideous mark was recent. Roman had seen it for the first time during Amanda's final mission and had wondered about its origin. Threader's scar provided Roman with an excellent target.

Using the point of his gun, Roman tapped the side of his own eye. "I approve of the look, Threader. Reflects the inner you."

Fury flooded Threader's face as he automatically reached for the disfigurement. Then in a millisecond the expression disappeared, replaced by a thin smile. "You've made quite an adversary, Cerberus. I shall miss that."

Very much aware of the bulletproof glass that separated him from Threader, Roman shifted until he partially sat on an adjoining desk to Kate's and shrugged, then jabbed again. "Too bad I can't return the compliment." With the Uzi now resting comfortably in his lap, Roman swung his foot casually. "I'll enjoy sending you to hell."

Threader laughed as he pulled a cigar from the inner pocket of his white suit. "I've manipulated you these past months, patiently, methodically. Savoring the challenge in destroying you bit by bit." Threader lit the cigar and took several puffs. The arrogance with which he paused told Roman that Threader believed he held a pat hand. "But now my patience is at an end. It's time to move on to more important developments."

Threader's gaze flickered to Kate. Roman maintained a bland expression, but inwardly his blood thickened. Out of his peripheral vision, he could see Kate discreetly checking the computer monitor. "Time, Doc," he demanded quietly.

"Ten, possibly twelve minutes," she whispered.

In ten minutes they could all be dead.

Time to call Threader's bluff.

He slid from the desk, the machine gun cradled in his arm, his finger resting on the trigger.

"Where are your guards, Threader?" Roman glanced around the deserted facility. "You aren't one to dirty your hands when it comes to a quick kill."

"You're correct, and unfortunately you will have to die quickly. You've left me no time to indulge myself." His voice showed real disappointment at that. "It's the screams, you know. The pitches are more exquisite sometimes than the most beautiful arias. Yours would have been one of those, Cerberus." He flicked an ash from his lapel. "Nevertheless, I have chosen to deal with you promptly, while my men are taking care of Prometheus." Threader glanced at the monitors. A flash of apprehension hit Roman.

"And Phoenix? Where is she?" Roman questioned, only partially drawing the older man's attention back. It wasn't good enough. Mentally Roman tossed in his ace. "Or does she still prefer to be called Amanda?"

Chapter Seventeen

Threader's head snapped around. "Well, well. I am impressed."

But not pleased, Roman thought.

"Are you aware Phoenix wants you dead?" He jabbed his cigar in Roman's direction. "It's true. She was afraid you would discover her new identity, even with the plastic surgery. I disagreed, thinking that self-pity had diminished your competence. I was mistaken." Threader's glance rested briefly on Quamar and for the first time acknowledged the man's presence. "But then, it appears that wasn't the only mistake I made."

Quamar, catching the arms dealer's gaze, shrugged negligently—the only movement he'd made since Threader's appearance. But Roman knew his friend—Quamar was content to wait for Roman's signal, his Uzi pointed directly at the observation room.

Roman addressed Threader in a friendly tone. "The solution wasn't difficult once I learned you'd adapted my system. Amanda was one of the few people who had the opportunity to copy the program. The fact that she'd lied about being incapable of breaking into your system made her the traitor.

"That and her new name." Roman flexed his shoulders, trying to ease the burden of failure that had just grown heavier with betrayal. "Phoenix. A mythological bird consumed by fire, only to rise later from its own ashes."

Threader smiled wickedly. "The charade was her idea, you know. Since the plan appealed to me, I allowed it," he explained, his voice indicating how much he enjoyed their sparring. "As she worked on the program, you hid in the jungle, waiting. Ironic, really. She was actually feeding me Labyrinth's secrets while you waited for information on my operations."

Something in Threader's voice tightened Roman's insides. For Amanda to betray her country, Threader must have controlled her with something powerful. "What did you threaten her with, Threader, to make her turn?"

Threader laughed. "Money."

Roman's nostrils flared in disbelief. Damn it, he couldn't have misjudged Amanda that much. But his constricted gut told him differently.

"Not everyone has such a strong sense of justice, Cerberus," Threader observed. "Phoenix is a greedy woman. Much more than you or Labyrinth ever realized or could afford." He rolled the cigar between his thumb and forefinger. He flicked the ashes onto the floor before smiling. "Didn't you ever wonder at how easily she placed herself inside the enemy's mind?"

He paused, almost as if he was letting them wait for the punch line of a joke. "It was because she *was* the enemy. If you think about it, the amazing part of this scenario was her performance as an ally."

"One minute to detonation." Quamar interrupted softly. Roman felt Kate step closer to his side.

"How does it feel, Cerberus?" Threader continued, unaware. "To know that these last months of agony you've been living through were for a woman who sold you and your country out for cold, hard cash?"

It felt like hell. As if Amanda's treachery had ripped out his soul. But he couldn't feed the anger, not yet, not until Kate was safe. Pushing the thought away, he carefully maintained an even expression. "And the woman in the courtyard?"

"The one you killed, you mean?" Threader chuckled. "I enjoyed that act of heroism very much, by the way." Then he waved his hand. "She was nothing more than a whore from Mexico City who happened to look like Phoenix."

Roman stiffened, letting his gaze drop to the gun in his hand. It didn't matter who it was, she was an innocent who died because of him.

Kate touched his arm but he didn't dare look at her. He didn't dare face the compassion he would see in those clear, gray eyes.

There was one piece of information still missing. Slowly he lifted his gaze. "Why?" he asked, a hint of steel underplayed the importance of the question. "Why the game of cat and mouse?"

Threader scrutinized the end of the cigar. "If it feed nothing, it will feed my revenge,'" he quoted Shakespeare quietly. Then he crushed the still-lit cigar in his fist and threw it against the window. Only then did he look up at Roman, the intellectual facade gone, replaced by demented fury.

Suddenly an explosion shook the ceiling. Threader's eyes narrowed briefly on the threesome before he stepped away from the window to the monitors. Roman glanced at Quamar and moved forward, his machine gun raised.

"Threader!" Roman yelled the name as he and Quamar opened fire on the observation room window. Bullets ripped through electronics and steel, shredding everything in their path. He barely noted the surprised scream from Kate. She'd covered her ears, but he didn't stop as he turned his Uzi on the surveillance cameras surrounding them. As the bullets poured from the gun, so did Roman's rage.

Within a few minutes the gunfire ceased just as abruptly as it began. He threw down the empty weapon and grabbed his pistol before pulling Kate behind him. Crouched to the ground, the three of them made their way to an exit at the far end of the lab.

"Once the system shuts down, the doors unlock." Roman's gaze pinned Quamar. "Then get her the hell out of here."

Kate felt the cold steel panels through her clothes as she sat huddled by a bank of equipment. She watched while Roman, balanced on the balls of his feet, squatted beside her and checked the ammunition clip in his pistol.

Kate didn't have to ask him what he planned to do.

"You didn't know, Roman," she said as she took in his rage with concerned eyes. "You thought it was her, they made sure of that. No one knew."

"I should have. If I'd realized sooner that Amanda was a double agent I could've stopped Threader months ago."

A tsking sound pierced the air. "And the fact remains, Katherine, a woman is dead and the great Cerberus failed in his duty to protect. Just as he's failed you." Threader laughed, the low-pitched tone sounded Vincent Price–like over the speakers. "Your weapons barely scratched the bulletproof glass, Cerberus. An amazing piece of equipment, is it not? Quite effective. It stops bullets as well as Halon stops fires."

Halon? Halon extinguished fires by reducing the oxygen that the flames fed on. Kate's eyes followed Roman's as they glanced over the ceiling. Spouts. Then with a jab of his finger, he indicated his discovery to Quamar.

"In several minutes you will begin to feel the effects." Threader was saying as the sound of hissing air filled the room. "Pity. I would have preferred our working together rather than watching your demise, Katherine."

Kate looked around the room, doing swift calculations in her mind. Threader hadn't lied. It would take a few minutes for the gas to reach them. The problem was she didn't think the system would crash before they suffocated. Even if it was close, she wasn't sure they could live on the difference.

Kate twisted around to face both men. "I need you to trust me, Roman." Her hands were icy as they grabbed his, but they were steady. Then her gazed locked on Quamar, silently pleading for help. The giant's expression flickered in response. She looked back at Roman. "And promise me that once you're free, you'll rescue me."

"What the hell are you talking—"

"Threader!" Before Roman could stop her, Kate sprang from their hiding place and ran toward the observation room. She heard Roman's bellow of rage but didn't dare glance back, understanding Quamar would keep him from coming after her. The giant knew as well as she did this was their only chance.

"As you know I've developed a process that slows matter-antimatter reaction," she shouted, then skidded to a stop in the center of the laboratory, placing herself in full view of the observation room windows.

There was a long pause. Long enough for Kate to think Threader was going to ignore her. Then the loudspeaker clicked on.

"Go on, Doctor."

"Marcus Boyd came to you because he discovered a secret I've kept hidden from everyone. Including the government." She drew another deep breath. "My experiments are further advanced than anyone believes. As of a month ago, I was able to maintain annihilation indefinitely."

Silence met her words, a long enough silence to allow her a short litany of prayers.

"If I promise to give you the formula, will you stop the Halon?" she prodded after a few moments.

"Oh, you will give me much more than that, Doctor. Understand?"

The greed in his voice coated the words like warm honey. She had him. "I understand." Relief made her slightly dizzy. Or maybe it was Halon, she couldn't be sure. "Stop the gas."

Threader studied her for a moment through the window. She met him stare for stare.

"You trust me to keep my word?"

No, she thought. "You trust me to give you the right formula?"

"Oh, yes, I can guarantee it, Doctor." With a nod, he walked away. Soon the hissing stopped and he reappeared by the windows. "Take the elevator directly in front of you. It opens into this room."

Time was precious and Kate needed to make every second count. As slowly as possible, she walked to the doors. She counted thirty seconds, and then punched the button. As she'd hoped, the elevator's descent to her level took several moments, giving her the opportunity to scan the room, wanting reassurance that the men were safe.

Suddenly Roman appeared not ten feet away from her side—out of Threader's view. His warrior's body poised and powerful, his eyes unblinkingly cold. Her gaze dropped to the gun in his hand, hanging at his side. Only the clenching of his jaw revealed the internal battle he waged. Instinctively, Kate understood he fought the urge to go with her, even knowing the surveillance camera i the elevator would give them away.

Fear, sharp and poignant, shot through her as the stee doors slid open. She caught the edge of one with a trem bling hand. Roman didn't move as she stepped on the el evator. Again she waited a few precious seconds befor hitting the button—it wasn't until after she'd dared t glance back at him. He hadn't moved, his face tempere steel, his eyes fierce. Only when the doors closed again di she lean back against the wall and curl her hand around th railing in desperation. *Please, let this work.*

When the steel doors parted again, Threader was wait ing for her, a gun pointed at her chest. "Hands behin your head," he ordered, all pleasantness gone. Slowly Kat complied.

He patted her down. "You disappoint me, Katherine. I' really thought that you'd started to care for me," he sneere as he straightened, apparently satisfied she was unarmed

She glanced at the weapon now prodding her stomach "I can see how devastated you are, Threader."

"My dear, you haven't really tasted true devastation That will come when Cerberus dies."

"No!" Kate didn't have to fake her cry of alarm eve though she'd expected Threader's betrayal. He grasped he hair and dragged her to a control panel hidden beside th monitors, then with a quiet deliberation, he flipped the fir protection switch.

Unable to stop herself, Kate watched the monitors for a sign of the two men below, hoping she'd given the syste enough time to crash before Roman and Quamar succumbe "You won't get the formula." She spoke the words qui

...tly, vehemently. The gas had stopped for three minutes, possibly four. But was it enough?

Threader turned to her and slid the muzzle of the gun down her cheek. "I'll take pleasure in proving you wrong."

Just then another round of explosions sounded. Kate's eyes darted to the TV screens just in time to see Cain dash across the compound.

Threader's gaze followed hers. "It looks like your brother is keeping busy. I imagine he's called for reinforcements."

"Brothers," Kate corrected, feeling unusually calm as she watched Ian follow Cain.

"No matter," Threader said angrily, then shoved her through the door and down the hallway. "By the time my guards finish with them, we'll be gone." Once again he gripped her hair, using the long tresses to drag her along and throw her into an elevator. Kate winced as her head slammed against the railing. She slid to the floor and shook her head, trying to stop the ringing in her ears. "You can't get away with this."

He hit the button with his fist. "I've already gotten away with it, my dear."

When the doors slid open to his study, he grabbed her arm and dragged her across the room before thrusting her into his throne chair. She cried out as her hip struck the desk, knocking a stone statue to the floor.

"Given the correct command, my system is designed to send all significant data to various satellite offices," he smirked, carefully keeping her pinned with the weapon.

Kate watched the computer with apprehension. Unnoticed, the virus would transfer with any data, infecting Threader's other computers.

Hurry, damn it. She bit her lip in frustration as Threader blocked the screen. The system should've started crashing by now.

"What the hell is this?" He leaned toward the computer, then twisted back toward her. "What did you do?" He screamed before leveling his pistol at her forehead. She could feel the cool steel digging into her skin. He clicked the hammer back. "Tell me!"

A gunshot exploded and Kate screamed. Thinking Threader fired, it took a moment for her to realize she was still breathing.

She opened her eyes to see Threader staring at his white silk shirt. A crimson stain spread rapidly across his chest. He swung his arm but was too slow. Another shot caught him in the shoulder, jerking him back. He coughed, then blinked, trying to focus as he looked across the room.

A woman stood in the doorway of the study. He streaked hair was coiffed smoothly in a severe bun that em phasized the tight black leather pantsuit covering her from neck to ankle. In her hand she held a large handgun pointed directly at the arms dealer.

"I underestimated your greed, Phoenix." He coughed again, and this time Kate saw the bubbles of blood on his bottom lip as he tried to raise his pistol. "I won't again."

The weapon tilted and for a second Kate thought he would fire. Then Threader's grip slackened and the pisto dipped, hanging from his fingertips. She watched the gu balance for a moment, then drop to the floor as he clutched the edge of the desktop for support.

"Even dying, your ego has no boundaries, Threader," came the dry reply as Threader collapsed behind the desk. Kate swung her head toward Phoenix, whose garish re lips curved with pleasure.

"I enjoyed that much more than I thought I would."

Gunfire sprayed the mansion's exterior. Phoenix crossed to the desk window and parted the heavy velvet drapes. Kate sank deeper into the chair and stared uneasily at the huge pistol trained on her heart.

"It appears he underestimated more than just me," Phoenix observed. Her eyes flickered over Kate before she peered out the window. "That's the sound of Threader's men dying out there. You'll be glad to know that Prometheus is kicking their butt."

"I am."

She studied Kate's defiant expression. "I'll bet you are, doll. Well, I'm not going to be around when he gets here." She let her hand fall from the curtain. "And neither are you."

Phoenix kicked Threader's body aside, the movement sending Threader's gun under his desk and out of Kate's reach. She braced herself to run. The risk of being a hostage outweighed her fear of being shot. Kate shifted her feet slightly, intent on planting them solidly in front of her, when her toe hit the small statue.

"I always wondered how Cerberus could fall for a mousy scientist."

Kate stopped, her full attention on Phoenix. "I don't know what you mean."

The other woman let out a deep, sultry laugh. "Then you aren't as smart as everyone thinks you are. He never talked about your relationship, but it was obvious he'd changed. Then Prometheus lost his girlfriend to a car bomb and Cerberus walked away from you. After, he'd lost the edge that forged his reputation."

Kate forced herself to breathe evenly. If what Phoenix said was true, then Roman had left to protect her. The last four days with him flooded her mind, but quickly she pushed them away. Now wasn't the time to think about what his actions implied.

Phoenix typed a few commands on the keyboard. "You are clever, aren't you? Not as clever as me, of course, but some."

Kate nudged the statue with her heel. "Roman knows you're the mole."

Phoenix glanced up, seemingly unimpressed with the information before a beep drew her attention back to the computer. "I expected him to figure it out sooner or later. If he hadn't been distracted with you, it would have been sooner. I guess I should thank you for that." Frowning, she typed in one more command. "Of course it would have helped if you'd managed to complete Nigel's research. Then I could've taken it from there."

With another small nudge, Kate felt the figurine tap the front leg of her chair.

"Damn it." Phoenix slammed her fist against the keyboard, startling Kate. "Congratulations, your virus did its job," she said as her finger tightened on the trigger. Kate froze. "Threader's business records, the research—everything—gone. But I'm sure you knew that, Doctor," Phoenix snarled. With her free hand, she shoved the computer off the desk.

Hope flared through Kate. If the files were gone, the security systems and power grid were next. Kate used the distraction to snag the statue.

"I don't like to lose." Phoenix's eyes narrowed. "So it seems we have a change of plans." She hauled Kate up, her face only centimeters away. "You've just become my insurance policy, doll."

Steel jabbed at her ribs and Kate tightened her hand on the statue. She wasn't helpless—she could fight. But if she hit Phoenix now, the gun could go off.

Suddenly the room went black. Phoenix jerked in surprise and stepped back. "What the hell?"

Kate twisted away from the gun, grabbing at it with her free hand, and swung the statue at Phoenix's head.

Phoenix's reflexes were lightning swift. She blocked the swing with a brutal hit to Kate's forearm. With a cry of pain, Kate dropped the statue but didn't release the gun, a reaction that probably saved her life. Using both hands, Kate pushed away the gun and plowed her shoulder into Phoenix, slamming her against edge of the desk. The gun fired, shattering the window behind Kate.

"You stupid—" Phoenix smashed her head against the side of Kate's face, but Kate still held on to the gun, wrenching it sideways as she tried to regain her balance. Another shot fired, ricocheting somewhere off the ceiling.

Desperately she tried to regain control as Phoenix's grip became more secure. She twisted Kate's wrist, and excruciating pain jabbed at Kate's arm. Phoenix wrenched the gun away.

"You lose, doll." Moonlight shadows danced across Phoenix's profile, revealing the pure evil underneath as she took aim at Kate's chest.

"Amanda!"

Kate heard Roman's scream and watched in numb horror as Phoenix switched targets, pointing the gun across the room. "No!" Kate cried and launched herself at the other woman, sending them both through the open window.

Chapter Eighteen

Roman watched in horror as the silhouettes of both women tumbled through the window. The draperies jerked, then ripped partially off their heavy rods.

"Kate!"

He slid across the desk, registering Threader's bloody body on the floor as he landed on the other side, and threw his upper body over the windowsill. In the darkness, he could barely make out a figure lying on the ground three stories below.

"Kate!"

"Down here."

The desperate whisper floated up from under the window's ledge, filling him with such relief his body trembled with it. He wasn't too late. With a curse, Roman tucked his gun into the back waistband of his pants. There was no time to call for help. He leaned farther out, ignoring the shards of glass that scraped his stomach, and balanced his weight with his good arm.

Kate lay flattened against the side of the mansion wall, her hands clasping the hem of the drapery, her back to the wall.

"Hurry, Roman. I can't hold on much longer. My hands—they're slipping."

"Kate, listen to me. If I pull you up by the drapes, you might lose your grip."

Roman shifted his body farther out of the window. She heard his belt buckle scrape against the ledge, then saw his face appear, the shadows obscuring his expression.

"I should be able to reach you." He clasped the windowsill with one hand. "When I tell you, let go and grab on to my wrist."

"I can't. I'll fall—" Her arms cramped, their muscles burning from the strain.

"Don't look down!" Fear infused the order as her head started to drop. "Look at me. Concentrate on me."

Kate whimpered, but her face remained tilted up, her head wedged between her arms. She could see his hand, coming within a couple of inches of her fingers.

"You're going to have to grab my wrist, sweetheart. My arm's injured so your grip needs to be strong. First one hand then the other. Get ready."

The air solidified in her lungs. *First one then the other.* "Now!"

She grabbed for his wrist with her right hand, praying for contact. She sensed the brush of warm skin and with it came a spark of relief. A scant second later she felt nothing but the night air. A scream exploded from her chest just as his fingers caught hers, firm, secure.

The other hand was easier. She let go of the curtain and locked on to his wrist. Slowly he dragged her up the wall. "Grab for the ledge, babe." Sweat trickled down his forehead and into the pained crevices of his face. "Swing your leg up."

It took Kate two attempts before she got herself up onto the foot-wide ledge. Each one, she knew, jarred his injury. Her body shook uncontrollably as Roman grabbed her

Bodyguard Rescue

by the waist with his good arm. He hauled her over the sill and gathered her close, ignoring the arm that hung loosely at his side.

"Jesus, Kate," Roman rasped against her ear. "Never again. Don't ever do that again." She nodded her agreement from under his chin, pretty sure that one dive through a window would last her a lifetime.

When she trusted herself enough to speak, she said, "I didn't think you'd find me so quickly." She shuddered and took a deep breath. "The power shut off just before we fell."

"You mean just before you dived," Roman corrected tightly. "The security system failed minutes before, unlocking the doors. Quamar headed for the compound to search for you, while I took the house—" His chest convulsed. "I could've been too late."

The *whop whop* of helicopters stopped Roman's next words. Kate turned her head in time to see three military choppers landing in Threader's courtyard. High-beam lights flooded the compound, then poured into the study. In their wake the gunfire ceased.

"Here comes the cavalry," she joked, her voice weak with relief. They were safe.

The increased tempo of the vein at the base of his throat told her Roman wasn't going to be distracted, even with being rescued. She resisted the urge to steady the pulse with her finger and instead braced herself, waiting. It didn't take long.

"Of all the—"

"Stupid," she inserted helpfully.

"That's not funny."

"I'm not laughing, Roman."

"You shouldn't have jumped her like that," he bellowed even as he gathered her closer. "She was a trained operative. One move and she could've tossed you over her shoulder and out the window."

"I wasn't thinking about her skills. She intended to shoot you."

"I can take care of myself. Unlike you." He paused, inhaling deeply. The skin tightened over the planes of his face as he struggled to gain some semblance of control. "I thought I'd lost you."

"I thought I was going to lose you, too." Kate tried to be contrite, she really did. If for no other reason than he had a valid point. She should have let him do his job. But if given the choice she'd do everything again to keep Roman safe.

"And Threader could have killed you! You can't protect yourself."

"I think I did a damn good job protecting myself...and you, too!" Kate stood her ground. "Besides, Threader's dead. Phoenix shot him."

The click of a gun reverberated through the room. "I believe you're a bit premature, Doctor."

Startled, Kate swung around, instinctively taking a few steps back. Threader had managed to drag himself into an upright position on the floor with his back braced against the throne chair. The helicopter lights from the window glinted off his pistol. Blood soaked his suit and shirtfront. No doubt any other person would have died with two bullets in him. For the first time in her life, Kate understood what it meant to make a devil's pact.

"As for your argument, my dear, I find it somehow prophetic." He took a shallow breath, and Kate could hear the death rattle from where she stood.

"Get behind me," Roman murmured from his position a few feet away, his body tensed in lethal lines. "Now."

"You do, Doctor, and I will be forced to shoot before he can pull that gun from behind his back." He directed his next words to Roman. "With your left hand, you'll never make it. She'll be dead. I've little time and even less patience." Threader's words slurred and he blinked, trying to maintain focus. Roman took a minuscule step toward her.

Bits of wall exploded next to Kate. "The next shot will be through her heart, Cerberus."

For a moment Kate thought Roman was going to ignore Threader's threat, but instead he remained motionless. Threader's gaze locked with Roman's before he smiled, sending more blood trickling from the side of his mouth. "I was there, you know, at the warehouse in Morocco, the night your team torched it. It took me a while to escape."

"If I'd known, you'd be dead."

Threader laughed, triggering a coughing spasm, but the gun remained leveled at Kate's chest. "Almost didn't make it. The explosion sent debris flying. I can still feel the hot metal searing my skin."

Roman flexed his fingers, waiting for the opportunity to strike. He might be slower with his left hand, but he was just as accurate. Only the knowledge that he couldn't beat a bullet stopped him.

"Every haunting second since then, I've lived with the deformity," Threader murmured. Roman could see where the situation was heading.

"So why shoot the doc, Threader?" Roman prodded, desperation serrating the antagonistic tone. "When *I'm* here. The man who ruined your plans. The man who made you a monster. Make it the final act of your play."

"Do not worry," Threader grimaced and shifted his body slightly, his breathing became more labored. "You see, I have no delusions about my mortality. I even welcome hell." He nodded drunkenly. "Because I'll be seeing you suffer as I have, Cerberus, living your own nightmare."

As Threader's words registered, a balloon of fear burst in Roman's gut. He grabbed for his gun and dove for Kate, knowing even as he shot Threader he'd been too late. In slow motion he saw Threader fire and heard Kate's soft grunt as the bullet struck. His own scream of agony was echoed by Cain's bellow of rage as his partner raced through the doorway.

Vaguely Kate registered the shots, then the shock of Roman's tackle. For a moment she was sure she'd been hit, but there was no sting, no pain. Nothing.

Kate started to tell Roman she was fine when fire engulfed her chest. Her body seemed to fold in on itself with excruciating pain. "Roman?" She reached out, grabbing air.

"Get help!" Roman shouted. To whom, Kate didn't know.

Somehow she'd ended up on the floor, not in his arms. He tugged frantically at her clothes, trying to get to her wounds. His face, grim and fearful, hovered only inches from hers. "It looks like he caught your spleen."

Something heavy pressed into her, sending another brush fire of white-hot flames through her stomach. A low moan escaped her lips.

"Baby, I got to stop the bleeding."

"Roman, I…" she whispered, unable to finish. The fire seemed to be lessening, leaving her weak.

"So help me God, don't you die! Do you hear me?"

Dying? So this is what it felt like, she thought. A dark, twirling mist slowly enveloped her, making her feel buoyant, pain free. The fire that seemed to ignite her a few moments earlier, seemed cool now, almost soothing. She closed her eyes.

"Damn it, Doc. Look at me!" Recognizing the desperation in his demand, she somehow managed to obey.

"Listen to what I'm saying," he said. The words were urgent, imploring. "God, Kate, loving you scares the hell out of me." Tears filled his eyes as he begged. "But losing you scares me more. You have to hang on. Understand?"

Because of the expression of raw anguish on his face, Kate tried to lift her hand to comfort him, but she had no strength. There was so much to say, but the mist increased, invading her vision. It swirled around her, sucking her into its depths, giving her only enough time to say what really mattered. "I love you."

Chapter Nineteen

Two months later

Kate's gaze drifted over the palm-fringed strip of white sand as she listened to the tranquil, rhythmic lapping of the crystal-blue water. A soft breeze, sweet with the scent of hibiscus, danced lightly across her sun-warmed skin, eliciting from her a sigh of pleasure. Paradise.

She'd spent the past few weeks walking the private beach, watching the gulls, welcoming their company as they circled, their somber wails mixing with the resonance of the rolling waves. In time she'd regained her strength, using the soft sounds and fragrances of the island to soothe, to heal.

Leisurely she ran a hand over her bikini-clad body. Gone were the bruises and ugly scratches. Except for the pink scar, her skin had tinted to a deep cocoa brown. Almost without realizing it, her fingers lingered over her concave stomach.

There had been no baby.

A familiar ache spread through her chest and echoed deep within her soul. With pure strength of will, she pushed the feeling away. She'd moved on, damn it. He had left and she had moved on.

It was hard to believe that a little more than six weeks ago, with her surgeon's blessing, her parents had flown her back from Mexico City to the States. Weeks spent in a private New York hospital had left her restless and empty. So much so that when she was finally allowed to go home, Kate realized it wasn't where she wanted to stay. Nor was she eager to return to the laboratory. Against her family's wishes, she packed some clothes and headed to the Caribbean, determined to spend her recuperation on some remote beach far from the mountains, civilization—and Roman.

He hadn't been there when she'd awakened in the hospital in Mexico City—only her family had been waiting anxiously by her side.

Hope that Roman would walk through the door kept her from immediately questioning Cain. But after a few days, the rejection was too much to bear.

She remembered the look of helpless frustration in Cain's eyes when she'd confronted him. Roman had left the hospital on business once she'd stabilized.

Once again love couldn't compete with Roman D'Amato's unyielding commitment to duty.

Kate stifled the nagging hurt, banishing it until tonight, where, in the darkness of her bedroom, she would allow the pain its freedom. The same way she had every other night since awakening in the hospital and finding Roman gone.

Quanar grunted, interrupting her thoughts. Dressed in a neon-blue Hawaiian shirt with white Bermuda shorts, the man represented a fashion designer's nightmare. She almost grimaced when he tilted back the floral flat-brimmed hat and came to stand behind her lounger. Only the shoulder holster and gun managed to keep him from looking like bad wallpaper.

It had taken a week for Kate to see through his facade

to the tranquil nature beneath. Since that time they had spent many hours playing chess and discussing various subjects, analyzing those they agreed on and debating those they didn't. Quamar sensed when she needed time to herself and when she needed a distraction from her turbulent thoughts. On those occasions he talked about his tribe or his fascination with ornithology and much to her surprise, a loving friendship blossomed between them.

Initially, when her brothers had insisted on Quamar becoming her chaperone, she had protested, arguing that the danger had passed. Roman had been the one who had killed Threader. Cain, hearing Kate's scream had rushed to the study, arriving just in time to see her shot.

With both Threader and Phoenix dead, Labyrinth had ferreted out Phoenix's informants easily. Two of the traitors had turned out to be Cain's secretary along with one of Jonathon Mercer's assistants. Even so, Cain and Ian remained adamant, believing time would reveal additional traitors. Quamar became Cain's backup protector just in case they proved correct.

"It seems you have company, Doctor." The lilting words startled Kate, bringing her back to the present. She followed her friend's gaze out to sea where a large white cruiser lay anchored. This was the first boat she'd seen anchored in her bay since she'd arrived, and a feather of apprehension tickled her spine.

"My job is finished. My debt repaid," Quamar said suddenly. The giant stepped into her line of sight, blocking the light with his shadow before flashing a toothy smile. "It is time for me to return to the desert and my tribe."

Kate sat up. "I don't understand. You can't go, Quamar." When the plea didn't work, she threatened, not caring how peevish it sounded. "You promised my brothers you would stay until I returned to New York."

Quamar sighed, a hint of sympathy in his dark eyes. "I only promised to keep you safe until my services were no longer required. And that time has come." He nodded toward the sea. "It was not a promise made to your brothers, although they took responsibility."

"Who—" It was then Kate saw a man wading through the surf toward them, his dark hair glinting in the sunlight, his powerful, well-muscled body encased only in tight black trunks that emphasized the easy, predatory grace in his stride. Roman!

Quamar leaned over and took Kate's hand. His large, warm fingers encircled the iciness of hers, startling her. His lips curved knowingly. "You are a rare jewel, Doctor." He kissed her hand, then released it. "I shall miss you."

Tears stung at the back of her eyes and threatened to choke her. "Thank you, Quamar. You are a true friend." She stood and hugged him.

"As are you," he murmured in her ear while returning her embrace. "Trust Allah." Then, with a quick wave toward the ocean, Quamar stepped back from Kate, salaamed and sauntered toward the beach house.

She turned back to the ocean, watching the white foam swirl around Roman's legs as he waded toward her with determined strides.

"Kate."

He was leaner than she remembered, but otherwise he looked the same. Longing tugged deep within her belly, and the self-betrayal sparked her temper. How could a man who had broken her heart still affect her so completely? Clearing her throat, she battled for composure.

At the sound, the lines of Roman's body altered,

tensed—subtly, but with her heightened awareness she noticed it. A horrendous thought occurred to her. "Did something happen?"

Startled at the obvious trepidation in her voice, Roman stepped closer, only to stop when Kate jumped back, placing herself out of reach.

"No, nothing's wrong." His features relaxed. "Everything is fine. We rounded up the rest of Threader's people a few days ago. It was simple actually, once we discovered Phoenix had left records."

"Then why are you here?"

"I missed you. I needed to see you."

"You've seen me, now leave."

His eyes grazed the minuscule pieces of white fabric that clung to her body. "We need to take care of some unfinished business."

"I don't understand," she said, as aware of the lie as she was of the butterflies in her stomach. "Threader's dead. The government took the formula and locked it away somewhere safe. I'm getting a much needed vacation." She nodded toward the boat. "It seems you are, too."

"That's one reason I'm here. One of many." He started to reach for her, then must have thought better of it. His arms dropped impatiently back to his sides. "But first we talk."

"Go away, Roman. I'm not interested in what you have to say," she responded quietly, fighting her own battle of personal restraint. "Your actions were explanation enough." Both times she'd trusted him, he'd let her down, sending her spiraling into an emotional hell that she'd had to claw her way back from. She wouldn't survive a third.

"Damn it, Kate. I won't hurt you."

"You're right—I'm not going to give you the chance.

It's over. You made your choice when you left the hospital for another assignment."

"There was no other assignment. Just some loose ends that needed taking care of. I wanted to finish it all before I came for you."

Came for her? To do what? Continue where they left off until he went on another mission? Fighting to keep her emotions hidden, she turned away, staring at the sand as tears flooded her eyes. Then a gentle hand caressed her back. She jerked away, falling to her knees.

"I can't. Not again." The words came out raspy, raw.

"Christ, Kate. Don't cry. Please." He fell behind her, spooning his chest over her back and wrapping her in his arms.

"Let me go." She elbowed him. "You've made your feelings about me crystal clear."

He gripped her tighter. "I quit Labyrinth."

Kate froze, unable to think, unable to believe.

"I love you, Doc." Turning her in his arms, he gently kissed her tears away. "Marry me."

She scrambled away, quickly putting the lounger between them, and shook her head vehemently. "No."

"You don't have a choice. I've got the license and we're getting married tonight." He circled the lounger slowly, his intent clear. "You're not getting away this time, Doc."

Her heart quivered, then flopped in her chest at the caveman routine. She took a small side step in her bungalow's direction. "I was never the one trying to get away."

"You're right," he admitted before he took a small step of his own, heading her off. "I was stupid to think I could stay away." The statement was deep and sensual, sending a ripple of awareness through her. "And I'll ask your forgiveness for that and much more—every time I'm buried inside you, loving you."

Her pulse pounded, sending thick, molten lava pumping through her veins. She forced logic to take control and took another step. "After everything, you can't expect me to be-lieve you," she said, even though her heart wanted to—badly.

"Yes, I can." Suddenly he stopped his pursuit. "Because I'll spend the rest of my life proving it, if you'll let me."

Kate's hand dropped to her stomach. The honey-dipped words turned her earlier butterflies into dive-bombers. How could she fight him, when he was all she'd ever wanted?

His gaze rested briefly on her hand before returning to hers with an intensity that probed her soul. "Are you…?"

"Pregnant?" she inserted quietly, following his thoughts. "No," she said, unable to keep the thread of disappointment from weaving its way through her response. She had wanted his baby. Desperately.

He must have heard the ache. "Ah, sweetheart, you will be soon." His eyes became hooded, like those of a hawk. "And it will be my pleasure."

The air around them crackled with sensuality, but she refused to give in to it—even knowing she'd lost. Her heart was his and gave her no other choice.

Only the how and the when were hers to choose.

Tossing her hair back like a true Scottish princess, she said, "I'll think it over."

"I mean it, Kate…" Roman started to argue until her simple statement hit him with the impact of a two-by-four. Relief rushed him from toes to throat, forcing its way out in a burst of laughter. "You'd better think fast."

"No. I'm not going to make it easy for you, Cerberus." She drawled out his name hauntingly, taking a cautious step backward.

He let the name pass, too pleased to fight over the trivial and took a step forward, stalking her. She took off for the bungalow.

Roman raced after her, the view from behind quickening his desire as well as his stride. She shrieked when he tackled her, even though he cushioned her body with his as they toppled into the soft bed of sand. After rolling her onto her stomach, he lowered himself ever so slowly.

"Seems to me," he drawled, enjoying the sensation of her bikini-clad derriere as it twitched against his groin, "we've been here before."

Kate stopped struggling, and a soft sigh escaped her lips.

"I love you, Roman."

The relief made him weak, then humble. For the first time, he could accept the words from her without feeling guilt. And God knew, he wouldn't have blamed her for not ever saying them.

Dropping her hands, he flipped her over and covered her completely, balancing himself with his arms. "I love you, too, Kate." He nuzzled her neck, inhaling her scent. "You should've made me suffer more after what I've put you through." He lay down beside her and drew her into his arms. "But I'm grateful you didn't."

"I couldn't." Tenderness shadowed her features. "When you suffer, so do I. The pain from that would be far worse than the pain of having you walk away again."

"Kate, I won't walk away again. I've been fighting my love for you since the day I saw your picture on your parents' mantel. When Threader shot you, all the feelings for you I'd tried to bury came back to haunt me." He caressed the soft line of her back.

"I had a lot of time to think about my past while I watched you in that hospital bed. I realized that the one thing I remembered most about my parents was the love they shared. With each other, with me.

"I hated the terrorists for taking my parents' love away. Uncle Joe had tried in his own way to replace it, but my world was never the same. In the hospital, I finally realized that in making the terrorists pay, they ultimately won. I was giving up my only chance to create what my parents had— the one thing I craved most in the world. Facing life without you, never to feel my child kick inside you or be able to hold your hand while growing old together—" he dropped his forehead to hers "—was more than I could bear."

If she hadn't loved him already, she would've toppled then. "Me, too."

"There's something else you need to know."

The words had an ominous ring, so she waited, not wanting to ask. Dread filtered through the love that had filled her only moments ago.

"For all intents and purposes, I've retired. But there will be times when Cain will need my help out in the field. Times when he'll only trust me as his backup. On those occasions I won't be able to turn him down, not if it means covering his back. Do you think you can handle that?"

She threw her arms around his neck, her breath hitching with relief. "I can handle anything, as long as I know you'll always come back to me."

The planes of his face softened. "Always, *mi amore*." One hand splayed across her stomach, only to stop abruptly when he encountered the soft ridge of scar tissue.

Pulling back, he looked at the marred skin with such intensity it left her cheeks burning with embarrassment.

"I'll never forget..." His voice trailed off as he took a deep breath. Then gently, almost reverently, he leaned forward and kissed the scar where the bullet had hit her.

"They're just scars, Roman," she said, trying to reassure him. She'd wanted to laugh, but then he suckled a cloth-covered nipple, and her bones dissolved into goo. One day she'd tell him how precious that pink line was to her. How it represented a new beginning. But now...now...

"Just scars," he repeated, the corners of his mouth tilting when he recognized his own words from the mountain.

"How, exactly, did you get them?"

"Well, you see," she whispered, pulling his mouth to hers, "I was playing racquetball..."

Like a phantom in the night
comes an exciting promotion from

® HARLEQUIN®

INTRIGUE®

ECLIPSE

GOTHIC ROMANCE

Look for a provocative
gothic-themed thriller each month
by your favorite Intrigue authors!
Once you surrender to the classic
blend of chilling suspense and
electrifying romance in these
gripping page-turners, there will
be no turning back....

HIE3

ATHENA FORCE

Silhouette®
BOMBSHELL™

The Athena Academy adventure continues....

Three secret sisters
Three super talents
One unthinkable legacy...

The ties that bind may be the ties that kill as these extraordinary women race against time to beat the genetic time bomb that is their birthright....

**Don't miss the latest three stories
in the Athena Force continuity**

DECEIVED by Carla Cassidy, January 2005
CONTACT by Evelyn Vaughn, February 2005
PAYBACK by Harper Allen, March 2005

**And coming in April–June 2005,
the final showdown for
Athena Academy's best and brightest!**

Available at your favorite retail outlet.

HARLEQUIN®
INTRIGUE®

Coincidences... Chance encounters...
It's what one Houston, Texas, firm specializes in.
Who knows what lies around the next corner...?

MATCHMAKERS
UNDERGROUND

Follow

AMANDA STEVENS

into the secretive world of the wealthy...
and the dangerous....

INTIMATE KNOWLEDGE
February 2005

MATTERS OF SEDUCTION
March 2005

Look for both titles
wherever Harlequin books are sold.

HARLEQUIN®
® *Live the emotion*™

www.eHarlequin.com

HIMMU2